BROKEN LINE

AN URBAN FANTASY

ANN GIMPEL

CONTENTS

BROKEN LINE

CATACLYSM SERIES, BOOK FOUR

An Urban Fantasy

By
Ann Gimpel

Tumble off reality's edge into myth, magic, and Armageddon

Copyright Page

In all my years as a Vampire, hundreds of them, I never imagined humans would be anything other than food.

Rich, pure, delectable blood. Prey that fought back never posed a problem. Mortals couldn't stand against those of us with supernatural ability. That world still exists, but it's taken a backseat to humans who've joined forces with turncoat mages. Mortals were never meant to wield power. Over the long haul, they're sure to be very sorry for the choices they've made.

Meanwhile, they're a huge pain in the rear and a threat to every type of mage, not only Vampires. Some days, I just want to go back to running my nightclub. *Ascent* is a "don't ask, don't tell" establishment. I never cared who frequented my bar, so long as they brought plenty of money and a powerful thirst for booze.

Maybe someday I'll be a humble innkeeper again, but it's

so far in the future I can't even think about it. Nope. For now, all I see is blood. Rivers of it, and not running down my gullet, either. On the plus side, I have good friends, powerful allies, and a Vampire who loves me.

We have to come through this unscathed. Have to. I'm Ariana Hawke, and I take care of what's mine.

Part of me can scarcely believe I'm writing this series. Vampires have been the bad guys in my Bitter Harvest series and my Gatekeeper series, and several others. Not so in the Cataclysm books.

Maybe I named the series what I did because turning Vampires into heroes was cataclysmic for me. Mortals are a sketchy lot. When the reality of magical beings grew a little too close, they banded together and fought back. Silly of them, huh? Even an army of humans isn't a match for a couple of determined magic-wielders, but they're going to have to figure that out on their own.

Ariana is a great heroine. I'm excited to tell you her story. And Nickolas is emerging as a Vampire I'd love to have next door. You know, for the clean-up work when things get dicey. Conan is perfect. He reminds me of my own wolves: noble, principled, and courageous as hell. Except he's not really a wolf at all...

If you're reading this, you've inhaled the first three books. Hang on for a wild ride as *Broken Line* keeps you guessing.

CHAPTER ONE, NICKOLAS

*B*riny ocean smells greeted me as our travel spell faded, spitting Ariana and me out a few kilometers east of San Francisco. I've never stopped missing the scent of the sea. It charmed its way into the core of my being during my years in Scotland before I was turned. Northern Italy—at least the part where Clan Giovanni's seethe was located—wasn't close enough to saltwater to carry that characteristic tang.

I still couldn't believe Ariana was mine. Truly mine for the rest of our immortal lives. The ramifications were staggering, and I wanted to spirit her away to a private spot, build us a magical tower, and retire there for the next couple of centuries. It might happen, but not anytime soon.

Not with a major war ahead of us. One where if we lost, we'd be in a world of hurt. These weren't run-of-the-mill mortals we faced, ones who'd learned what they knew about supernatural creatures from television and the Internet. Nay, we faced men and women who were part of a paranormal task force. While far from naïve, they didn't know as much as they thought they did about us. Hopefully, we could capitalize on their relative ignorance. A similar effort had gone well in Seattle, but San Francisco's squad was over ten times the size.

Even if there were 5000, we'd blast through their ranks. We had to. The early battles in any war are critical. I was a knight before I was a Vampire; it's how I know these things.

In a far more pleasurable vein, Ari and I had made love for hours, until it was time to meet up with everyone east of San Francisco. We could have kept going for days. Months. Sex with another Vampire is unbelievably erotic. It's not just the blood that's mixed in, but the entirety of the experience. We can push limits like no other magic-wielder. Just culling up memories of all the ways we'd pleasured one another made my cock shoot to attention. As if I hadn't come so many times I'd lost count.

Focus, an inner voice hissed.

I considered telling it I was smitten, and Ariana eclipsed everything, but the task that lay ahead was daunting. Indulging in lusty imaginings was counterproductive. I aimed to ensure she and I had all the years I planned on. For that to happen, we needed to get through the series of battles to come.

Not just this one, but all of the others that followed. I've always had a practical bent. I understood full well we'd be up to our fangs in conflict until mortals backed down. They'd made the mistake of their pathetically short lives when they got greedy and didn't want to share Earth with anyone magical.

That lesson should sink in damned quick, but I had a feeling it might take years and millions of dead before humans recognized their mistake. We'd lose dozens of mages along the way, and even one dead magic-wielder was unacceptable to my way of thinking. Strange I'd feel that way, since most mages view Vampires as one step up from pond scum.

Ariana glanced around, her blue eyes narrowed in thought. She's almost as tall as I am with a sinuously muscled frame, high cheekbones, a regal forehead, and full, sensual lips. Her waist-length black hair had been woven into braids and tucked out of the way. Both of us wore dark clothing. We were warded, but eventually we'd drop our invisibility casting, and the fewer who saw us the better. We stood on the edge of a grassy verge. In the distance, a sign read Tilden Park, our agreed-upon meeting place.

"Appears we're early." Ariana ran her tongue over her lower lip. "Too bad. We could have snuck in one more—"

I captured her hand and placed it over the bulge in my pants. "Hush, darling. I'm having hell's own time as it is not dragging you into that thicket over there."

Silvery laughter rustled through my mind. "No one can see us. Why not right here?"

"Don't tempt me, wench."

More laughter as she wound her arms around me and crushed her mouth over mine. Licking, sucking, biting. The brush of her fang tips nearly did me in. For long moments, we lost ourselves in a hot, sweet kiss. The points of her nipples pushed against my chest, and where she straddled my thigh her heat seared me.

Before I gave in and shoved a hand between her legs, I dragged my mouth from hers. She nuzzled my neck and murmured, "Yeah. I get it. We're in a strange place, vulnerable as fuck. But damn it, Nick, you're hotter than a Times Square Rolex."

I'll be the first to admit modern terminology flummoxes me. Despite my cock beating like a second heart where it curved against my belly, I managed, "Huh? Times Square is in New York, and Rolex makes watches, but…"

After a final hip butt, she untangled her legs from mine. "Something stolen is said to be hot. People steal Rolexes all the time, and—"

"Got it." I grinned at her. Being with her, kissing, talking, fondling felt right, perfect, but we had to pay better attention. Mortals might not know we were here, but anyone magical would feel emanations from our spell—and from us.

Groups of people walked by, some with dogs on leads. Others sat at long tables chatting up a storm. "Maybe not the best place to have selected as a rendezvous spot," Ariana said softly.

Once I wasn't transfixed by the wonder of her in my arms, I'd been thinking the same thing. Pheromones and the unique musk of sex clung to us. I was making a point to breathe just to keep savoring them. A uniformed guard, or maybe a policeman, rode through the various groups on a bicycle, stopping to talk with them. One by one, people rose and strolled toward the park gate where I'd seen the sign.

"Mmph. Must be closing time," I murmured.

"Makes sense," Ariana said. "They usually shut down public gathering spots at dusk."

A woman angled her head our way. She must have heard voices, but of course she couldn't see us. With a slight shrug, she hurried toward the entry point. Hooking a hand under Ariana's arm, I tugged gently, and we hurried uphill from our current location. A thick grove of eucalyptus trees provided some cover.

Before we got to the top of the hillock, I felt the distinctive bite of Witch and Sorcerer power and changed course to intercept it. Portals formed within a tangle of birch and aspen trees, disgorged mages, and were eradicated as soon as they'd done their job. Not everyone was warded, but I bit my tongue. These were allies, many of whom weren't overly fond of Vampires. I wouldn't make any friends by chiding them for being sloppy. Shifters and Sidhe joined the newly arrived.

Percy, a Sorcerer I worked with at Ariana's nightclub, *Ascent*, strode to us. Over two meters tall and built like a tank, he cut an imposing figure in his customary tartan, linen shirt, and sandals. Grey stubble was showing on his shaved head, cheeks, and chin. He nodded and ran shrewd blue eyes over the gathering crowd.

"I have the personnel info. Their system was eminently more hackable than Seattle's database," he said, not bothering with telepathy. No reason to since the park must have emptied of everyone but us by now.

Other mages drew near, forming a rough circle around us. I exchanged greetings with those I knew, as did Ariana.

"There you are, mate," Clive exclaimed. Another clan

Giovanni Vampire, he'd come to the States with me a hundred years before. Blond, striking, and charming, he had a ready smile that concealed his fierce nature. He glanced from Ari to me, nostrils flaring. A knowing grin formed as he put two and two together.

"Congratulations," he said and pushed between us, wrapping an arm around my shoulder.

"He was worth waiting for." Ariana grinned back. Her words sent waves of delight coursing through me, and intensified the push-pull of wanting to ravish her and needing to sharpen my concentration and make certain I didn't miss anything on the eve of a major skirmish.

Leaning into her, I whispered, "Thank you."

"None needed," she whispered back. "What I said was true."

Clive rolled his eyes and made a snorting sound. "Not sure which is worse," he muttered, "the two of you lusting after each other or the two of you now you've gotten a taste of the merchandise."

Percy chuckled. "That's a good one, son. I'll have to remember it."

Clive was diplomatic. He didn't bristle at being called "son," neither did he mention he was a hell of a lot older than he looked.

"Where's everyone else?" I asked after minutes ticked past and it became clear no one else was arriving.

"We talked about deployment earlier today," Percy said without detailing exactly who "we" referred to. "What we came up with was if over 2000 of us aimed for Tilden Park, someone would be sure to notice. Even having 500 of us here is risky. This region is thick with turncoat mages—and others who don't have a stake on either side. With the current problems, they're bound to be on the lookout for alterations in the status quo."

"Point taken," Ariana replied. "Thanks for not chiding us for being absent from the war powwow, but are the others not coming?"

"They're nearby," Percy said, "in four groups about the size of this one. They already have their assigned targets. Once I've parceled out tasks here, we'll let them know and launch."

"Did we tap any local mages to help?" I asked.

Percy nodded. "We did, indeed, but only those I've known for a long while. Tough to tell who to trust these days."

"No shit," Ariana growled. "Many have to be working for the other side."

"My concern too," Percy concurred, and added, "Where's Conan?"

"Good question." Ariana gave a slight shrug. "Haven't seen him since before the club closed last night."

"I'm sure he'll show up." I raked a hand through hair that needed to be bound up and tucked out of the way. If anyone could take care of himself, it was Conan, a shapeshifting mage who usually favored his dire wolf form. Guardian magic was powerful, and Conan was heir apparent to his tribe.

"Not much we can do about Conan's absence." Ariana looked straight at me. I knew her well enough to read concern in her finely honed features and blue eyes.

"Have you tried raising him with telepathy?" Percy pressed.

Ariana shook her head. "We didn't want to risk any more magic than was necessary to transport ourselves here."

"Good choice." Percy made come-along gestures with both hands, and everyone pulled in close enough to listen.

Over the next quarter hour, he handed out assignments. Because the San Francisco Paranormal Task Force was so big, we were working in pairs, not trios like we'd done in Seattle. Granted, three of us to one cop had been major overkill in some instances, but not quite enough in others. Three of our targets had escaped and had to be run down.

It was when I'd discovered Vampires were as big a bunch of turncoats as other mages who'd sold themselves to mortals for devil-only-knew-what inducements. I could have lived out my years without that prime bit of knowledge. It made me ashamed.

Not much love lost between Vampires, particularly those from different clans, but I'd assumed we had a sense of decency and sufficient integrity not to sell out to mortals. Crap! They're food. We control them, not the other way round.

"Erm, I almost hate to ask," Clive spoke up, "but has anyone heard from the Kelpies?"

I'd been wondering the same thing myself, but I'd been content to let sleeping horses lie. The Scottish water horses were definitely a mixed bag. Stronger than fuck magically, they were dicey allies since none of us trusted them.

"Nope," Percy said. "I was getting around to asking you about them. You three were the last ones to talk with them.

This isn't the type of undertaking where they can just pop in unannounced."

Interesting. Not much got past the big Sorcerer. He must have known about our chat in the alley behind *Ascent,* although this was the first he'd mentioned it.

"Oh, we can't, eh?" a strongly accented British voice inquired. Along with it the brine-smell of the nearby sea intensified tenfold.

"Well, I'll be damned. They were hiding." Ariana didn't even try for subtle.

"Poor choice of words, Vampire," the voice continued.

Kelpies swarmed downhill toward our group, hoofs clattering against the rocky ground. Even in human form, they retained their horse's feet. Even though we numbered in the hundreds, and they were perhaps only twenty-five or so, the fine hairs on the back of my neck rose. Once upon a time, Ariana and I had a discussion about who inspired fear most effectively: us or them.

My vote went with Kelpies.

Ariana crossed her arms under her breasts. "If you don't like my words, Kelpie, pick others."

"We were observing," another of the Scottish water horses said. "Making certain we'd come to the proper decision."

Percy strode to the Kelpies, planting himself firmly in front of them. "And your choice was? I'm inquiring because I'm in charge of strategy, and we had one mapped out that will need some alterations if we're to include you."

I was trying to decide if any of the Kelpies were the ones we'd talked with behind *Ascent.* It was impossible to determine since they all looked alike with long, tangled black hair, dark eyes, and burly builds. Garbed in leather and chains and tatted up, they looked like a bad-boy motorcycle gang, but an eerily beautiful one. They shared that otherworldly trait with Vampires.

One Kelpie took a step forward until scant centimeters separated him from Percy. The Sorcerer held his ground. "We shall assist," the Kelpie announced, "but we will do it in our own way."

"Which is?" Percy spun one hand in a circle.

"We will march on their offices and wreak havoc," the Kelpie replied. "You only selected cops; we will destroy everyone else. Including all their electronics."

Percy cocked his head to one side. "I'd been planning to finish sabotaging their databases, but that could work," he agreed.

"It will work," the Kelpie said. "Timing is essential. Your operation must be well in hand before ours begins."

I took a few steps until I stood next to Percy. "Forgive my ignorance of the extent of your power, but—"

"Nothing can harm us, Vampire," the Kelpie said. "Not lead. Not iron. Not silver. Our only weakness is a limit to how long we can remain human."

"Even that's not a weakness," another Kelpie snorted, and brine bubbled from his nose. "So what? We gallop back to the nearest water. Ought to scare a few mortals half to death."

"Where is the guardian?" the first Kelpie asked.

"Why does it matter?" Ariana skewered him with her direct gaze.

"We liked him," the Kelpie said. "Him joining forces with Vampires went a long way toward validating yourselves in our eyes."

"Yeah? Well, we love you right back," Ariana sneered.

Percy sent a pointed look skittering her way. "How will we communicate with you?" he asked the Kelpies. "Does telepathy work?"

The water horses dropped into their own language, a combination of clicks and clacks punctuated by the occasional whinny. They seemed to be arguing. It was hard to tell. Finally, the one who'd spoken first withdrew a polished piece of white quartz from a pocket. About the size of a chicken's egg, it was lit with a soft inner glow.

"Take this," he said. "When it is time, speak into the stone and say *now*."

Percy took it between two fingers as if he didn't trust its magic. I didn't blame him. "Just now?" he raised his bushy eyebrows. "Any particular language?"

"Aye, just the one word. Use whatever language strikes your fancy, Sorcerer. We know them all," the Kelpie replied.

Just as they'd done on the first occasion I'd met with them, the group vanished in the time it took to blink my eyes shut. One moment they were there, the next the only evidence of their presence was hoofprints in the dirt. The brine smell remained, but it too was fading.

Percy stared at the glowing stone. "Seems too simple," he said.

"Do you suppose it's some kind of tracking device?" Ariana asked.

He shook his head. "I'd feel that kind of energy. This

reminds me of the North Sea, all pounding water and storm-tossed waves." With a small shrug, he dropped it into a sporran wound around his waist by a leather cord.

"Best get moving," I said.

"Yeah, it's going to be a long-ass night," Ariana muttered.

"Only if our prey eludes us," I replied. It wouldn't take long to kill one mortal, unless said mortal was armed with charms making him immune to Vampire persuasion.

Or had a sidearm loaded with silver bullets.

"I'm working with Clive," Dee called out. A necromancer Witch, she'd moved past her initial distaste for Vampires, but Clive can be a charming fellow when he puts his mind to it.

Black hair in a geometric cut framed the Witch's stark cheekbones. Olive skin, black eyes, and pronounced bone structure confirmed her Indian heritage. Medium height, she was thin with ropy muscles that hinted she might be stronger than she appeared. Tonight, she wore her usual tattered jeans and a denim jacket.

"Sounds good to me." Clive trotted to her side. "We make a great team."

She smiled back. "We do all right together."

"Everyone ready to roll?" Percy asked.

Amid a sea of ayes and yesses, the teams teleported away. I set a spell in motion to take us closer to our assignment, one Thomas McMurdy, a deputy police chief in charge of the Paranormal Task Force.

"They assigned the head honcho to us," Ariana said.

"Means they trust us to not fuck it up," I told her.

"Then we'd better not. I'll manage our warding." Her

fangs dropped, making her so irresistible breath would have swooshed from me if I'd been the breathing type.

McMurdy was supposedly off duty, so I brought us out about half a kilometer from his home.

"Wow. Are you sure this is right?" Ariana craned her neck around taking in huge houses with extensive landscaping.

I'd memorized the address and rattled it off.

Ariana dragged her phone out and tapped its display. "Yup. Right place."

"Why did you think it might not be?" I asked, wondering if she didn't trust my navigational ability—or my magic.

"Because cops don't make this kind of money," she replied. "Nowhere near it."

"Maybe he married money," I suggested, relieved her concerns didn't revolve around incompetence on my part— and grateful I hadn't launched into a diatribe rebuking her for not believing in me.

"Possible, but my first instincts say he's on the take. Cops are in a unique position to make far more than their salaries on the side."

"That's the house." I pointed to a multi-story brick affair partway down the block. "Shall we sneak round the back and do some sleuthing before we barge inside?"

"Man after my own heart. Hang on a moment. I want to shore up my warding. In case he's playing host to mages—or has them on retainer as watchdogs."

I wrapped an arm around her shoulders. Once she nodded, we glided silently up the neighboring home's driveway and cut across a short fence separating its backyard from McMurdy's. The portion of the house facing the street had been dark. Not so back here. Light flooded from several street-level windows.

We settled between two large trees. Scanning through warding is a neat trick. I was just drilling a small hole in Ariana's protective layering when my nostrils filled with fur and wet rocks, the scents of guardian magic.

A large dire wolf padded toward us, his black-and-silver pelt glistening in muted light from a partial moon. *"You can't do this,"* Conan told us. *"Not alone. A veritable army resides within."*

"We have to do something," Ariana replied in kind.

"We would have figured out McMurdy wasn't alone," I inserted, wanting to make certain Conan understood we were neither helpless nor stupid.

"Maybe yes, maybe no," Conan said. *"His bodyguards include a guardian."*

"What?" Ariana clapped a hand over her mouth. *"Sorry."*

"How is that possible?" I demanded.

"Long story," the wolf said. *"No time for it now, but I have an idea I'm fairly certain will work."*

Ariana looped an arm around the wolf's neck and hugged him. *"Let's hear it,"* she told him. *"I want to get this show on the road."*

CHAPTER TWO, ARIANA

Conan's power wrapped around us. I'd come across him centuries before when he was a scrawny puppy on the run from his people. Except then, I'd had no idea he was a guardian. I'd just believed him some arcane variety of shapeshifter. He'd used me, selected me on purpose because guardians loathed Vampires and someone like me would be the last place they'd look to find their missing spawn.

He may have made me believe he needed my protection, but the true winner in our long partnership was me. Fresh from beheading Mistral, my maker, I'd been drifting and unsure where to go next. I'd gotten away with my crime, but it didn't make plotting a course for the rest of my life any easier. In that way, Conan and I had helped one another.

Much of what I am today is a direct result of Conan's unstinting faith in me. And I like to think he's benefited from our association too. He must have, or he'd have been gone long since.

The pulse of his magic was almost as familiar as my own as he swept Nick and me along with him. I had a feeling where we were going, and the wolf didn't disappoint me. Veils parted, and we entered the realm of the dead right next to a length of glowing golden rope stretching to infinity in both directions.

Conan's magic is linked to the ley-lines. He draws energy from them, and they respond to his call. *"Can we talk down here?"* I stuck with telepathy in case the answer was no.

"Yes," Conan replied. "The hum of the lines will shield whatever we say to one another."

"How do you know there's a guardian in that house?" Nick asked.

Conan growled, and Nick revised his question to, "Did you sense one of your own in the building, or did someone tell you they were there?"

"Both, but not in that order." Conan was still growling. "I barely caught up with the two of you. Started at the club and then went to the park."

"If there's a guardian up there"—I pointed above my head—"presumably they can tap into the ley-lines too."

"Not nearly as well as I can, and not at all if I marshal their power first." Conan sounded determined.

"How many others do we face?" Nick asked. It was a good question; I kicked myself for not inquiring first.

"Twenty. One Sorcerer, one guardian, the rest Sidhe from the dark court."

"We're good," I muttered, "but maybe not that good."

"Which is why—" Conan began just as the distinctive crackly feel of guardian magic blasted me from all sides.

Fearing attack from the treasonous fucker in league with McMurdy, I threw my magic wide open summoning destruction and balancing it between my outstretched hands.

"Save your firepower," a familiar voice snapped.

"That's Fairclaw," Nick sputtered.

"Good guess, Vampire." A large silver wolf trotted nimbly the length of the ley-lines with another hot on his heels. I recognized Moonglow, Conan's mother. Conan's given name was Moonwraith, but he hated it. I'd named him the day I found him and only discovered his true name recently.

Both wolves sprang from the lines amid the shimmer and shudder of magic. When it settled, they wore their human bodies. Fairclaw's silver hair had been braided with jewels. Moonglow's snow-white tresses hung loose to the ground. Both guardians were naked. I'd never seen them in any sort of clothing.

Fairclaw's striking face was screwed into a disgusted expression, as if he'd bitten into something indescribably bitter. "I didn't believe you," he sputtered and faced Conan.

"I did." Moonglow nodded at her son. "You'd have no reason to make up such a heinous tale."

"Can we skip the family drama?" I inquired. "Which guardian fucked you behind your backs?"

Fairclaw cast an annoyed look my way and said, "Tone it down," in a pained voice.

Charm oozed from Nickolas. I recognized a subtle mesmerism casting. "We have work to do, people." He adopted a tart tone but was diplomatic enough not to add what he had to be thinking.

Guardians were a huge pain in the ass. Except for Conan.

"The only reason I told you anything is we require help." Conan looked from his mother to Fairclaw and back again. "I don't have any interest—or investment—in how you punish Darksword, but the mortal who gathered mages to his side must die."

"He isn't our problem," Fairclaw said stiffly.

Something about his attitude got to me and I marched right in front of him, pushing Conan a few inches over. "Now you look here," I began, ignoring his features darkening into thunderclouds, "everyone in that fucking house above us are our problems. Your magic is just as vulnerable as everyone else's, never mind you started with more than most of us. We have to win this war, and since you're here, you're going to help us with this one teensy task."

Nick flanked me, offering support. What came out of his mouth surprised me when he said, "Even the bloody Kelpies are hoof-deep in this mission. If they can lay aside whatever reservations have kept them aloof forever, surely you can see your way clear to fight side by side with us for the next hour or so."

Shock etched into Moonglow's timeless face. "Kelpies, you say? How in the goddess's name did they get involved?"

"A Vampire invited them." Nick smirked.

"You promised aid at a long-ago meeting," Conan reminded them. "Now is a good time for a down payment on that pledge."

Moonglow stepped closer. "I will fight alongside you.

Fairclaw and I originally thought to shanghai Darksword and be done with things, but now I have a deeper understanding of the problem." She turned her amber gaze on Fairclaw.

After a lengthy pause, he bared his teeth and snarled, "Aye, I will fight."

Moonglow crooked a finger at me and Nickolas. "Come close, you two."

"Why?" I asked. She'd saved my life once, but I didn't trust her.

Her mouth curved into a knowing smile. "Oh ye of little faith. I shall weave protections so I don't end up having to purge either of you of silver poisoning."

"Thank you." Nick turned to face the guardian.

After a short pause, I did the same.

Conan glided next to his mother. "I do not know this casting."

"Open your magic to me and learn it," Moonglow suggested and raised her arms in front of her. Light flowed from her outstretched fingertips.

My skin felt one size too small when her power washed over me. Not unlike a vast wave, smelling of fur and damp rocks, prickly warmth started at my feet and swished over my head. Not too bad, all in all. I kept waiting for the other shoe to drop, but it never did.

If guardians could truly protect those like me from silver poisoning, it was quite a gift. Moonglow took a step back. "There. It is done."

"How long will it last?" Nick asked. Damn, he was Johnny-on-the-spot with relevant questions tonight.

Moonglow drew her white brows together. "Hard to say. At least a few hours, perhaps as much as a day."

I glanced at Conan, who nodded slightly. It meant he could replenish his mother's casting when we needed it. "Do we need a plan?" he asked.

"Why would we?" Fairclaw dropped into his wolf form. The ley-line nearest him began to vibrate.

"I'll manage the lines," Conan said and began a soft chant.

With a sputtery, popping sound, the line first buckled and then broke, pointing straight up. Riding on guardian enchantment and the power loosed by the ley-line, we shot upward. My fangs dropped, and I rekindled the destructive magic I'd summoned earlier. Next to me, Nick did the same.

A large, fancy room formed around us, but I wasn't interested in what it contained. Mages shot to their feet; power arced around them as they readied themselves to fight us. Our arrival shouldn't have come as a surprise. Surely, they'd felt the disturbance when the ley-line broke.

"One enemy at a time," Nick told me and threw himself on a Sorcerer stirring up something in a kettle suspended over a fire burning at one end of the room. Nick keeps a blade. I need to do the same. Fangs are great, but nothing like a weapon when I'm trying to rip enough shit apart to end someone.

Energy from the ruptured line poured into the room. I had no idea how the guardians had managed it, but they had. I sidestepped a volley of Sidhe destruction and launched myself at the nearest one. No time to fuck with mesmerism. The Sorcerer already lay twitching in a pool of blood, and

Nick had moved to his next victim. Unless the guardians had something unexpected up their sleeves, this was going to take a while.

Killing immortals isn't easy. I have to break enough they can't fix the damage with magic. A cacophony of wolfy snarls erupted. I couldn't take my concentration away from my victim, but I didn't have to. Fairclaw and Moonglow—and maybe Conan—were meting out punishment to their own.

Sidhe power ripped at me. How in the fuck was he managing to do jack? I had him pinned, and blood poured from three gaping holes I'd torn in his throat. I'm slow on the uptake. The mage twitched in death throes before I understood it wasn't him but one of his companions who'd targeted me by wrapping what were starting to feel like silver bands around my torso.

Were it not for Moonglow's protections, I'd have been in a world of hurt. Convinced my work with target number one was done, I launched myself at the next nearest Sidhe. It was uphill work since I had to punch through enchantment to reach her. Miniature lightning bolts flew from her hands as she tried to keep me at arm's length. She'd seen what happened to my last target.

Perhaps she had better instincts, quicker reflexes, or a more finely honed survival instinct. I'd come out of the blue and tackled the dude I'd ended. It was looking like he'd be the only freebie on today's menu. I enjoy a challenge, but not ten in a row—especially if I can't get close enough to fang them.

I dove forward; she parried my momentum with more magic. And then we did it again. And again. Sidhe and Fae fight dirty like that—because they can. Their magic is strong, relatively speaking. Frustrated by my lack of progress, I bared my fangs and hissed.

The fucking bitch laughed at me. Laughed. That did it. My next lunge was powered by fury. I broke through her barrier, but not without cost. My skin felt like it was melting, aching and burning by turns. No matter. I got my hands around her neck long enough to fang her good.

And then I tore her neck halfway round. Blood shot everywhere, but blood is my go-to place. Slippery, thick, reeking of minerals, there's nothing like it. Except this blood wasn't for me. Still riding on rage, I twisted her head all the way off and chucked it across the room.

A quick glance told me Nick was mowing through Sidhe like nobody's business. Quick and efficient, he'd amassed quite the body pile. What happened next was my own fault. I shouldn't have allowed Nick's gorgeous, blood-embellished face and body to divert me.

A quartet of Sidhe divebombed me from the corners of a square. They were on me so fast, I barely saw a blur before they tossed me on the floor. I smelled silver. Of course, they'd assume they could dart me or wave a flagon of powder under my nose and I'd be a goner.

I felt the sting, but instead of getting worse, it stopped there. Relief was heady. Being told I was safe—and actually testing it and finding it true—were two different things. Maybe I could employ my newfound invulnerability to my advantage. The Sidhe had wrapped silver bands around my lower arms and dropped a small bar of the shit on my chest. They were holding me down, so I pretended to be fading. I made what I hoped were pitiful mewling sounds and writhed in their grip. Convinced I was on my way to turning into a pile of moldy bones, they backed off.

Fuckers. They had ringside seats to what they assumed would be a spectacle.

I'm quick. Supernatural strength and speed make up for Vampires' relative lack of magical ability. But still, I had to plan this to make certain I could pull it off. Feinting left, I twisted in midair and drove my teeth into the nearest Sidhe. I aimed for the middle of the back of her neck. She wasn't expecting it and squealed like a stuck pig. I'd have laughed, except my mouth was full.

I didn't even try for elegant. While the other three were processing why I wasn't dead yet, I let go with my mouth and twisted the gal's head all the way round until I heard vertebrae crack. For good measure, I drove my fingers into her eye sockets until I hit gooshy brain matter.

"Why you goddamned bitch," a man growled and grabbed my arm.

"What? Don't like being outsmarted?" I leered and felt blood dripping off my fangs onto my chin. Good. I wanted to look like something out of his worst nightmare. Not that he'd be around long enough to cull up any more nighttime imagery.

Taking advantage of his proximity since he was dumb enough to still be hanging onto me, I pulled back against his grip. When he lunged forward, I switched direction and tore most of his neck off. I'd been hoping for a last friendly curse or two, but all I got were gurgles.

Chucking him aside, I straightened and glared at the

other two. Both men, they were backing away from me. I curved my hands into fists and raised them in front of me. "Come on, you lily-livered jerks. You don't get to run. Not after selling your souls to mortals." I spit bloody phlegm on the floor between us and added, "How in the fuck could you do that?"

"What we do is none of your affair," the one on the right said.

"When it butts into my business, yeah it is," I shot back.

The yapping and snarling from the wolves had gone down a few decibels. I figured Darksword was either dead or not far from it. Sure enough, Conan leapt onto one of my assailants from behind. A single snap of his huge jaws severed head from neck. I threw myself on the fourth guy. Maybe watching his compatriots die had cut the heart out of him because he didn't even fight back.

"You're no fun." I kicked his almost dead form once half his blood had soaked into thick carpets covering the floor. He was too far gone to answer me. McMurdy faced some major cleanup before this house would be habitable again. Yeah. Tough to gin up any sympathy for him.

"That's all of them." Nick materialized next to me.

"Did you kill McMurdy?" I demanded.

Nick shook his head. "Didn't find him."

I scanned the sea of fallen bodies. "Doesn't make sense. Why would he have all these mages here if not to protect him?"

"Let's do a better job hunting," Conan suggested silkily.

The other three guardians were gone. We didn't need them anymore. In a backhanded way, I was grateful to

Darksword. If he hadn't been a part of this sketchy charade, Fairclaw and Moonglow wouldn't have been willing to lift a claw to help us. Well, perhaps Moonglow would have chosen to help her son, but Fairclaw definitely marched to his own drummer. If something didn't further his agenda, he walked away.

"I already scanned for anything alive," Nick told the wolf.

"As did I," Conan replied. "Who's to say all those mages didn't shield McMurdy somehow?"

A familiar thumping sound started up and then grew louder. I bolted for the front door yelling for Conan to follow me.

"What is that?" Nick shouted over the noise of helicopter blades.

"Helicopter. It's a kind of aircraft. Bad news for us. McMurdy's leaving. Must have had a heliport on the roof. Figures that fucker knows how to fly them. He's probably some kind of ex-commando."

"Aye, and I might have understood one word in three," Nick muttered. "Just tell me how to stop him."

"Our magic won't touch him," I growled and hoped to hell Conan could leverage something to disable the bird.

Conan woofed sharply. I recognized that bark. He was alerting me to something. Even though I was nearly to the door, I cut hard left into a room that had been converted into an armory with enough firepower to stop a rebellion in a banana republic. It was impressive, but I didn't have time to gawk.

I may have been slow on the uptake earlier, but I didn't

need instructions. I grabbed a long-range rifle fitted with an infrared scope. Luckily, the clip was attached and full. Normally, my luck didn't run this strong, but I wasn't about to complain.

Nick whistled and grabbed a rifle of his own. Seconds later, we made it to the front yard in time to see a UH-60 Black Hawk lifting off. Lucky for us, the thing required a short lag time for the engine to get the blades turning. I shouldered the rifle and switched the scope on. I've never been much for firearms, but it was a pretty big target—so long as my bullets traveled that far.

Nick had already opened fire. I joined him. A whoosh of power from Conan added either oomph or direction to our efforts. Doors were popping open all over the neighborhood.

Of course they were. My fangs were still on display. Nothing I could do about it except hope the relative cover of night would be on my side. What the fuck was wrong with all these looky-loos? Most sane mortals would keep a stout door between them and the mess unfolding in McMurdy's front yard.

I heard the rumble of machine gun fire. It took a moment to register McMurdy was shooting back. The craven bastard. What he should have done was stick it out and fight. Only cowards ran.

Our next volley of bullets was accompanied by a blast of guardian magic that nearly knocked me to my knees. Screams rang out from many directions; they told me McMurdy's bullets had found homes in civilian bodies.

Ha! Let him explain that one to his superiors. A low booming thundered toward me, followed by a detonation that made my ears hurt. Above us, the Black Hawk turned into a fireball. Flaming debris rained down. At least the humans weren't screeching any longer. They were smart enough to retreat—and I bet my ass more than one were dialing 911.

Meant we had to exit stage left. "Time to leave," I said.

"What about the guns?" Nick asked.

"We bring them with us," I told him. "Our prints are all over them, and there's not time to wipe them down."

"Look!" Conan jutted his snout skyward.

It took a moment peering between the wreckage of the chopper, but then I saw it. A goddamned parachute. "Fuck! He punched out."

"Nothing we can do about it," Conan said.

Sirens cut the night, growing closer fast. McMurdy was a big cheese. Naturally, his fellow dicks, er cops, would come on the run. Guardian magic wrapped around Nick and me. When it cleared we were in *Ascent's* stockroom still clutching the rifles. We reeked of blood and were filthy, but now wasn't the venue to address either of those issues.

Nick balanced the stock of his gun on the floor and turned to me. "How in the hell did McMurdy get out of that flying deathtrap? I'm assuming the floating thing had him in it."

Conan padded to his bucket and slurped water. I felt tired. We'd failed. McMurdy was still in the game, which meant our job wasn't done.

"Ariana?" Nick prodded.

I turned to him. "Yeah. I heard you. The short answer is it was a military helicopter. My bet is McMurdy served in some of the world's hellholes. Since he knew how to pilot the craft, it means he also was trained in how to parachute out of it in case it was shot down."

"So he's alive?" Nick raised a coppery brow.

"Unfortunately, yes," I replied.

Conan glided back our way, water sluicing off his muzzle. "What do you want to do?" he asked.

"We have to go back and finish this," Nick said. Conan woofed agreement.

"Yeah, no choice there." I closed my fangs over my lower lip. "And sooner rather than later. McMurdy will have a whole hell of a lot of explaining to do since he opened fire on civilians. I'd rather catch him before he launches into a pack of lies that gets everyone even more fired up about hating mages than they already are."

Shoving a bank of shelves out of the way, I opened a trap door leading to a half basement and chucked my rifle into it after checking the safety was engaged. Nick did the same. I'd come up with a more permanent solution later, but for now, no one would find them.

"Where are we going first?" Conan asked.

"Back to his house?" Nick suggested.

I nodded. "With all those dead mages, the last thing McMurdy would want is for anyone to come inside. We have to start there so we can track where he went."

"Do we need anything from here?" Conan asked.

I went to my desk and dug through a couple of drawers until I came up with my Gerber Ghoststrike knife and its ankle holster. For some reason, its particular alloy blend didn't bother me. I'd never used it for much of anything beyond keeping unruly customers in check since showing my fangs wouldn't have been in anyone's best interest.

After clipping it into place and dropping my trouser leg over it, I nodded at Nick and Conan. "Move 'em out. Or I can handle the travel spell."

Conan whoofed laughter. "You sound like those bad Westerns you like to watch."

"Aw geez, and here I was trying for the bad World War II films I also inhale like blood-porn."

"There's a lot for me to catch up on." Nick grinned.

As a unit, Conan and I said, "Not."

We were still laughing when the wolf's spell caught us up. If I had to go into battle, I had the best companions ever. I'd have said something, but I couldn't come up with anything that didn't reek of schmaltz. Besides, they probably knew without me saying a word.

CHAPTER THREE, NICKOLAS

The reek of burning wood and something acrid that might have been plastic singed my nose before our surroundings grew clearer. The airborne thing must have hit the ground in multiple spots and caused fires.

Just when I thought I was making progress categorizing everything new that had sprung up during the century I'd moldered in stasis, an item like the helicopter crossed my path. I'd seen a few when I'd lurked at airports deciding if I could force myself to board a plane, but other than that I knew nothing about them. Apparently, one had been waiting on the roof of McMurdy's house. It suggested they didn't require long stretches of asphalt to land and take off.

Trees took shape around us. We were behind McMurdy's house not far from where we'd begun our attack. Thick, greasy, black smoke hung a meter or so off the ground. Raised voices came from the direction of the street. No one sounded like they had anything under control.

"I'm ordering you to allow me to leave," a rough male voice rasped.

"Ha. Maybe we got lucky," Ariana murmured.

"Sorry, sir," another man retorted. "I have orders. Surely you understand orders."

"What I understand is I was defending myself," voice number one ground out.

"Maybe so, sir"—a woman stepped into the breach—"but you put civilian lives at risk. Two people are dead because of what you did. Fifteen are wounded."

"Eh, collateral damage. You should have been in Iraq, sweetie."

After a momentary pause, the woman stood up for herself. "Do not patronize me...sir. Our orders are to hold you here until someone relieves us."

A long, rustling sigh was followed by, "Look, sweetie, er lieutenant, I'm sorry. I have important matters to attend to. My entire task force was set upon tonight, and—"

"This conversation is over, sir," a new male voice that oozed command clipped off the words.

"They're not pleased with him," I noted. "Perhaps we can leave it to them to punish him?"

"Not a chance," Ariana said. "Even if they charge him with something, they'll allow him to remain free on bail, and then he'll run."

"It's not my first choice," Conan said, "but let's move a bit closer."

"You can kill him from here," Ariana mumbled.

"True, but don't you want to watch him die?"

"Aye, I do. Shall we?" I wove warding around us, so we'd

remain invisible after we left the trees. Once it was as robust as I could manage, we moved to the side of the house.

Sure enough, a man with cuffs circling his wrists stood off to one side. Someone had looped a length of chain through the cuffs and around a nearby pole supporting a streetlight. We still had a few hours before dawn eroded our power. The street, which had been empty, was full of official looking cars. Two ambulances were just pulling away from the curb, sirens blaring. I assumed it meant those within required immediate care.

"Two choices." Conan switched to telepathy.

"And they are?" I asked.

"Drop him in his tracks, or kill him and move him...elsewhere."

"Oooh, I vote for door number two," Ariana said. *"If he vanishes, it should really freak them out."*

Guardian magic built around us with its characteristic scents of fur and wet granite. We also reeked of blood, but it wasn't part of Conan's casting. I considered offering carte blanche to my power, but the wolf hadn't requested assistance. Perhaps it was simpler for him to stick with his own talents.

A couple of the cops milling about must have sensed something because they stopped what they were doing and glanced from side to side.

"Almost," Conan murmured, followed by, *"Now."*

The magic he'd been husbanding gathered momentum and arrowed straight for McMurdy. The head of San Francisco's paranormal task force was oblivious—until the last possible moment. I'd have had more respect for him if he'd gone out quietly. Instead, he squealed like a gutted pig, screaming for the other officers to protect him.

"From what?" a female cop inquired acidly. "Having bad dreams, McMurdy?"

"No, you stupid twat. They finally fucking found me," he yelped.

"For Christ's fucking sake—" the woman began. Her words halted abruptly as McMurdy's form took on a luminous aspect and then winked out as if it had never been there. All that was left were the cuffs still tied to a nearby light pole.

Half a dozen uniformed police rushed forward, pawing the air where McMurdy had been. "Damn it." A man stepped closer and retrieved the handcuffs. He shook his head. "All this supernatural mumbo-jumbo gives me the creeps."

"Me too," the woman said. "Did his task force really take it up the shorts tonight?"

The man turned to her and nodded. "Yeah. Something like 80 percent of them are dead."

Even from where we stood several meters away, I saw color drain out of her face. "But that's almost a thousand cops."

"It is," he concurred. "Now buck up and get back to work, Eisley."

Still looking shaky, she snapped off a salute and a pallid, "Yes, sir."

I herded us back behind the house and asked, "Do we want to look through the place before we leave?"

"Grand idea. It's probably the only chance we'll have." Ariana nodded briskly.

"The rest of them will be too spooked to cross the threshold," Conan agreed.

We let ourselves into the basement and hustled up the stairs. To be on the safe side, I scanned again for anything living and came up with zilch. I wasn't certain what we might find, but the best way to know your enemy is to spy on them. Surprising the things that crop up.

After a fruitless search, we ended up in what appeared to be a library on the top floor. Ariana pounded on a keyboard, trying to get the computer to disgorge its secrets. She didn't labor very long. "I'm not Percy," she said, "but we can bring this with us."

Meanwhile, I'd been pawing through the desk and come up with a bunch of electronic adjuncts. "How about these?" I held up a handful of plastic cylinders in several colors.

"Yeah. We want those. They're flash drives. And that thing in your other hand is an external hard drive. Any more of those?" Ariana furled her dark brows.

I dug through a welter of paper and came up with four more, dropping everything into my pockets as I went. "Almost daybreak," I reminded her.

"As if I didn't know," she mumbled and tucked the computer box thing under one arm after yanking wires out of it right and left.

Guardian power rose so fast it felt like a sucker punch in my guts. "We're about to have company," Conan said. "We could take a stand, but it's better to be gone."

The transition to *Ascent* was seamless and so quick I

didn't get to ask, "What do you mean by company?" until the stockroom shaped up around us.

Conan shook himself; black and silver fur flew through the air. "Mages, probably Sidhe, were teleporting in."

Ariana set the computer on the floor. "Mmph. Like as not they were after the same things we took." She turned to me. "Good thinking on your part to case the joint."

Her compliment pleased me, and I rifled through my pockets, dropping flash drives and the other larger things on her desk. My clothing had stiffened from dried blood. "What are the chances of a shower and fresh clothes?" I asked.

"Pretty damned good." Ariana chuckled.

"I'm leaving," Conan informed us. "We did good tonight, but we have to be back at this very soon. Before they have a chance to rise in force against us."

Ariana placed her hands on her hips. "Are you going to see Fairclaw and Moonglow?"

The wolf barked once. I took it as a yes. Apparently, so did Ariana, because she added, "See how they feel about doing a little more wet work."

Lupine laughter rippled from the wolf's throat. "All the work we ever do is 'wet.'" He smirked.

"Not true," Ariana retorted. "Your mother saved my life."

It was enough information for me to interpret "wet work" as killing. Conan was absolutely correct. Striking fast and hard was effective when followed up with more fast and hard—until the enemy begged for a truce.

"Regardless. I will find you later." Conan turned and walked through a rent in the air, making me wonder why guardians ever bothered with portals. Clearly, they were more for show than a necessity.

Ariana had tugged out her phone and was tapping on its display.

"What's up?" Percy's deep voice boomed.

"Hacking," she told him. "Lots of shit for you to decrypt."

Her screen went dark, and Percy strode through *Ascent's* back door, muttering, "Damn it. I was aiming for inside." He kicked the door shut behind him and looked from me to Ariana and back. "Rough night?"

"You could say so," Ariana told him. "How'd things go for you?"

"Good," the big Sorcerer replied. "Easy. Almost too easy."

"Any losses on our side?" Ariana asked.

He nodded solemnly. "Aye. A Witch and a Druid that I know of."

"Crap," Ariana muttered. "I suppose it's not a bad ratio—two to a thousand—but I'd have liked it better if we hadn't lost anyone."

Percy whistled. "A thousand? Where'd you come up with that figure? Have you talked with some of the rest of us?"

"No. Not other mages, but from what we overheard, we killed close to a thousand of their absurd task force tonight," I told him.

"Overheard from whom?" Percy angled his head to one side, eyes narrowed in concentration.

"Long story," Ariana replied. "The intel is solid, but it

will keep until all of us are together. We knocked off the top dude, but it wasn't easy."

Percy's keen blue eyes scanned the room, zeroing in on the pile I'd left on Ariana's desk. "Are those the drives?"

"And this." Ariana bent to tap the black plastic box. "I tried, but it's pass coded and beyond me."

"I'm sure I can convince her to yield her secrets." Percy smiled. "Women like me."

"What's next?" I asked, confused by his assignment of gender to a plastic box.

Percy shrugged. "Good question."

"We weren't sure how tonight would go," Ariana said, "so we didn't plan beyond it. Stupid of us. We should have. The club is closed for a few more days. Can we get a critical mass of us in here right after sunset to plot our next moves?"

"I'll do what I can to spread the word," Percy agreed. "Just so I'm clear, this is McMurdy's computer?"

"Presumably," Ariana replied. "We had to fight our way through twenty mages—including one guardian—to get to him."

"Even then, it wasn't straightforward," I spoke up.

"I would like to hear the story, but not right now," Percy said. "Anything I should know about the electronics?"

"They were popular," I told him. "After Conan killed McMurdy and spirited him to another location, mages converged on his study. Luckily, we got there first."

"What's in his computer must be important," Ariana spoke up. "Otherwise, no one would have given a damn about leaving it for others to sift through."

"Did you have to fight the second set of mages too?" Percy set his mouth in a tight line.

I shook my head. "Conan sensed them and got us out of there fast."

"Pfft. So this McMurdy person was working closely enough with immortals for them to protect him," Percy mumbled thoughtfully. "And there was even a guardian in the mix?"

"Yeah. Goes without saying his kinsmen were less than pleased by that development," Ariana said. "They helped us, but mostly they grabbed their traitor and made off with him."

Percy gathered all the bits and pieces I'd carried and dropped them into a cloth bag. Next, he picked up the computer. "Really only need the drive," he said, "but it's simpler to take the whole thing. Look for me around six. Hopefully, I'll have some answers." Turning, he walked toward the door, opened it, and left.

"Feel like some blood and cleaning up?" Ariana asked.

"In that order," I told her. "Not much point washing up before we go kill something."

"In the old days"—she smiled at me—"we'd celebrate by draining a mortal. I miss those times."

Moving until I faced her, I wrapped her in my arms. "I miss them too, but having you makes up for everything."

Tilting her head back, she locked gazes with me. "Silver-tongued devil."

"That's me all right. Your spell or mine?"

"I'll take us so long as you keep holding onto me."

"My pleasure." It would take more than the army of mages we'd already faced to force me to ever let her go.

The day was drizzly and overcast, annoying for anyone but Vampires since we welcome any kind of shielding between us and the sun. "You've been quiet," I said to Ariana after we'd chowed down on a collection of small game—and one small deer. We were in what I assumed was her usual feeding spot not far from her house.

"Yes, I suppose I have been quiet. I'm refueling and thinking." She tossed a racoon on top of a pile of other corpses. Conan would help himself to the leavings whenever he returned.

"About?"

She rolled her shoulders back and swiped an arm across her bloody fangs. "Mostly, where we go next. Between the prison breakout and mowing through two paranormal task forces, we've definitely got them on the run."

"Do we?" I pulled my fangs in and waited. I was done eating. Much as I wanted to divest Ariana of her clothes and feel the sweet sway of our bodies grinding together, this was a conversation worth having.

Ariana glided in front of me. "Say what you're thinking."

"All right. Seems to me if we had mortals riled up, San Francisco's task force would have been more of a challenge. Our particular target was guarded, but none of the others seemed to be."

"What makes you think that?" Ariana asked.

"If they'd been on edge, they would have been harder to take down. We wouldn't be looking at two of ours versus a thousand of theirs."

"Humph. See what you mean," she mumbled. "It's

possible McMurdy always kept an assortment of mages in residence, although the thought makes me sick."

"Doesn't sit well with me either," I retorted, "but the worst were the treasonous Vampires from our last mission. The one before this one."

"Let's not go there." She raked a hand through her hair, smearing still more blood. With everything we were covered in, a few more streaks were meaningless.

"All right. What do you think about...?" I angled my gaze toward the sound of running water. This part of North America had nearly as many rivulets and creeks as the Highlands.

A soft smile altered her fierce expression. "It will be cold, but there's a cave behind a small waterfall."

"Great. It will shield us from the day." I bowed low. "After you, *Cara*."

Rather than moving ahead of me, she linked an arm through mine, and we strolled through thick undergrowth that crunched and squished beneath our feet. A fast moving creek came into view. It was lovely with large flat rocks, clear water, and even the flash of a few fish as the current carried them from pool to pool.

Letting go of my arm, Ariana sprinted forward and sloshed through water that sometimes hit her midthigh. A shimmering cascade reflecting blues, greens, and violets in a kaleidoscopic array lay just ahead. She pushed forward until she stood under it, letting the torrent sluice over her.

It looked refreshing. I hustled to her side and let the falls clean my hair and pound some of the blood flakes off my clothing. "Brrrr." I grinned.

Ariana smiled back. "Just like the good old days, eh?"

"In my 'good old days,'" I retorted, "we heated water over the fire."

Silvery laughter warmed me. "Yeah? How'd that work? My memory is the damned tub was nearly stone cold by the time it got full. Besides, my family were peasants. We couldn't afford anything as fancy as a copper bathtub. First time I saw one was in the seethe. Come on, let's get these clothes off. They weigh a ton."

"Clothes off eh, wench? Thought you'd never ask." Slipping and sliding on mossy rocks, I ducked beneath a natural rock archway and followed her behind the falls and into a decent-sized cave peppered with limestone formations. The roar of the water was muted in there.

"Are you going to stand around all day?" she demanded. Her garments were already off and tossed over a few rounded rocks. In the muted light of the cave, her skin took on an ivory hue, lending her the air of a renaissance statue.

"You're so beautiful." I drank her in, from long legs topped by a vee of spiky black curls to flared hips, to high, full breasts with puckered nipples. Her midnight hair dripped water onto the rocky ground.

"I'd like a chance to see if I was hallucinating last time you took off your clothes." She ran her tongue over her fangs. All the blood had washed away, and they were shiny white, deadly and alluring.

Bending, I unlaced my boots and levered them off, tipping them to pour water out. Next, I removed my jacket and shirt and chucked them over a nearby rock. They were still streaked with enough blood to merit a trip through

Ariana's washing machine. Before I got a chance to undo the fastenings on my trousers, she bolted toward me and threaded her arms around my back, nails digging in.

The press of her nipples against my bare chest was incredible. I covered her mouth with mine, licking, sucking, and biting. She gripped handfuls of my hair as she slid her hands beneath it and cradled my head. My cock pushed into her stomach, so hard it ached. The wet material in my pants was uncomfortable. Shoving a hand between us, I made short work of my zipper and freed my unruly appendage.

Ariana ripped her mouth from mine and untangled her hands from my body. "Wahoo! Cock's out. You beat me to it, but I'll take my victories any way they fall."

"Wait. Come back here." I started after her, but she'd turned and bent over a handy rounded boulder that was just the right height. Her ass spread, offering me a view of her swollen sex. The air thickened with musk and wildflowers, Vampire pheromones.

I surged forward, intent on burying myself hilt deep in her amazing body, but first I wrapped my arms around her and filled my hands with her too-good-to-be-true breasts, pinching and rolling the nipples. She moaned and writhed and butted her hips backward into my cock.

"If I'd known you were going to tease me"—she twisted to toss a coquettish glance over one shoulder—"I'd have climbed on and been done with things."

"We can do it that way too. Next time." Wrapping a hand around my shaft, I settled it at the opening to her body and rubbed it in small circles. The motion sent waves of lust crashing through me.

"Nick!" Clive's frantic voice blasted into my head.

For a moment I flirted with not replying. Not until Ariana and I were done, but something about his agitation told me I had to respond. *"Aye. What?"*

"Kelpies. They have Dee and me, and—"

Christ. Goddammit. Fuck. *"And what?"*

But he didn't say anything else, mostly because the connection had been severed. Probably by Kelpie magic.

Ariana groaned and jackknifed her body out from under mine. "I heard that," she said. "We have to find them."

My brain was still addled with lust, but it was clearing fast. "We should let Dahlia know, and we need dry clothes."

"All of the above," Ariana agreed glumly and snatched up our discarded clothing and shoes. "Damn it. I was enjoying myself."

"Makes two of us, *Cara.*"

The feel of her magic enveloped me. When it cleared, we stood in her living room, and she was sprinting for the laundry area. The whir of machinery told me she'd done something to our soaked things. When she returned, she dropped an armful of clothing next to me, and a towel.

"These should fit," she said. "Not much to be done about your boots."

"They'll dry on my feet," I mumbled, not bothering to add that no matter how bad things got here, they were never as severe as they'd been during my years as a knight.

"Do you think you can find him?" She toweled off and dragged clothing over her body.

I did the same. The pants were a little on the short side,

but they'd do. "I'm not sure," I told her. "Clan bonds are strong."

"But Kelpie power is probably stronger." She shook her head. "Let me raise Dahlia."

"And then we'll leave." I laced my wet boots over the dry pair of stockings she'd given me while she employed telepathy. It must have gotten the coven mistress's attention because Dahlia catapulted into the room, her large raven, More Than Never, riding on her shoulder.

Tall and gaunt, the only thing exuberant about the Witch was clouds of spiky, red hair. Her tresses stuck out at all angles and hung to the middle of her back. She had eyes the shade of uncut emeralds and a sharp face that was all planes and angles. Her usual ragged jeans hugged her long legs, and a worn nubby sweater hung to hip level. Scuffed brown leather boots hit her mid-calf. On a shorter woman, they'd have reached knee level.

"Surely Clive said more than that." Dahlia spun one hand in a circle.

I shook my head.

"Well, crap." The Witch paced back and forth. Eying me, she asked, "What's your plan?"

"Get as close as we can to where he and Dee were in the Bay Area and track them."

"Geez, may as well hunt for a needle in a haystack." Dahlia frowned. "Wonder what happens if we mix our magics?"

"I'm game," I told her. "Let's find out."

"Can you go outside?" She glanced Ariana's way. "My

connection to earthbound power is stronger without walls between me and it."

"Won't be a problem," Ariana said. "Let's get moving."

"That scroll," I spoke up. "The one that had information about Kelpies. We should take another look at it."

"Why?" Dahlia demanded. "The trail will grow even colder than it already is."

"I agree on that part," I told her, "but I know less than nothing about them. We need to find their weaknesses."

"If they have any," Ariana muttered.

"Aye, well, five minutes on this end of things won't make much difference." I crossed the room, withdrew the scroll from its spot, and unrolled it on the coffee table. I wanted to get going too, but we couldn't afford to make any mistakes. No one that I knew of had ever taken on Kelpies and walked out winners on the other side.

Not if the legends were to be believed.

"*L*ook here." I pointed. "This is the most promising idea we've come across."

"Because it's the only one," Dahlia noted sourly.

"Don't quibble." I bent over the spidery script. Last time Nick and I examined this scroll, we'd had quite the difference of opinion about its translation. We couldn't afford any miscalculations about this section.

Nick squinted at the cracked vellum. "What do you think this word is?" He pointed. "And this one?"

The raven had curved its talons around the edge of the table and was peering at the scroll through keen avian eyes. "Salt," the bird croaked in response to Nick's question. "Salt and blood."

Dahlia stroked the bird's shiny black feathers. "My take too," she told her familiar.

I uncurled my back from where I'd been bent over the

aged lore book and stood. "So if we mix salt and blood and iron filings, we might have a chance."

"According to whoever wrote this," Nickolas said.

"It's all we have to go on." My reply may have been on the testy side, but my body still hummed with wanting him. My plans had been sex in the cave, followed by sex in my bed, followed by a tryst in the bathtub... I had to get over myself and suck it up. Clive and Dee needed us. Even I wasn't heartless enough to keep on keeping on in the face of someone else's misfortune.

"Salt and blood are simple to obtain," Dahlia said. "Where will we find iron filings near here?"

"Not so much finding iron, it's ubiquitous," I replied. "It's the filing it into shards that poses a problem. For us."

"Yeah. Not quite as bad for me," Dahlia agreed. "You get the salt and blood in a few beakers. I'll be back in a few minutes with iron to add to them."

"We'll use test tubes with stoppers," I told her. "The glass is close to unbreakable, and they're not likely to leak."

"What? Did you used to teach chemistry?" The Witch's mouth twisted into half a smile.

"Nope, but they come in handy for a lot of things, and I got a good deal on a box of a hundred a while back."

The answer seemed to satisfy the Witch because she winked out of sight. I'd actually purchased them to give myself to-go doses of blood for nights when I was too busy to hunt, but the Witch didn't need to know that teensy bit of "too much information."

Nick was still hunched over the scroll. "It appears if we

sprinkle the mixture in a circle, the Kelpies won't be able to break through."

"It can't be that easy," I mumbled. "Remember that Kelpie in Tilden Park? He said metal doesn't faze them."

"Maybe it's the mixing it with salt and blood," Nick replied. "Salt circles keep ghosts out of places."

"Hopefully, we'll have an opportunity to see if it really does work." I sent an attempt at a smile his way. "There's still the problem of locating Clive and Dee."

"Been thinking about that," Nick said. "They're probably close to the ocean."

"Why there and not some big lake?" I asked.

"Kelpies prefer salt water. Says it right here." He stabbed a finger at a spot in the scroll.

I stooped to read over his shoulder. Sure enough, his translation meshed with mine. "Much of the lore associates them with some loch or other," I said.

"Aye, I know." Nick shrugged and got to his feet. "This is why I wanted to take the time to at least look at the scroll. Also, when we were talking with them at that park before we went after McMurdy, one of them said something about switching to horse form and heading for the sea."

I'd forgotten that part, but it came back to me once Nick mentioned it.

It surprised me when he put his arms around me and tipped my chin up so our eyes met. "I love you, Ariana. Sorry about all this."

I cradled the side of his face. "No apologies. We'll do what we have to, although I didn't see this one coming. I figured mortals would fight back—once they had time to map out a strategy—but Kelpies?"

"We knew we couldn't trust them." Nick snapped his fingers. "Their part in last night's mission. Did anyone ever find out if they did what they said they'd do and wiped out everyone they found in the task force's headquarters?"

"Not sure. Let me raise Percy. If anyone would know, it would be him. He had the communication stone to let them know when to move out."

"Aye, but I had the sense that bit of quartz wasn't exactly a two-way device," Nick said.

I'd already raised my mind voice. *"Percy?"*

"Aye. What? Your computer project is giving me heartburn."

"Did the Kelpies ever check in with you?"

After a pause, Percy said, *"Now that you mention it, they did. According to them, they flattened the task force offices and everyone in them. Plus all the electronics. Why?"*

"They have Clive and Dee," Nick jumped into the conversation.

"What does that mean?" the Sorcerer demanded.

"I believe they're being held prisoner," Nick clarified.

"Fuck. That's not good. But not surprising, all in all. Kelpies were an unknown quantity. Is there anything you need from me?"

I exchanged glances with Nick. It would be potentially helpful to have Percy hunt with us, but we needed to know what was in McMurdy's computer too. *"We're going to ride to the rescue. I hope. We'll keep you in the loop,"* I told him. *"How close are you to hacking into that CPU?"*

"Not close at all," he growled. *"Whenever I think I'm getting somewhere, the damn thing threatens to enter autodestruct mode."*

"Keep chipping away at it," Nick said. *"Dahlia's back, and we're going to get moving."*

"You know where to find me." Percy signed off.

"So they did what they said they would," I mused. "Why in the fuck would they have set their sights on two of ours?"

"Eh, I can think of lots of reasons," Nick replied. "Primarily, Clive getting in their faces about what he viewed as double dealing."

"Where do you want me to put the iron?" Dahlia asked. The raven cawed from her shoulder.

"How about if you take it outside?" I suggested. "Hold on. We'll be right there with the test tubes, and then you can add your iron to them."

I hurried to the kitchen and dug through a cupboard, dredging out the box with lab-grade test tubes. It didn't take long for Nick and I to add salt and blood to three of them.

"I hope our blood works," Nick said as he licked a wound in his wrist to seal it.

"Mmph. Well, it didn't say human blood, just blood," I replied. "Besides, our blood was human once."

Nick chuckled. "Not for a very long time, but I like the way you think."

We walked the tubes out to Dahlia and stood a few feet away while she sifted iron filings into them. The contents bubbled and took on a rusty hue. Once she had the stoppers back in place, she handed one to me and the other to Nick.

"What was that you were saying when I arrived?" Dahlia asked Nick.

He turned to face her. "Clive was less than pleased when it became obvious the Kelpies had used him. Probably made him feel quite the fool."

"I don't get it," Dahlia said. "We used each other."

Nick screwed his mouth into a scowl. "Not the Vampire worldview."

"Regardless." I stepped into the fray. "We need to determine who Clive and Dee were assigned to snuff out. Once we know, we can get close to where they seized their target."

"It was a woman named Aira Bolis," Dahlia said. "Dee is one of mine, and I knew all my Witches' assignments."

"Was Aira working? Or at home?" Nick furled a brow into a question mark.

"Wait a sec." Dahlia dredged a cell phone from her back pocket and scrolled through screens. "Bolis is a detective, and she was off duty."

"Means she could have been anywhere," I muttered.

"We could start with her house," Dahlia suggested.

"Good a place as any," Nick agreed. "You have the address?"

The coven mistress offered a parody of a smile. "Of course, I do. Hang tight, and I'll take us there. Ward yourselves."

Daylight would take a toll. "I'm going to grab a hat and gloves," I said. "Back in a flash." Nick hadn't asked for them, but neither did he refuse the set of raggedy garden gloves I tossed his way. His hands are a lot bigger than mine, but I figured the stretchy canvas would fit well enough.

The herb-infused scents of Witch magic wafted around us, and we traded the thick evergreens that surrounded my home for aspens and birches and concrete. I had no idea which city we were in, but a narrow street was dotted with one-story bungalow-type houses. Everyone's yard was well-maintained, which suggested the folk who lived here weren't poverty-stricken.

No one reacted to our sudden appearance, which meant no mages were nearby. Lots of other people, though, hurrying this way and that. From the angle of the sun, I guessed it must be around three. Good. Dusk wasn't all that far away.

Dahlia herded us around the back of a beige house. Not much of anywhere for us to take cover since someone had turned the rear yard into a garden with rows and rows of vegetables. Resigned to hanging onto my ward—and wasting magic doing so—I scanned the house as slyly as I could manage.

One lifeless mortal lay within. It suggested Bolis was dead, but we had to check to make certain it was her.

"*Come on.*" Nick gestured.

No doors were set into this side of the house, so we unlocked a window with a small shot of power, clambered through it, and nearly fell over a woman sprawled in a very small pool of congealing blood. Yeah. Waste not, want not. Human blood has shifted from normal fare to a delicacy. The cop's ID dangled from a hook on a nearby wall.

"It's her, all right." Dahlia leveled a kick at the corpse. "I hope she suffered."

It didn't look like it to me, but I kept my counsel. Fang marks in Bolis's neck indicated Clive had dined. Death by Vampire is a dreamy affair. For all I knew, the cop had gone out in a blast of ecstasy.

I felt Nick deploy tracking power. He didn't have to say a word. Dahlia and I followed him as he went back through the window and melted from street to street. It appeared Clive and Dee had stuck to back roads, but I'd be damned if I could figure out why they hadn't gotten the fuck out of there. Their job was done. No reason to stick around.

The stench of the North Sea hit me like a wall. *"Kelpies accosted them here,"* I said.

"Not so simple," Nick replied. *"My money is that Clive reached out to them. He had a way to locate them once, and like as not, he deployed it again."*

"But why would Dee have agreed to such a foolhardy plan?" Dahlia rolled her eyes. More Than Never squawked, but she shushed the bird.

"Why else?" I mumbled. *"She's in love with him. Or in lust."*

I waited for Dahlia to stumble, to say something that would really offend me. Like she'd thought Dee had better sense than to fall for a Vampire, but the coven mistress wisely kept her mouth shut. Who knew? Perhaps she'd had her own share of ill-advised liaisons. Back in the day, we didn't mingle with other mages. Hell, they thought we were abominations. The worst of the worst.

Times had changed. A lot.

Ignoring our conversation, Nick was a hundred yards ahead, moving steadily. Not fast for a Vampire, but grass wasn't exactly growing under his feet, either. I sprinted after him with Dahlia just behind me. She lacked my supernatural speed, but her long legs partially made up for it.

"Do you think he'll be able to find them?" she panted, reminding me of one more benefit of my non-breathing physiology.

"Even if he can't track Clive, the Kelpies left a scent trail half a mile wide," I told her.

"There is that. Even I can follow it."

As we loped along, I sorted landmarks and decided we had to be on the west side of Oakland, headed for Alameda. Unfortunately, the clouds had parted, and I felt the bite of sunlight through my hat and on my gloved hands. The nasty orb was sinking toward the western horizon, but not quickly enough to suit me.

We'd flanked Nick long since. His face was set in stern lines. I wanted to ask what he was thinking, but it could wait until after we'd located our friends. The next quarter hour passed in relative silence. We made better time than if we'd been a vehicle. Rush hour had turned into a twenty-hour-a-day affair in this part of the States. We wove through stalled lanes of cars, moving west the whole time.

Maintaining a ward was starting to drain my power, particularly since I'm not at my best when the sun is out. Nick jumped a six-foot chain-link fence and landed on a beach littered with the detritus humans love to leave behind. Wrappers. Glass. Plastic bottles and bags. The tide was coming in. It would cover up some of the mess, but whatever got dragged into the ocean didn't solve anything. It just kicked the can down the road.

Mortals were pigs, and they'd done nothing but grow worse.

Crap. My mind was wandering. I reeled it in and scented the air. Kelpies—three of them—Clive, and Dee had stood in this very spot perhaps an hour-and-a-half before, but the track came to a crashing halt, almost as if the Kelpies had chosen this beach to obliterate their presence.

Nick skidded to a standstill. No one was anywhere near us, so he shelved telepathy and said, "The easy-to-follow part of their trail peters out here. I'm going to loose my ward. If we're quick about it, no one is near enough to notice."

"They must have gone somewhere." Dahlia sounded exasperated as the power concealing her dissipated.

"Probably teleported," I mumbled, grateful to not expend any more of my dwindling magic on mind speech or warding. "If Clive summoned them, somehow. Why can't we do the same?"

"I have no idea what he did," Nick admitted. "We lack names, which are essential to all the summoning castings I'm familiar with."

The raven hooted, sounding more like an owl. Dahlia glanced at it, and herb-saturated magic vibrated around them as they conversed. From the feel of it, they might have been arguing. I'd spent enough time around the bird to appreciate its keen intelligence. It might be bonded to Dahlia through some arcane witchy ritual, but he thought for himself—or perhaps herself.

The raven launched itself from Dahlia's shoulder, cawing up a storm before shooting skyward.

"What's he doing?" Nick asked.

Dahlia screwed her mouth into a worried expression. "First off, my familiar is female. All Witch familiars are. More Than Never is calling other birds. They may have seen the Kelpies, and it's a sure bet if there really are a hundred of them in the vicinity, some bird will know where they live."

I thought back to my conversation with a few Kelpies in the alley behind *Ascent.* "I believe they said that number was scattered along the western coastline."

"Doesn't matter," Dahlia retorted. "More than a single Kelpie would be cause for birds to sit up and take note. They're better than you think at keeping tabs on potential sources of food."

It took me a moment to make sense of what she meant. "So Kelpies don't eat all of what they kill?"

"Exactly." The Witch nodded. "They toss chopped up carcasses into shallow waters knowing full well predators will soon render them unrecognizable."

"Yeah well, I bet that's not working as well for them as it once did." I blew out an unneeded breath. "What with DNA testing, the cops don't require much of someone to ID them."

Nick wrapped a hand around my lower arm. His touch was both welcome and reassuring by turns. "Probably, the water horses are just doing what they've always done. They're not being kind by leaving spoils; neither are they being especially careful."

I nodded. It made sense. All of us had traditional

methods, techniques we'd learned along the way. The whirr of wings filled my ears. Where a single raven had left us, several dozen birds winged our way. Mostly gulls with the odd hawk mixed in.

Dahlia crouched in the sand; one by one birds landed forming a rough half circle in front of her. More Than Never resumed her spot on her mistress's shoulder. I glanced around us. While we three wouldn't have flagged anyone's attention, the avian conclave, reminiscent of a scene out of the movie, *The Birds*, would surely draw the click of someone's phone camera.

The birds cooed and chirped. Dahlia replied in kind. As the odd conversation played out, twin lines formed between her brows, and her eyes developed a pinched expression. As quickly as they'd come, the birds leapt upward, wings beating the air for purchase. Feathers fluttered around us.

"Well?" Nick asked after they'd left.

"There's a condemned aquarium perhaps half a mile south of here. Kelpies have claimed its lower level." Dahlia switched to telepathy.

Good call on her part since a young blonde woman toting a fancy camera with a huge lens ran toward us. "I got it all on video," she crowed, "with a few great stills mixed in. Are you a bird caller? Or bird whisperer? Or something like that?"

Dahlia rose to her feet and smiled pleasantly. "What's your name, child?"

The gal, who looked about eighteen, colored. "Laurie, and I'm scarcely a kid."

Dahlia raised her arms in front of her, fingers moving in

an intricate pattern. Rosemary and cinnamon thickened, along with the bite of Witch magic. "Laurie. You will forget everything you saw. Before you leave, you will erase the media card inside your camera. Do it now, and then you may go."

The girl's blue eyes widened as she fell into trance, pupils dilating. "Yes, Mistress," she murmured and bent over her camera. I heard the electronics hum as she erased her SDHC card. Moments later, she turned and walked toward the same fence we'd cleared to access the beach.

Dahlia dusted her hands together. "Should take care of that little problem," she said.

I didn't think it worth mentioning there may have been other, less obvious, photographers trolling the beach. "A lot of oddballs live in this region," I mumbled. "Probably no one would think twice about what you did."

"Eh, you never know. Better safe than sorry," Dahlia replied.

"Let's find that aquarium." Nick set a course down the beach. "What exactly is it?"

"A place where aquatic life is on display for the public to come through and gawk at," I told him.

He stopped walking long enough to turn and stare at me. "So a zoo, but for fish?"

"And otters and seals and octopi. Anything that either lives in the sea or eats from it," I clarified.

"Did more than one bird notice the Kelpies?" Nick asked Dahlia.

The witch nodded. "Yeah. Most all of them did. They're quite a spectacle once they turn into horses, and a condemned aquarium would be perfect since it's bound to have underground water channels they can access."

"Are we going to waltz in and demand they return Clive and Dee?" I asked.

"Not with three of us and goddess-only-knows how many of them," Dahlia replied.

"We'll go inside and see what develops," Nick said. "I'm looking forward to getting away from daylight, and they don't have a bone to pick with us."

A hulking gray building came into view. It was easy enough to see why it was closed. One corner had fallen in. Probably the foundation had eroded from long exposure to saltwater. The front door sported an enormous padlock.

Dahlia spoke a word that made my bones hurt, and the lock sprang loose. "Impressive," I said.

"Witches are not weak." She turned her green eyes on me. "Some of us could have done with more rigorous training, but we can accomplish more than most other mages believe possible. While we're at it. I am not leaving without Dee."

"Good to know," I muttered and followed her and Nick through the door. Freed from its lock, it creaked in the wind.

CHAPTER FIVE, NICKOLAS

A large open room with a rounded ceiling sported paper murals depicting different types of marine life. I started to call to Ariana to shut the door, but she pulled it closed. It might not stay that way minus its lock, but we wouldn't be here all that long.

I hoped.

The windowless interior was a welcome change from being outside. If I never saw daylight again, it would be too soon to please me, but I was being a prima donna. I'd do whatever I had to, today and in the future. The odds of my efforts not including trips during daylight hours were thin.

Before we had a chance to move beyond the foyer, I heard the clip-clop of horse hoofs. At least it simplified our task. We didn't have to find them or lure them out. I understood perfectly. If anyone unauthorized had entered my seethe, I'd have greeted them before they made any progress through my domain.

"So much for the element of surprise." Dahlia stopped and turned toward the sound of approaching horses. In one fluid motion, she whipped out her test tube and sprinkled its contents in a ragged line between us and the approaching Kelpie.

I'd hoped for a few moments to decide on a course of action. Part of me was furious at Clive for not just killing the cop and getting the fuck out of there. What had he been thinking to summon the Scottish water horses for a cozy spot of tea and crumpets?

Worse, why had Dee gone along with it? She might be smitten, but she was also level-headed. A necromancer Witch, she herded the dead, a task requiring patience.

I'd find out soon enough, and I quashed my first instinct, which was to leave Clive to chip his own way out of the mess he'd made. Two Kelpies pranced into view. They wore their men's bodies, and I had no idea if we'd talked with these two before. They all looked disturbingly alike. Rather akin to an endless batch of twins.

"You've come in search of your kin," one of the Kelpies said.

"We have," Dahlia concurred.

"You've gone to a lot of trouble for naught," the other Kelpie noted.

"Why?" Ariana asked. "Surely, you don't have any need for a Witch and a Vampire."

"We didn't believe we did," the first Kelpie said, "but the Vampire was enough of a wise-ass, we decided to incorporate both him and his wench."

"That would be Witch to you," Dahlia snapped. More

Than Never flew in circles above everyone's heads screeching her disapproval.

"Witch. Wench." The Kelpie shrugged. "They kind of sound the same."

"What exactly does incorporate mean?" I asked and withdrew my own test tube, ready for anything.

"What did it mean in your seethe?" the second Kelpie asked.

"That we'd turned them," I told him.

The Kelpie grinned at me, showing his squared-off teeth. "Smart Vampire. Smart in some ways, maybe not so bright in others."

"What are you inferring?" I wanted to throttle him, but anger wasn't my friend. Not when I needed a clear head.

"If the contents of the cylinder in your hand matches what Witchy-Babe spilled on the floor, don't bother."

"Aye," the other Kelpie cut in. "The lore is rife with Kelpie-antidotes, except none of them work."

Ariana sashayed closer, hips swinging. "Back to your, erm guests. We don't exactly understand," she purred. "Vampires are the only mages who drain and renew."

"Are you certain of that?" The Kelpie nearest her snaked a hand forward. She evaded his touch.

"Yeah," she said. "Quite certain."

"We're...experimenting," the other Kelpie said. "Or we will be once we've had a chance to study the problem."

More Than Never divebombed the Kelpie, beak aimed for one of his eyes. The Kelpie shouted an unintelligible word, and the raven changed course. After a few desultory flaps, she landed on Dahlia's shoulder.

The Witch strode until she stood toe tip to hoof with the Kelpie who'd mentioned experiments. "You will not subject my Witch to any of your machinations. Return her. Now."

"And if I choose not to?" The Kelpie was almost simpering, an odd display for such a bully-boy.

"There. Is. No. Choice." Dahlia inserted spaces between her words.

"What are you planning to do, Witch?" the other Kelpie sneered. "Sic your bird on us again? You saw how well it went the first time."

More Than Never clacked her beak a few times but didn't show any sign of leaving Dahlia's shoulder. What in the hell had happened when the Kelpie aimed magic her way?

"A word if I may?" I kept my tone smooth, civil.

"If you must, Vampire," the same Kelpie said.

If I'd needed to breathe, I'd have sucked in a breath and puffed it out long and slow. "I am asking you to forgive my kinsman. He is young and somewhat naïve. I have no idea what he did to annoy you, but I will accept a geas to set matters right. Surely, there's some boon I can provide you?" After inserting a pause, I added, "Dead bodies are rather my specialty."

A muted snarl from Ariana told me she did not approve of me groveling, but I wasn't. Not exactly. I was bartering. Everyone has a price. I was homing in on the Kelpies'.

"What if we wanted her?" The Kelpie Ariana had teased, pointed dead at her.

"I'm not for sale," Ariana growled. "Not to you or anyone."

"Nothing more to talk about, then," the other Kelpie said. "It's the female Vampire or nothing."

I closed the distance between him and me. "She is my mate," I thundered. "Pick something else."

Both Kelpies burst into braying laughter. My hands curled into fists; my fangs dropped. If Ariana hadn't made a grab for one of my arms, I'd have launched myself at the Scottish water horses, outcome be damned.

"You're lying," one of the Kelpies managed through snorts and whinnies. "Your kind doesn't pair bond any more than we do."

"It is unusual," Ariana said smoothly, "but Nickolas is my mate. Test my words with a truth casting if you don't believe me."

"We should not have to prove anything to them," I ground out through clenched teeth. "What in the fuck did Clive do to piss you off?"

The Kelpies exchanged glances. "Summoned us as if we answered to him."

"How is that different from what he did the first time he reached out to you?" I inquired as I worked to rein in my temper.

The Kelpie nearest me said, "The first time, we were intrigued."

"Plus, he had something we potentially wanted," the other one added.

"And this time?" Ariana furled both dark brows.

"He had the audacity to rebuke us for not being forthright with him." The Kelpie who'd answered pushed straight dark hair over his shoulders.

"Ha," the other Kelpie added. "As if Vampires are poster children for honesty."

Anger threatened to swamp me. Starting in my toes, it rolled through me like white-hot fire. If it hadn't been for Ariana's hand still clutching my biceps, I'd have forgotten our objective and hurled myself at him.

"You can dun us all you want," Ariana told him, "but we are aboveboard in our business dealings. It's only with mortals that our morals slip a wee bit."

"Humans aren't worth the skin bags that contain them," one of the Kelpies said.

"At last"—Ariana's voice was smooth, laced with a calming infusion—"we agree on something."

I was grinding my teeth together so hard my fangs were making divots in my chin. I retracted them and relaxed my jaw enough to say, "Let me be certain I have this straight. You didn't care for Clive's...message, so you took him and his Witch companion prisoner?"

"It's how we operate." The other Kelpie nodded as if to say, business as usual.

"Vampires don't exactly have much moral high ground to stand on," I began, weighing my words carefully, "but how about if we bring you a nice, newly dead mortal."

"How newly dead?" the first Kelpie asked.

"Piss on that." His companion rolled his odd eyes, so dark it was impossible to tell where iris and pupil met.

"What then?" I pressed. Everyone has a price. If I kept after it, they'd tell me theirs.

"Ten live mortals," he said, his gaze boring into me.

I narrowed my eyes. "Five, and we have a deal."

"Seven. Last and final offer," he said.

"Done." I stuck out a hand.

"Wait!" Dahlia squawked. "Where in the fuck will we find seven humans to sacrifice?"

I glanced her way. "We missed a few cops earlier tonight."

"So we did," she agreed. "Finding them could prove...difficult."

"Not our problem," the Kelpie who'd been bartering with me said.

"A deal is a deal," the other one chortled.

I felt them draw power to leave and cried, "Hold it right there."

"You don't order us about," one blustered.

"Aye, it's how your clansman fucked himself," the other added.

"Point of clarification," I said. "We bring you live humans, and you release our companions immediately."

"You're no fun," one of the Kelpies muttered.

"That was the agreement," I told him.

While he was dithering, probably questing about for some caveat I wouldn't like, the distinctive feel of Conan's magic filled the large, empty chamber. This was one of those times the guardian didn't bother with a portal. He simply shot through a gap in the ether, landing on all four feet. Hackles raised, he growled menacingly.

"Guardian." One of the Kelpies almost bowed. Guardians had that effect on everyone.

"What is this crap?" Conan demanded and snarled louder.

"We engaged in a bit of creative negotiating," the other Kelpie replied. "Everyone is delighted with the outcome, and—"

Conan woofed, drowning him out. "Release the Witch and Vampire now."

"But we haven't received our promised spoils," the Kelpie protested.

"Are you suggesting my associates aren't honorable?" Conan showed a whole lot of teeth.

"Nay. Of course not, guardian."

"Go get them," Conan continued. "Or I will release them myself."

"No need to get riled," the Kelpie said. The air thickened and filled with the salty tang of the North Sea. When it cleared, Clive and Dee ran toward us.

Dee threw her arms around Dahlia. "I am so sorry."

"Apologize later," Dahlia snapped. The scent of an herbal infusion replaced the mineral smells of the sea.

Ariana understood they were leaving and called, "Meet at the club around six," after their dissolving forms.

"We should get going too," I told her, fully aware we had work to do before we could teleport back to *Ascent*.

"What about our side of the bargain?" one of the Kelpies demanded.

"You'll get your sacrifices," Conan said. "They might not still be alive, but you'll get them."

"Not nearly as much fun," the other Kelpie groused.

"Maybe not," Conan told him, "but they're still food. No need to play with your entrée before you eat it."

The analogy was depressingly similar to what we did

before we drained someone. I turned to Clive. He was staring at the floor. "I'm sorry," he mumbled. "I miscalculated. If we still had a clan house, you'd have every right to toss me out."

An idea percolated, and I said, "How about if you apologize to the Kelpies?"

His head snapped up, neck corded, jaw tight. I saw in his blue eyes he'd rather die than abase himself to a Kelpie, but it had merely been a suggestion, not an order. I followed it up with, "You've caused us a hell of a lot of unnecessary trouble, Clive."

"Aye. I get that part," he said. Rolling his shoulders back, he turned to face the Kelpies. "I, um, I'm sorry. My attitude was not the best."

"Try inexcusable," the nearest Kelpie advised.

Clive nodded. "I didn't think I was that bad, but I can see where you would have. I was put out because I felt used, but it didn't give me a right to ride in on a high horse. No pun intended." A muscle danced in his clenched jaw. "I am very sorry. I put my clan lord and his mate at risk, and a Witch I care very much for."

"What is this?" One of the Kelpies shook his thick, unkempt head of black hair. "The Vampires I've known don't love anything but blood and lots of sex."

"Kind of like us," the other Kelpie snickered.

"Aye, well perhaps we're evolving." Clive shrugged. Turning to me, he added, "I will provide whatever you promised them."

"How about this?" the first Kelpie said. "One live mortal, and the slate will be clean."

"Done." Clive summoned a teleport spell.

I clamped down on a spate of directions. Clive had made a grave error when he attempted to hold the Kelpies to answer for what he considered quite the shortcoming. Because he was still treading shame-filled water, he'd be especially careful coming up with the Kelpies' plaything.

Still growling, Conan trotted to the Scottish water horses. "It pains me to say this, but we must continue our alliance. You are not done with that obligation."

"Not a problem, guardian," one of them said.

"Aye, we had a fine old time tonight," the other cut in. "Let us know when the next battle is."

A portal formed. Clive emerged with an unconscious man dressed in a uniform slung over one shoulder. He dumped it in front of the Kelpies.

"Where'd you find him so fast?" Ariana asked.

"Went back to my target's house. I figured other cops would be there to check on her, and I wasn't wrong."

"You got lucky," I told him.

He displayed a smile laced with a flash of his old cockiness. "After the rest of tonight, mate, wouldn't you say it's about time my luck started running on the good side of the fence?"

"We're not done with this topic," I told him. "Did anyone see you?"

Clive shook his head. "Probably scared the pants off them when that bloke"—he jerked his chin at the comatose officer—"vanished from their midst."

"Means no mages were amongst them," Ariana spoke up. "Or they'd have cut right through your illusion."

"Feel free to stick around," one of the Kelpies said, "but we're off to enjoy our gift."

"How will we find you?" I asked.

"He knows." The nearest Kelpie flapped a hand in Clive's direction before hefting the cop over one shoulder and clip-clopping out of the room.

"We're leaving too," Conan said. The unique prick of his power surrounded the four of us as he herded us back to *Ascent*.

"Things got better after you showed up," Ariana said to Conan.

"Did they?" the wolf woofed. "I didn't notice."

She hooked an arm around his thick, furry neck. "You wouldn't have since you weren't there before. It appears they respect guardians."

"Aye, and the rest of us can piss up a rope," I muttered half under my breath.

"Most mages recognize our magic as superior," Conan said. "But that isn't the issue here. The Kelpies trust us."

"Why?" Clive asked.

"Because we allowed them to live when we had the opportunity to wipe them out. It was long ago, but immortals have deep memories. Much like today, we struck a bargain with them. They'd been experimenting with a few mage-lines as breeding stock. We put a stop to it. The agreement was they'd stick with mortal women."

"What they do with them isn't all that swift," Ariana grumbled.

"Conan shook his shaggy head. "Humans aren't our province. Kelpies don't produce very many young, and the odd woman who vanishes, sacrificed on the altar of continuing the Kelpie line, isn't especially important."

I agreed with him. My view of mortals had shifted from a partially symbiotic relationship to seeing them as a scourge. A quick glance at a wall-mounted clock told me it was late afternoon. I wanted a spot of time with Clive before I did anything further. Crooking a finger, I said, "We're going to that flat you rented."

Ariana looked from me to him. "Can you be back here in an hour?"

"Probably sooner than that," I told her and launched a teleport spell. I'd stopped by the flat a time or two since Clive rented it, but I had yet to spend a night there. The apartment took shape around us.

"Look, mate, I already said I was sorry. To you and the Kelpies." Clive cast a diffident look my way. Except I knew him well enough to recognize rebellion simmering beneath the surface.

"Whatever were you thinking?" I kept my voice quiet. The old me, the one who'd been a master Vampire, would have been up in his face yelling. Or worse, draining him enough to make him remember why it was good to follow orders.

Clive squared his shoulders. "Vampires should have equal standing with any mage. Hell's beacons, Kelpies are on everybody's blacklist. They even make us look good. I kept coming back to how they'd played me, and it didn't sit well. Dee and I kicked it around."

"Surely, she didn't think hunting them down was a good idea," I broke in.

"Nay, she didn't, but she stuck by me." He frowned. "Dahlia looked angry."

"She was," I affirmed. "Dee is part of her coven. It's not so different from being part of a seethe."

"Should I say something to Dahlia?"

"Probably wouldn't hurt, but your injured pride is a low priority."

"Aye. I get that." He clasped his hands behind his back. "What's our next objective? Will we be returning and picking off the ones we missed last night?"

"I don't think so. We killed around a thousand."

Clive whistled. "Dee and I were wondering about that. How many did we lose?"

"Two that I know of."

"Excellent. We did better than I thought we would."

I nodded slowly. By anyone's estimation, last night had been a stunning rout for the opposition. "The part that bothers me most is how entrenched mages are in human affairs. My target was surrounded by twenty immortals including a guardian."

Shock widened Clive's blue eyes. "A guardian, you say? How'd that go over with the other ones?"

"Predictably." My tone was dry. "But were it not for their assistance, we'd have failed to secure our assignment. As it was, he escaped in one of those winged craft things and somehow survived even after we'd shot it out of the sky."

"What happened then?"

"Conan moved him to another spot and finished him off."

"At least that last makes sense, but we slept too long," Clive mumbled.

While I agreed with him, there wasn't much we could do to alter the situation—other than soaking up every detail as fast as we could. "Our target was the head of the task force," I went on. "Ariana was pretty sure he was on the take because his house was so grand."

"You mean accepting bribes? Officials have been doing that since money was invented," Clive noted sourly.

"Aye. It's exactly what I meant." I switched gears. "How'd you raise the Kelpies?"

"Fair enough. First time, it was sheer, blind luck. I traveled to the ocean and sat in the sand watching the waves. It's not new for me. I used to sneak away from my blacksmith chores to the shoreline. The North Sea is wild and unpredictable. Watching its ebb and flow reminded me not to get too caught up in my day-to-day miseries. And gave me the courage to stow away on a barge headed for southern waters."

"So that's how you got to Italy."

"In a series of hops and jumps, aye," he said. "Back to the Kelpies. They hide themselves in the surf, but if I used my third eye, I could find them well enough. Several were slicing through the waves, braying like donkeys and spewing brine. I walked nearer and invited them to talk with me."

"That was when you made assumptions that didn't pan out." I sent a pointed glance his way.

"Aye, but it was also when they told me which telepathic frequency would work to talk with them. At that time, I had no idea they were going to show up at the club." He jimmied a stone from a pocket. It resembled the one Percy had been given last night in the park.

"Telepathy, but with a few add-ons," I noted.

Clive nodded.

"Ready to get back to *Ascent*?

His irresistible grin formed. "That's it? No thirty lashes at dusk? Or a vestal virgin's blood?"

I grinned back. "Don't tempt me. I've always wanted to find one of those vestal virgins. Their blood is supposed to be ambrosial."

"Mind if I try to run Dee down before I show up?"

"So long as you don't take too long about it," I cautioned.

"I won't. Just want to see if she's still pissed at me."

I started to tell him he could charm the socks off anyone, but held my tongue. Clive was going into this relationship in a one-down position because there was never any love lost between Witches and Vamps. He knew as much, but it hadn't deterred him.

"She must be quite special."

"She is to me. See you soon, mate."

I wandered around the flat for a few minutes thinking about Ariana and *Ascent*. It would be closed for six more nights. I didn't think it would be enough time, but maybe I'd be surprised.

I was just readying myself to leave, after changing out of my borrowed garments into something that fit me better, when the musky wildflower scent of Ariana bombarded me.

"Darling. What a pleasant surprise." Scooping her into my arms, I kissed her. After a perfunctory kiss back, she wriggled out of my grasp.

"Not so pleasant, or I wouldn't have come after you. Conan had it out with the guardians," she said.

"And?" I girded myself for the worst.

"They blamed him for Darksword's defection."

"How? That doesn't make any sense."

"Yeah, well it gets even murkier. Apparently, Conan challenged Fairclaw to the magical equivalent of a duel when Fairclaw gave him a raft of shit. Conan won, and now his kin are demanding he take his rightful place at the helm. Meanwhile, Fairclaw formed his own contingent and is vowing revenge, and—"

"Whoa." I held up a hand. "Their timing is terrible. We can't afford to get sidetracked by an internecine war. What's Conan going to do?"

"Not sure, but I wanted you nearby—in case something unexpected happened."

"Like what?"

Her fangs had dropped; it told me how unsettled she was. "I have no bloody, fucking idea," she said. Magic built around her as she readied a travel spell. *Ascent* was plenty close enough to walk, and dusk had fallen.

"Let's walk," I suggested. "Good opportunity to clear our heads, and it won't be but a few minutes longer."

She dismantled her casting, and I followed her out the door, locking it behind us. Not that there was much in the flat worth stealing, but I didn't need any additional complications—like tracking down a thief and making him sorry he'd ever been born.

I was worried about Conan, more worried than I'd let on to Nick. Part of my anxiety stemmed from the years when I'd mothered him. He hadn't actually needed me then, neither did he need my protection now, but I couldn't turn off my caring and concern for my longtime companion. My brother in everything but blood. I could see advantages to him taking over as prince of the guardians. Maybe. It depended on how much cooperation he could gin up.

If Fairclaw was going to subvert him at every turn, the first few years would be a rocky tenure. By then, we'd have either won or lost the war with mortals. Part of me felt selfish for resenting anything that diverted Conan's attention away from fighting. The group needed him. We were stronger together. The other half of my brain was quick to step in and correct me.

Not selfish. Not at all. If humans prevail and magic dies, nothing will be left for anyone, magical or not.

Clive hadn't been at the flat when I'd gone after Nick. I wanted to ask how their meeting had gone, but it wasn't my affair. Yeah, I was still partially sunk in our old ways, but Vampire clans kept to themselves, and Clive was blood-bound to Nick's seethe. From the looks of things, Dahlia had been far more perturbed about Dee's role in the Kelpie mess than Nick was about Clive's.

I knew less than nothing about the inner workings of a coven. Did Dahlia have the power to force Dee away from Clive? So long as Clive's interest in the Witch was genuine, I hoped not. I rolled my mental eyes at how far afield I was getting. This was so not my business.

My own liaison with Nick had yet to be tested. We'd said most of the right words, but as Vampires we lacked any type of ceremonial ritual to bind us together. We could get married the way mortals did, but it didn't feel right to borrow customs from creatures we held in contempt.

We landed in *Ascent's* main room. It was rapidly filling with exuberant mages. They had every right to be jubilant. We'd struck three significant blows in quick succession. The question was what we'd do for an encore. And the one after that and the one after that. Last night had made it painfully clear we needed a fully formed battle plan.

"Are you all right?" Nick asked near my ear.

"Yes in some ways. No in others."

"Know what you mean." He dropped an arm across my shoulders; I leaned into him.

Percy stormed through the front door, a mixture of worry

and anger streaming from him. I remembered McMurdy's computer. And the magical scanner. Percy's plate had been more than full, and it appeared he hadn't exactly been rolling box cars.

The Sorcerer's gaze fell on Nick and me, and he pointed at the stockroom. I got the picture and bolted that way with Nick right next to me. Percy dragged the door shut and draped a sound screen around us. Interesting. Clearly, he wanted to shield our conversation, even from the other mages pouring into the club.

"The computer was a find," he said without preamble. "Question is what we do with the information. It's deucedly disquieting."

"Tough for me to imagine anything worse that what we already know," I said and girded myself. Usually, Vampires don't use labels like "good" or "bad" when it comes to information. We just float with the punches. All my years in close proximity to mortals must have made me soft.

No more. I was done thinking like a human. Fuck them all.

"Whatever this is, let's hear it." Nick stood straight. I was proud of him. His let-the-good-times-roll attitude reinforced my resolve to be a Vampire first. Everything else would fall into line if I could remember that part and put it into action.

"A very quiet workgroup was formed nine years back," Percy began. "It included the leaders of every major country and their top genetic scientists. For the first year, they hunted—unsuccessfully I might add—for an antidote to magic. Something they could sprinkle on us from planes that would render us powerless."

"What?" I sputtered. "That's worse than that stupid scanner."

"Aye, the scanner was a fallback arrangement, but let me tell this in order," Percy said. "Once they failed to concoct an antidote, they moved to spying on many mages for the purpose of ferreting out a way to force their cooperation. Many died rather than sign on as agents who would spell destruction for their own kind, but there are always weak links."

He blew out a tense breath before continuing. "It was the beginning of mages perverting their own magic to destroy others with power. Witches were of particular interest because—"

"Of their charms," Nick cut in sourly, followed by, "Sorry, I'll shut up."

Percy nodded. "Aye. The charms were a real draw. It didn't take too many threats before Witches were on government payrolls all over the world. The workgroup is still meeting regularly. That's one scrap of good news because we can launch an attempt to infiltrate the discussions."

"So it's all part of the same strategy?" Nick sounded furious. And incredulous. "When Roseann told me about mages working for humans in Europe, I assumed they were freelancing, separate from our problem on this side of the Atlantic."

"Pfft. Wouldn't it have been peachy," Percy mumbled.

"How often do they meet?" I asked.

"Quarterly for the large group," Percy replied, "but there

are smaller subsections that meet monthly. One holds conference calls each week."

"Let's get moving hacking into that one. You can manage it, right?" My computer skills weren't up to it, but Percy's might be.

He shook his head, dashing that hope. "I can try, but it's remote. My guess is they're shielded both electronically and with magic."

"What does the weekly group do?" Nick asked.

"They monitor data from the scanners that are rolling out, which brings me to my next point. I didn't suddenly fall into a pit of extra time, but the scanner problem rose to the top like rotten cream. I admit I was curious after I ran a few experiments with the one Dee got hold of. It won't be overly hard to design a spell to shield us from it."

"But?" I spun one hand in a circle. I knew Percy well enough to recognize he'd left a few things out.

"The spell is a real power hog. Only a few of the strongest of us will be able to manage it and still have magic left over to do anything."

"How long before an average mage would run dry?" Nick narrowed his eyes in thought.

"Maybe an hour, which would be enough to move away from the scanner, but the most critical part is I need to design an alarm that senses when we're approaching one of the infernal things."

"Is that possible?" I asked.

"Aye. But only because of a couple of the flash drives Nick gave me. They have the schematics, all the elements contained in the design."

"So you didn't actually need the scanner itself?" I sought clarification.

"Not really, but it's always good to have a prototype to run tests on."

I absorbed what he'd said. No wonder the cavalry had shown up in force to make certain McMurdy's computer and peripherals didn't fall into the wrong hands. Like ours, for example.

"We have to tell everyone." Nick spoke slowly. "It will alter our next steps."

"Will it?" Percy angled his bushy brows upward. "The way I see it, we have a few additional tasks on our plates, but we have to keep on keeping on. If we back down now, humans will assume they won."

"Which wouldn't be so bad," I said. "We could simply wait them out were it not for their pet mages."

"If we keep kicking holes in their ranks in this country," Nick said, "it might have a trickle-down effect on other nations aligned with the U.S."

"You can bet they know what happened here," Percy said. "With the communications network they have in place, an alarm probably sounded around the globe right after we broke those New Age mages out of lockup."

A sharp knock pounded on the stockroom door. Without bothering to wait for us to answer, Ruby twisted the knob and stood in the doorway staring at us. "What the hell? Did someone die?"

"We'll be right out," Percy told her.

"Good. Everyone's waiting. By the way. Where's Conan?"

"Not sure." Damn it. He'd left again.

I expected Ruby to hound us for details about why we looked so apprehensive. Instead, she turned and walked back into the club, heels clicking on the wooden floor. Smart Fae. Some news can wait.

"I'll tell everyone what I found out," Percy said in a flat, no-nonsense tone. "Many minds are better than a few in this instance."

"Fine with me," Nick agreed. "I'm still figuring out how to leverage your new information."

Percy strode past us; the buzz of his deep voice told me he'd begun talking. "That weekly phone meeting," I said, keeping my voice low.

"What about it?" Nick turned to me.

"We need to find out who's on it that's reasonably close to us."

A corner of his mouth twitched. "We ambush them and take their place."

I nodded. "Yup. About the size of it. Might not be as simple as all that, but it seems doable."

"If Percy has a list of participants, it would help." Nick had adopted his thoughtful expression, which meant his mind was clicking along at a mile a minute.

"He must. Otherwise, he wouldn't have known about the meeting schedule at all," I offered hopefully. Pretending to be someone else had a bunch of potential pitfalls, particularly if the group employed voice tracings. If I was in charge of security, I'd have put some fail-safes into operation to ensure the integrity of the discussion.

Except it appeared the group had formed years back,

maybe not this weekly one, but people got sloppy after time passed and nothing untoward cropped up.

"Ariana," Nick was saying.

I gathered my far-ranging thoughts and focused on him. "This thing is big enough, we have to alert other Vampires," he said. "Even if they don't want to help out—and they may well not—it's their right to know how close to the edge of annihilation we're treading."

"Do you have a way to reach Roseann?" A flash of jealousy stabbed me out of nowhere. It had zero placc here, so I quashed it as best I could.

He shook his head. "I asked for a cell number, but she said it was better if we made a clean break of things." His beautiful mouth took on a wry expression. "Particularly considering I'm a wanted man in Europe."

"There is that," I agreed. We moved into the main part of the club in time to hear the last part of Percy's talk. For once, silence reigned. I got it. The whole specter of being spied on —and for nearly a decade—was creepier than hell. Maybe a list of all of us resided on one of the flash drives. Surely, Percy wouldn't have had time to look at them all. Not with everything else he'd been doing.

Dahlia stepped forward. I scanned for Dee's energy and was relieved to find her at a table with half a dozen other Witches, presumably sisters from her coven. Whatever had passed between her and Dahlia didn't include her being sequestered in the guild house.

"While your message is annoying and unnerving," Dahlia said in her smooth contralto voice, "it changes nothing, other than now we know more about the parameters of what stands against us. We threw down a gauntlet when we broke those mages out of lockup. We have to keep the pressure up, or all our hard work will have been for nothing."

A thunderous wave of assent rolled through the club. It provided a focus. We'd deal with punishing those responsible for the complicated plot to destroy us either by proxy—as we murdered their foot soldiers. Or maybe not at all. It was tempting to react, but the coven mistress had a level head.

When the furor died down, Nick glided to the front of the room and stood next to Percy. "This may not sit well with most of you, but we need all the help we can muster," he told the group. "I'm going to rustle up as many Vampires as I can find for whatever we choose to do next."

"We need a whole lot of nexts," Percy broke in. "At least three more targets. Ideas, people?"

If I'd been mortal, I'd have exhaled slowly. No one pitched a fit about Nick's announcement. I saw a few grimaces, but they vanished fast. Mmph. Maybe the others were more used to us than I'd imagined. It felt odd to view myself as an ambassadress of goodwill for my kind, but we needed all the breaks that fell our way.

Side conversations had blossomed. Figuring out what to do next wasn't easy. We'd pretty much ridden the paranormal task force horse into the ground. The other ones scattered around the country would be nailed down like Fort Knox. Besides, we'd proven a point by dismantling two of them. We needed something bigger.

Something new.

I scrabbled behind the bar for a marker and trotted to a

whiteboard hanging near the entrance. Usually, it contained the evening's beverage specials. "Toss out possibilities," I shouted encouragement. "I'll write them down."

Twenty minutes later, we had quite a list, but the candidates fell into distinct categories. I whistled to get everyone's attention. Once the group quieted somewhat, I raised my voice and pointed to the board. "Nice work, everyone," I said. "We have communications targets, government targets, and financial institutions."

"Communications, first," Ruby yelled.

"Aye, then finance," Percy spoke up.

"Government last?" I scanned the crowd and saw heads nodding.

Christa, a seer for the Fae, sat on the bar, legs dangling. She angled her head and asked, "Government, as in DC?"

"Aye," Percy answered her. "Not much point mucking about with local institutions." He paused to take a measured breath. "But once we're thorough knocking out communications networks—including all the cell phone providers—and dismantling banks, we may not need to converge on Washington."

"We get the money, right?" Ruby's wings fluttered with excitement, her fascination with gold shining through loud and clear.

"Evenly divided, Fae." A Shifter sidled to where Ruby stood and locked gazes with her.

"Stuff it," I shouted. "No point haggling over something we don't yet have."

"Yeah," the Shifter—a youngish-appearing man with white hair, sky-blue eyes, and a rangy build—replied. "But it's good to get the bones of these things tacked down ahead of time. Especially when Fae are involved."

Ruby hissed at him before she said, "Love you too, dickwad."

"Communications, people." Percy pounded a huge hand on one of my new wall panels. It made a hollow booming sound that shut everyone up fast. Once he had what looked like undivided attention, he ticked items off on his fingers. "Internet. Phone systems. Television. Radio."

"Post office," a Witch called.

"Eh, they're on their way out, anyway," Ruby answered.

"Well, if they're all that's left, they won't be," the Witch countered.

"Good point," Ruby acceded.

I offered her kudos for knowing which beach to bleed on. Clearly the USPS wasn't it.

"There aren't more than a dozen primary Internet service providers in the U.S.," Percy said. If we start with them and sabotage the main fiber optic cable trunks, it should create enough panic to make a point."

"How will they know it was us?" Dahlia asked.

"I'm planning to crash one of their weekly phone meetings," I told her. "While they're reeling, I can toss out something subtle like maybe mages are turning on them, er us."

Percy turned his blue gaze on me. "It's exceedingly dangerous, Ariana. For one thing, if they figure out you're not whomever you're impersonating, the electronics can lead them right to you."

He'd brought up a particularly good point. "Erm,

yeah. I'd have to do this before all the ISPs went dark. Or the group wouldn't have a way to finesse their meeting." I turned a ten-thousand watt smile his way. "Maybe we could leave whichever one they're using for last?"

"Or we could wait until you're done," he told me. "Easier that way."

"What about the scanners?" Dee asked. "If we're going to be out in the field chopping through fiber optic cable trunks, which are enormous, we run the risk of discovery before we've done much damage."

Percy started to say something, but Nick held up a hand. "I was thinking about the scanners. Rather than each of us launching individual protections, isn't there some mechanism that would simply disable them? Perhaps not permanently, but for some period of time?"

Conan melted out of shadows. I had no idea how long he'd been here, or if he'd only just arrived. "Guardians will manage the scanners. They have a particular noxious scent that we can detect."

"Can you knock them out of action?" Nick asked.

"We should be able to, but it's important to make certain no more are produced."

"I know where they're making them," a Witch from a Nevada coven that had disbanded called. "Tried to break in there, but there was too much metal."

As soon as she mentioned it, I remembered the tale she'd told. She'd gone after a prototype intent on examining it, but failed to obtain one.

"Tell me." Conan lifted his snout in her direction. Once

she was done describing a warehouse on the outskirts of Las Vegas, he said, "Is it the only place?"

She shrugged. White hair rippled around her shoulders. "Maybe not, but it will put a hole in their plans."

Conan turned and walked through a slash in the ether that absorbed him.

"What's he going to do?" the Witch asked.

"Destroy the building," I told her. "He made short work of a maximum security prison that was mostly underground, so he shouldn't have any trouble with a warehouse."

"How do we know the other guardians will buy in to his offer about the scanners?" Dahlia asked.

I hesitated, not wanting to say anything about Conan or his possible new role in guardian circles. She was waiting for an answer, so I settled on, "I trust him. He wouldn't have said he could do something if it weren't within his ken." My reply seemed to satisfy her.

"Back to the ISPs and fiber optics," Percy said. "While the lot of you were talking, I compiled a list and identified the primary fiber optic trunks in the country. There are a few more than I'd expected, but nothing we can't handle."

I waited while he assigned mages to several work groups before I tapped his arm and asked, "Where'd you leave the electronics from McMurdy's?"

"At Rob's. He's still working on them." Percy turned so we faced away from the others. "Are you certain you want to do this?"

"Yeah. Damned certain. Maybe we'll learn something."

He narrowed his eyes. "Let's see. The weekly meeting will be tomorrow afternoon, Eastern time. It's that one or nothing because I want those ISPs well on their way to ruin long before next week rolls around."

"Got it."

"Where will you do this?" Percy nailed me with his inscrutable gaze.

"Not *Ascent*. Not my home." I chewed my lower lip, feeling the press of fangs.

"Also not your usual computers," he reminded me.

And then I recalled my original plan. "I'll figure out which of the contingent is female and close enough for me to slip into her home and take her place."

The big Sorcerer nodded tersely. "No halfways, Ariana. Kill who you have to and get in and out clean. Will Nick be with you?"

I shook my head. "Gotta do this one myself. Besides, Nick's hunting down other Vampires."

"Best to you. I'm as close as telepathy if you run into trouble."

"Maybe. Depends how far away I am. I'll let you know what happens."

Percy turned back to his emerging work groups, and I found Nick. He'd been talking with Clive. "I'm out of here," I told them.

"Not by yourself, you're not," Nick said firmly.

"Yeah. This time I'm going solo. You have a job to do. So do I. We'll connect once we're done."

He threaded his arms around me and kissed me once, hot, hard, and full of promise. When he lifted his mouth from mine, he said, "Do not take chances."

I grinned and stepped from his embrace. "I'm a Vampire.

Chances define us. Best of luck finding more Vamps. Bunches of us are scattered through the States, but you might want to start in New Orleans. My job will be done by tomorrow night. I'll meet you either here or at home."

"Might take me longer than that," Nick cautioned.

"Do you have a plan?" I asked.

Clive nodded. "The basic structure, aye. Nick thought Clan Ravnos would want to know some of their ilk had gone rogue."

I thumped his chest with an index finger. "The not taking risks goes both ways. There's a good chance Clan Ravnos gave their blessing to anything that would throw human blood their way."

"Vampires in Louisiana would scarcely benefit from sheep on this side of the country," Nick said. "We'll exercise due caution, though."

"There's a good chance other clans know something about what's going on," Clive cut in. "The days when we closeted ourselves in clan houses are long gone."

"True enough," I replied. "But the only clan left besides Ravnos is Tremere. Clan Hawke and Clan Giovanni are ancient history."

Before I could change my mind, or lose myself in another kiss, I pulled magic, intent on teleporting to Rob's small studio. With Clive's and Nick's admonitions to watch my back ringing in my ears, the nightclub shimmered to nothing, replaced by Rob's cluttered living room.

"Humph. Wondered when one of you would show up," he mumbled. Garbed in his usual faded dungarees and flannel work shirt, he sported a full beard that was mostly black with silvery strands mixed in. His dark curls were cropped short and surrounded his head like a corona.

I shook off the dregs of my spell and positioned myself to look over his shoulder. Rob wasn't much of a talker, so he'd appreciate me reading and drawing my own conclusions.

He tapped the display with an index finger. "Here. Right here is more than enough to make me want to start slinging power around."

"Yup. I want all of these fuckers dead too. Did you find the drive with their meeting notes or schedules or composition?"

"Aye. What are you planning?"

"Better if you don't know."

He cast a sidelong glance my way out of bloodshot pale-blue eyes, scrabbled through a pile of flash drives, and handed me one. I had no idea how he figured out which was which. They all looked the same. "Read through this first," he said gruffly and tapped his monitor once more. "Then you can decide what you want to do next."

"If you're trying to dissuade me—" I began.

"Wouldn't dream of it," he cut in dryly. "But it's wise to know as much as possible about what we face."

His words made me ashamed of my bristly outburst. I was already in position, so I began at the top of the screen determined to glean what I could from the purloined drives.

CHAPTER SEVEN, NICKOLAS

The stench of rotting vegetation surrounded us. I'd done my best, but I'd teleported Clive and me into a swamp. The ruins of what had once been a manor house rose a few meters away. Vines and thickets grew up and over walls that had once been cream-colored.

The air was damp, heavy, and sticky. Insects buzzed, but they didn't bother me. With the unerring instinct common to living creatures, the flies and mosquitoes knew we were dead. I could see where it would deter mosquitoes, but flies loved to lay their eggs in dead flesh. Perhaps they saw us as an exotic no-man's land. Not exactly dead, but not alive enough to bother biting—or nesting in. Regardless, them leaving us be was a plus.

We squished through knee-deep water angling toward the plantation house. I figured it had to have a road on its other side. A spot we could get our bearings and scan for other Vampires. The muted snap of jaws reminded me alligators trolled these waters. Unlike insects, they'd consider us fair game.

Until we ripped a few heads off.

Clive chugged ahead and up steps to what remained of a wraparound veranda. Tugging off one boot at a time, he poured water out of them. "What do we really know about Clan Ravnos?" he asked. "Other than their general reputation for being nasty."

"Not much," I admitted as I emptied my own boots and put them back on. "But their clan is apparently still intact, which is more than I can say for ours or Clan Hawke."

"True enough. Where should we look first?" Clive squeezed water out of his lower pant legs. I did the same. The material was heavy, and it would take a while to dry. A long while in this hot, damp climate.

"Maybe we won't have to search for them," I told him. "I'm hungry. Let's kill something. It will serve two functions."

"Brilliant! We get dinner, and it might draw them because we're poaching."

"Exactly," I replied. "If we get lucky, they'll hustle on over to chase us off." I made my way around the house, climbing over fallen trees and stomping through thick, gnarly vines with long thorns.

Clive leapt over the last swathe of greenery to a dirt road, muttering, "Finally."

"New Orleans, the city part, isn't anything like this," I told him and spun a net to lure game. Regardless of whether the Clan Ravnos Vamps came running, everything went better after fresh blood.

A pile of carcasses grew as we fanged whatever walked into my snare. After a time when we simply fed, Clive lifted his mouth from a large snake and said, "You're worried about her, aren't you?"

I didn't have to ask who he meant. "Aye. Of course I'm worried."

"What exactly is she doing?" Clive tossed the snake aside and upped the hypnotic waves flowing from him, waiting for the next candidate to cross his path.

"Pretending to be someone else."

Clive nodded. "Seems like it would be simpler now than it used to be. Given you can hide behind an electronic wall."

"Except she has to do away with the one she's impersonating," I pointed out.

"So? She'll be eating better than us." Clive offered a bloody smile.

The snap of large jaws was suddenly much louder. I'd been crouched over a scraggly rodent, but jumped to my feet, grabbed one of the creatures I'd drained, and tossed it toward the noise. Scales rustling over branches added to the clank of teeth gnashing together.

"What are they?" Clive asked.

"Alligators. Let's knock them out. It's easier than feeding them."

The dank air thickened with our mesmerism casting, and a thick purple river flowed outward. Claws scrabbling on wood told me the opportunists were scaling the steps, following our path around the falling-down mansion. Sure enough, a snout shot toward us. Long and menacing with a million teeth and small eyes set off to the sides.

Clive whistled. "Damned impressive. Never seen one outside of pictures in books."

The lead alligator almost made it to the road before he collapsed, head lolling, jaws still snapping weakly. Five more heaved themselves through the dense vegetation behind him before succumbing to the same fate.

I bent to run my fingertips over the closest one's scaly hide, impressed by its bulk and sheer killing potential. "I suppose they thought they'd get a free meal."

"Speaking of free meals," a voice laced with acid said, "you're on Clan Ravnos land."

I spun toward the voice in time to see four Vampires saunter through the mist. Three men and a woman sashayed forward. I had no idea what the allure of leather was, but this batch were dressed much like the Kelpies had been with leather pants, high boots, and vests that hung to hip level. Black shirts peeked from beneath the vests.

"Since when do Vampires wear uniforms?" Clive asked. The question could have been innocent were it not for the mocking tone in his voice.

I winced. Not the best foot to lead with. I started to approach them, but thought better of it and said, "I am Nickolas Giovanni. Clive is part of my clan."

"From everything we've heard, your clan died out half a century ago," one of the male Vampires said. He didn't offer a name, and I didn't ask.

"Unfortunately, your information is correct." I bobbed my head. "About a hundred years ago, I came to the States with two clansmen hunting for new recruits. We ended up in stasis to escape dark sorcery. I didn't realize my clan had been set upon until quite recently."

"Are you looking for a new affiliation?" the woman purred. Pheromones wafted from her as she tested the waters.

"Nay. Appreciate the offer, but we have news and a request," Clive said.

"They can wait," the woman said firmly and glided closer to Clive, her intent crystal clear. We've never been shy about public sex, and she wouldn't have even bothered moving out of sight of the rest of us.

I waited to see what Clive would do. A quick fuck wasn't exactly on the schedule, but I could use the time to talk with the other Vampires. He turned the full power of his charm on the woman. "So flattered, lassie, but I'm promised to another."

Her warm smile faded; the tips of her fangs retreated. "Bullshit," she said succinctly. "We don't roll that way."

"Our clan always was different." Clive managed to sound both proud and sorry rolled into one. "Nick is mated to another Vampire, and I'm as good as mated to a Witch."

"Pfft." The female Vampire flapped a hand Clive's way. "Passing infatuation. You'll get over it, and I know exactly how to speed things up." She pulled her vest open, but before she could drop it onto the ground, Clive shook his head.

"You're exceptionally beautiful, darling. Perhaps if I'd met you first... But I didn't."

"Get back here, Laura." One of the men snapped his fingers.

She trained dark eyes crackling with irritation his way, but eventually she complied, stomping toward her clanmates.

"Why are you here?" one of the other men asked.

"Two reasons," I told him. "We're gearing up for several major confrontations with mortals. If we don't take a stand, they'll keep right on co-opting mages to do their bidding."

"Not our assessment," the Vampire retorted. "Humans come. Humans go. This batch will get over their false impressions soon enough."

"They've developed a scanner that identifies mages," Clive added.

The Vampire who'd asked me why we were here doubled up a fist and punched the air. "Yeah. We know about it. They've been pouring into New Orleans. We're destroying them as we locate them, but it takes a while."

"Back up a minute," the Vampire who'd ordered Laura to stand down barked. "You said 'we're gearing up.' Your clan is no more, so who's we?"

"An all-mage group representing every discipline," I told him.

His eyes widened. The others took a step back. "Since when do mages do anything together?" he demanded.

"Since now," Clive said.

"But all the other mages hate us," Laura spoke up.

"Some still do." I faced her, appreciating her beauty. Red hair swung around her shoulders in thick curls. I'd been unsure how serious Clive was about Dee, but I wasn't wondering any longer. Using as few words as possible, I sketched out how Ariana had parleyed *Ascent* into a safe haven where all mages were equal.

"So you want to know if Clan Ravnos will help?" one of the men asked once I was done.

I nodded. Behind me, the rustle of scales told me my mesmerism casting was fading. "What do you want to do about them?" I glanced over my shoulder.

"I've got it." Laura strode around us. I heard the clunk of something heavy as she cracked skulls open.

"You said two things," another Vampire noted. "What was the second?"

"You won't like it," I warned him.

"Maybe we already know," he countered.

I thought about it and was quite certain they didn't. "When we were slicing holes in Seattle's paranormal task force, two of our targets got away. Because they could have identified us, we had to take care of them."

"Short version." The Vampire snapped his fingers. The off-hand gesture was beginning to irritate me.

A glance at the sky confirmed dawn wasn't far off. It meant I had to get Clive out of here soon. "All right, short version," I agreed. "When we found the targets, they were in league with three Clan Ravnos Vampires."

"You're making that up," the Vampire growled through fangs that had clicked into place.

"Wish I was," I told him. "Test my words with a truth casting if you wish. Up until then, I'd been proud Vampires hadn't sold out to mortals. After discovering I'd been wrong, I felt ashamed. So humiliated, I failed to mention it to the all-mage gathering."

"What'd you do to them?" he asked in a tone that could have meant anything.

"Killed them." I squared my shoulders, waiting. The proper course would have been returning them to a Clan Ravnos seethe to face justice, but it hadn't been practical.

After a long pause, he snarled, "Good. They deserved it."

"Can we count on your clan's aid?" Clive asked.

"Hard to say," the Vampire replied. "We need to discuss it with everyone. It's nearly daylight. Wait out the day in our seethe, and we'll have an answer for you."

"Just so we're clear," I said. "We will not be joining your clan."

The Vampire who'd been talking with us tossed a full-fang grin my way. "We're not so bad. Once you get to know us."

"We appreciate the offer to bide through the daylight hours," I told him, sidestepping the issue of their reputation. "If you decide to aid our cause, perhaps you could get the word out to the rest of your clan houses."

"If we decide to help, we will do that."

I nodded his way. Their offer of shelter through the day wasn't without risk. "Will you require our presence to answer questions?" I asked.

"Nay. We have all the information we require—" he began.

"The hell we do," one of his companions broke in. "I want to know what you've done so far and what your multi-mage group has planned for the future. Also, a single pet Vampire, this Ariana Hawke, is one thing. How will Witches and Fae and Sidhe, and Shifters feel about far more of us?"

I shrugged. "They didn't bat an eye when we teamed up with Kelpies. Shouldn't be a problem."

"Kelpies?" Laura yelped. "Now there's a story I want to hear. They nearly had me when I was quite young, still human, and living near Fort William."

"It's decided then," the Vampire who'd indicated they had all the information they needed said.

It seemed to be, but I wasn't any more at ease about waltzing into their clan house than I'd been earlier. "Tell us where to find you," I looked from Vampire to Vampire, establishing eye contact and hopefully trust. Although the latter isn't an especially hot commodity among our kind.

"Follow the River Road toward town. When you get to Marvel Lane, turn right. We're the house standing by itself next to an old graveyard at the very end of the lane," Laura said.

"We'll be along soon," I told them.

"Of course you will," one of the men said. He and the other three turned and walked back into thick mist rising from the damp ground.

"What do you suppose he meant by that?" Clive asked.

"Only that if we don't show up, they won't help."

"They didn't seem all that bad," Clive ventured. "What did you think?"

"They seemed like Vampires. No matter how we dress things up, when you slice to the heart of things, we're all pretty much alike."

"Well, they truly didn't know about their errant clan members," Clive murmured.

"My take as well," I told him.

"How are you thinking this will play out?" Clive settled on the bulk of a dead alligator.

"What do you mean?" I sank into a crouch across from him.

"If Clan Ravnos says they'll help, what exactly will we ask them to do?"

"They get to choose where they'll fit best," I told Clive. "For example, the communications and financial parts seem like they'll be mostly computer manipulation. I'm no good at that, and neither are you."

"The next big battle will be in Washington, right?"

"If things go that far."

Clive made a snorting sound. "What about Clan Tremere?"

"We should rustle them up too, but I don't know where to start looking."

"Maybe Clan Ravnos will?" Clive ventured. "Except it's precarious ground. Even mentioning the other clan could make them change their minds about extending aid."

I nodded. It was dangerous ground, indeed. Who knew how much bad blood flowed between the two clans? Back in the Old Country, Clan Ravnos had alienated nearly everyone with Clan Tremere only a step or two behind.

"We're not exactly team players," I muttered.

"We didn't used to be," Clive corrected me. "We've been doing all right in that regard lately." An aria trilled, and he reached into his coat pocket, coming up with a ringing phone. After fumbling about a bit, he stumbled on the right spot on the screen and said, "Aye?"

A moment later, he handed the phone to me. I looked at the display and saw Ariana's name. "I'm here," I said.

"Why didn't you answer your phone?" she sounded tense.

"Because the sound is turned off."

"It's not much good that way," she groused. "How are you two doing?"

"Make it so I can hear," Clive spoke up.

"We're doing all right," I told her. "Where's the speaker function?"

She walked me through activating it and then said, "Define all right."

"They're thinking about it," I told her. "We're supposed to show up at their clan house in case questions crop up."

"Not sure I like that part. About their seethe," she clarified.

"I'm not totally comfortable with it, either," I told her, "but they were shocked about the Vampires we found in Seattle. That was genuine."

"Do you suppose you could break loose sooner than tonight?"

"If I don't go after Clan Tremere. What's happening." My words may have been casual, but she needed me, trusted me enough to reach out. It highlighted our brand new commitment to one another and made me long for her.

"This will be cryptic," she warned, reminding me the phone in my hand wasn't to be trusted with sensitive information.

"I understand."

"I located my objective. I may need assistance carrying out my plan."

"How many?" I asked. If she was asking for backup, it meant more than one mortal stood in her way.

"Four that I can tell, but all of them are...special."

Fascinating. Not human after all. Special probably meant they were magic-wielders. "Your target, is she...special?"

"Yes."

"Is there any other possibility?" I wondered if there might be an easier constituent for her to tackle.

"Nope. This is the only woman."

"What time do you need us?" Clive asked. His blue eyes gleamed hotly, and his fangs had dropped in anticipation of carnage.

"Four my time at the latest. It's two hours later where you are."

"We'll be there," I told her.

"Thanks. Knew I could count on you."

A rectangle that announced the call had ended flashed on Clive's screen. He pocketed the phone and said, "Maybe you might want to engage the sound on yours."

It was a good idea. I located the phone, saw Ariana had tried to call me three times, and scrolled through settings not finding what I wanted.

"It's on the side," Clive said. "Upper left has a switch."

"Fuck. I must have found it to shut it off."

"Aye, none of this is obvious." Clive sounded as empathetic as a Vampire could, which is to say not very.

"Come on." I stood, intent on finding the Clan Ravnos

seethe and wrapping things up there. If we got back to the Seattle area early, it would give us more time to plan Ariana's strike.

The edges of the night sky were turning pearlescent with the coming dawn when we located Marvel Lane. The sign was faded, but I'd been following Vampire spoor, which made the sign extraneous.

"What's up?" Clive asked. "You've been quiet."

I stopped walking. "Something about this doesn't feel right to me. The closer we get to their clan house, the weirder it feels."

"Which part?"

"For starters, we were hunting in their territory. They mentioned it at first, but not again."

Clive glanced down the street and frowned. "You're thinking we'll have to pay the piper?"

"I'm thinking they'll couch it as a deal. Join their clan or pony up the usual price for poaching."

Clive's blue eyes widened. "Combat to the death? Surely, they wouldn't be that stupid. Not with everything that's facing us."

"Makes very little sense," I agreed, and then added, "Also, they never did much more but prevaricate over the question of aid."

"Mmph. Early on, one of them said they didn't believe mortals posed much of a threat, no matter what they did."

I nodded. "They did, indeed. It's a classic Vampire worldview."

The more we talked, the more concerned I became. We were running a fairly tight time clock as it was. I did not want Ariana to have to face the mage and her associates alone. She'd wait for me, but if I didn't show, she'd go by herself. I should have asked if Conan was part of her strike plan, but I hadn't.

"There you are." Laura's rich deep voice snagged my attention. She strode toward us wrapped in a green shawl that covered head and hands. "Josh sent me to guide you."

As if I required a guide to find a seethe. I swallowed a tart rejoinder and turned so I faced her. I wanted her to believe me, so I held her gaze with my own. "Something's come up. My mate called, and she needs my assistance."

"Good enough." Laura transferred her scrutiny to Clive. "I'm still craving some one-on-one time with you, my little hunk. We can play until your master gets back."

Ever the charmer, Clive ran his fingers through her thick hair. "Can I take a rain check, sweetheart? The reason Nick and I were standing here is we were strategizing. He and I are most of what's left of our clan, and—"

"I understand. You can scarcely refuse if your master requires you." Laura trailed her fingertips down Clive's arm. "Rain check it is. What shall I tell Josh?"

I rattled off my cell number. "Have him call me if he has questions. Assuming things don't turn to shit tonight, I can return tomorrow. Or maybe a delegate from your clan could meet us in Seattle."

"We'll let you know." She leaned forward and smushed her mouth over Clive's.

He didn't exactly push her away, but neither did he encourage her. I'm not sure she even noticed. She was so taken with him, anything shy of outright rejection wouldn't have registered.

I readied a travel spell. It was close to launch when another Vampire from the ratty mansion on the river pelted toward us. "Goddammit, Laura. You were supposed to escort them home, not fuck them in the road."

She extricated herself from Clive and turned to face him. "They can't stay. I was just saying goodbye."

"What do you mean, can't stay? They have to," he thundered.

Vampire power sheeted from him as he attempted to hold us in place. If he'd been stronger, it might have been a contest. As it was, his efforts weren't much more than an annoyance, but reinforcements were on their way. I felt them closing on our location.

It clinched my uneasiness. I shouted, "Laura has my cell number," just before I loosed my spell and teleported the fuck out of there.

"What in the hell was that all about?" Clive asked as the walls of our flat formed around us.

"They had plans for us," I said tersely. "Ones they clearly didn't bother to communicate to Laura."

"Even I figured that part out. Do you suppose we'll hear from them?"

I shrugged. At this point, I didn't care. Not that honor and integrity are Vampire slogans, but being used rubs me the wrong way every fucking time. "I have no idea," I told him. "Do you have something dry I could borrow?"

"Sure, mate."

I trailed after him to his bedroom and noticed he'd

amassed a respectable collection of garments. If I ever got a spot of time, I needed more than borrowed clothes from Ariana and the items in the cave and her washing machine.

As we were cleaning up and dressing, he asked, "How'd you know they were up to no good?"

"I didn't. Not for certain, but they didn't come by their shoddy reputation for nothing. If they'd truly been interested in fighting mortals, they'd have had plans percolating. Adding a couple of capable Vampires to a seethe would be a coup. I didn't see them letting us walk away without arguments. Even if we won a duel over the poaching issue, we would have lost because the rest of the clan would be out for our hides."

"No way to come out ahead, eh?"

"About the size of it." I perched on his bed and put my soaked boots back on. They'd dry on my feet. Eventually.

I didn't want to think about Clan Ravnos any longer. They made me tired. And pissed. This wasn't about them. None of it. If they couldn't let go of their immediate desires to focus on the big picture, we didn't need them as allies.

"Nick?" Something about Clive's question suggested this wasn't the first time he'd said my name.

"Aye. Ready. Let's figure out where Ari is and join her."

CHAPTER EIGHT, ARIANA

The more I thought about Nick and Clive going into the Clan Ravnos seethe, the antsier I became. But there wasn't anything I could do to help. Other than drop my project and teleport to New Orleans. I stared at my phone. Should I call him back? If I did, what would I say? I'd already urged caution. He didn't answer to me, nor should he.

Finally, I dropped the phone into a pocket. Nickolas had been taking care of himself for a long time. I needed to trust he'd figure things out.

Rob dropped a bottle of beer next to me. "I'm leaving soon, but you're welcome to stay."

"Thanks, but I need to shove off too." I got to my feet. I'd been sitting long enough, my limbs were stiff. I shook out each leg and straightened my back, while taking a good hard look at Rob. His usual sanguine demeanor was all but gone. Lines etched into his forehead and around his blue eyes. I'd have asked where he was going, but it was none of my business.

"Are you still determined to crash the teleconference?" he asked.

I nodded. "It will be harder than I thought."

"Yeah. I overheard your conversation with Nick. Are you sure one of the other participants wouldn't offer you simpler access?"

"They're all men."

"So? Have Nick do the talking."

I raked a hand through my hair, surprised when my fingers snagged on tangles. Surely, it hadn't been that long since I'd brushed it. "That could work, unless someone asks him a question." I winced. "Erm. That didn't exactly come out right. Nick is plenty smart, but there's a lot of modern shit he doesn't know about, and..."

Rob curled a hand around my upper arm. "Ariana. What's your goal?"

"To listen in and plant seeds that will sabotage their scanner project."

"The listening in part is simple. In terms of the other, I'm not sure anything you could say would even get anyone's attention without outing yourself."

I shook my hair over my shoulders. "Maybe it would be good for them to know the jig is up. That they've been discovered, and—"

He moved his hand from my arm and held it in front of him, fingers spread. "Nay. It's too soon."

I drew back. "What do you mean too soon?" More words

wanted out, ones that said he had no right to dictate my moves, but I sat on them.

"Those bloody scanners are our primary threat. We need to destroy or deactivate them. If we show our hand too soon, while hundreds of those infernal contraptions are being put into service, we'll push mortals to accelerate their timetable. Once they get aggressive with their new toys, it will blow everyone's cover."

"And then we'll have another problem on our hands," I muttered.

"Exactly." Rob's mouth was set in a tense line. "Fighting while remaining hidden is much easier than fighting in the open. Not that we won't reveal ourselves when we pick up staves and plowshares, but at least we won't have to go off-world to plan our offensives."

His reference to archaic implements amused me. I considered telling him I'd be leaving a trail of four dead bodies, but decided to keep my mouth shut. The fewer who knew what I was up to, the better. Not that Rob was any kind of threat, but anyone could be tortured.

"Not sure if Percy told you," I said, "but Conan is destroying one of the places they make scanners. For all we know, it might be the only one."

Rob slitted his eyes my way. "That's great as far as it goes, but it won't impact the ones that are already in service or on their way to jurisdictions that bought them." He paused long enough to suck in a breath and blow it out. "I still say they're our top priority."

"It's a start," I insisted, feeling defensive of Conan.

Rob flashed a rare smile and tossed a hard drive into a pocket. "Aye, and a decent one. Our paths will cross soon. I found a buyer for Nick's gems. Should have funds later today."

"I'll let him know. Thanks for the beer and a spot to work."

"You've done a lot for us when you didn't have to," he said before turning and walking out the door, which clicked shut behind him.

For some reason, I'd been expecting him to teleport. It wasn't quite midday. I had plenty of time, so I returned to Rob's primary workstation and sat on a rolling stool. The bit he'd wanted me to read had been unnerving, so much so I'd skimmed parts of it, while an internal voice chanted, *"Yeah, yeah, yeah. Blah. Blah. Blah."*

I owed it to myself—and Nick and everyone else—to do a more thorough job. So I settled in, determined to read through what appeared to be a manifesto created by the secret task force that had formed years before. It appeared the master document had been added to from time to time because inserts carried different dates and initials.

The list of principals was at the beginning. Some had been lined through. Had they died? Or been subsumed by disgust and quit? I voted for the former. Anyone who'd drunk enough Kool-Aid to sign up in the first place probably wasn't about to have a change of heart. It would be like a Vampire concluding they'd made a mistake years after they accepted someone's streaming wrist in the first place. Something about the transformation made us not look back.

Not all newly turned Vamps made the transition, but it wasn't because they decided Vampires were inherently evil.

Nope. A few never made it past the impulse control phase. Master Vampires differed in how much latitude they offered. Mistral's fuse had been on the shorter side. If a freshly turned recruit didn't get it together within six months, he destroyed them.

Christ! My mind was wandering. The stark words scrolling down the monitor bore bleak testimony to how much mortals hated magic. What a contrast to a couple of hundred years back when humans left offerings for the Fae and Sidhe and paid homage at ceremonies like Beltane and All Hallows Eve.

I turned back to the working document that defined our enemy. It reminded me of Hitler's final solution, except mages were the target, not gypsies and Jews and Catholics. Because we weren't exactly helpless—ergo, not material to march into death camps—the founding fathers had been wary.

They'd taken care to recruit a few mages from the get-go, absorbing knowledge to inform their staged strategies. Anger rolled through me, making it tough to concentrate. My fangs wanted out, so I let them drop. A few self-serving dickish mages had created the substrate that could be the undoing of us all. I hoped they were proud of themselves. It made my plans to mow through the four standing between me and the teleconference much more appealing.

I scrolled up and looked at the list. Had mages been given founding member status? Probably not, but I did a computer search for the original fifteen names anyway. I'd expected it to be harder, but I didn't need to hack into any confidential databases to locate any of them. And a few, like the jerk who'd been president then, didn't require me looking him up.

I moved the cursor back to my spot in the manifesto. At least my anger had ceded centerstage. In its place sat revenge. I'd personally kill every one of the fuckers who'd thought this up in the first place. Of course, the poison had spread as the plan progressed. They'd needed some elements —like the scanners—that hadn't yet been developed.

Driven by a sick fascination, I kept reading. Two elements came through loud and clear. They viewed any magic-wielder as a threat, even the mages they'd coerced into helping them. It was tough to feel sorry for the stooges, but they were slated for the chopping block as soon as their services were no longer required.

Ha! Bet it was news to them.

And potential leverage. They were well-positioned to wreak havoc—if we could lure them back to our side. The second component was whoever had designed this planned for it to outlive them. Succession policies were laid out. Apparently, it never occurred to the original group that their overarching goal—annihilation of magic—wouldn't be universally welcomed.

I covered the last few paragraphs, but didn't find what I sought. The group had no idea they were signing their own death warrants—and those of the entire population of Earth —with their despicable scheme.

Staring at the screen, fingers splayed over the keyboard, an idea swatted me right between the eyes. It was so straightforward and elegant, I was amazed I hadn't thought of it before. Of course then I hadn't had access to the document in front of me. It would be simple to harness the power of the Internet to splash the manifesto—and its associated names—all over the place. I could send it to every news outlet, along with a nice little note explaining exactly what the death of magic would mean to mortals.

I brought up a fresh screen and started composing, but stopped myself. This wasn't only my decision. I needed to float it past the group. And that wouldn't happen until after I'd crashed the teleconference.

Clicking and saving, I emailed the document to myself. Next I slid the flash drive with all the teleconference information into a slot and copied it as several PDFs, which I also emailed to myself. Satisfied I'd done what I could, I turned off Rob's computer and stood.

Should I go to *Ascent* or home? I opted for home. A shower and fresh clothes would go a long way toward making me feel better. Slogging through the human-developed "final solution" to magic had made me feel dirty, like I'd taken a bath in pig shit. My magic was a bit on the sluggish side. It reminded me I needed to feed. Instead of my house, I aimed for my favorite spot in the nearby woods and gorged on rodents while I did my best to clear my mind of the trash I'd been subjected to.

A short woof told me Conan had found me. He must have been at the house waiting. He dug into the carcasses I'd chucked into a handy pile. For a while, I drank and he ate. At the point when he'd left *Ascent*, he'd been on his way to deal with a manufacturing site for scanners. I waited for him to say something, but when it seemed he wasn't inclined to offer up details, I asked, "How'd it go?"

He looked up from where he lay on his belly, the wreckage of a fat raccoon between his front paws. Blood streaked his muzzle and paws. "It's gone. Along with everyone in it."

"Did you suck them through the ley-lines."

Conan shook his head. "Something about the scanners wouldn't have played well if I'd cast an unmaking spell through the lines. I used magic to blow the thing sky high." Getting to his feet, he padded closer to me.

"Something's bothering you. What is it?" I asked.

"Not ready to talk about it."

A mini-pep talk about collateral damage died before I could give voice to it. Besides, it wasn't Conan's style to waste energy feeling sorry for something he'd done. Which meant it must be something else.

"How'd your research go?" he asked me.

I sketched out what I'd found. He started growling long before I was finished. I knew exactly how he felt. "Do the other guardians know anything about the covert task group?" I asked.

"No idea. Even if they did, Fairclaw would have discounted it. His position hasn't wavered. Mortal activities aren't of interest."

"But they have to be," I insisted. "If they manage to force all of us to leave—"

The growling morphed into a snarl. I suspected his changing role in guardian circles was what was eating at him. It wasn't a problem I could help with since I thought all his kinsfolk sucked. Except perhaps Moonglow.

"Are you still going to pretend to be that other mage?" Conan asked.

"Yeah. Nick should be back in time to come with me. Clive too. There are four magic-wielders in her house…" I left it there. No need to spell out my intent.

"I'm coming," Conan said.

"Glad to have you. Always." I dug a hand into his thick neck ruff. There were many questions I hadn't asked, like what would happen if he picked up the leadership mantle for his kin? My guess was he wouldn't be spending much time with me any longer, and it made me sad. I didn't need him in the same way I needed Nick, but Conan and I had history. He was one of the very few creatures I trusted implicitly.

The wolf went back to eating. I made a run for the house. The sun was actually out today, and my hands were turning red. I opted for a shower. It was quicker than a bath, and I wanted to tack down locations for the original founding members of the anti-magic coalition. Maybe once I was done with the call, I could kill a couple of them—for starters. I hadn't bothered to retract my fangs, and they pressed against my chin, eager for action. After culling through my wardrobe, I settled on black pants, a black shirt, and a black scarf around my head. After braiding my wet hair out of the way, I secured the scarf.

Conan had come in while I was cleaning up, but Nick and Clive were in my living room too. Both sat on a sofa sipping tea.

"You're early," I exclaimed, followed by, "Why?"

"Can't trust Clan Ravnos," Nickolas said.

"What a surprise," I muttered.

"Aye, indeed," Clive chimed in. "They talked a good line, but never really committed to anything."

"How'd you get away?" Conan asked.

"Easy. We stopped half a kilometer from their clan house," Nick said. "To kick things around. Didn't take long before I decided leaving was the best option. I had a teleport spell well in hand when a bunch of Ravnos Vamps headed our way."

"So, did you actually talk with them?" I asked.

Clive nodded. "Earlier. We started in a swamp with a decaying mansion. Nick thought if we fed, we might draw their attention, and it did."

"Aw crap," I mumbled. "Poaching is a high offense."

"Aye, but they didn't harp on it," Nick said. "Mostly, because they were hoping to force us into their clan house. They knew what happened to mine."

"Originally, we agreed to spend the day at their seethe," Clive added. "Once we got close, though, Nick thought better of the idea."

"They have my cell number," Nick said. "In case they have a burst of patriotism toward other mages."

"Not holding my breath." I couldn't resist rolling my eyes.

"Neither are we," Clive tossed out.

For the second time that afternoon, I went over the materials we'd lifted from McMurdy's house.

"That's just creepy." Clive shook his head.

"Bastards! They've been watching us all this time." Nick's fangs were on display.

"Mortals have always watched us," Conan pointed out. "But their attention didn't used to carry malevolent intent."

"I say we kill them all," Nick growled.

"I'm in," Clive said. "Hell, those Ravnos fuckers might be too. If it meant buckets of human blood."

"Don't forget the Kelpies," I said sweetly.

"See? Lots of allies." Conan stood and fluffed out his coat.

"Any leads on Clan Tremere?" I asked.

"Nay," Nick replied. "After our run in with our Ravnos brothers, I lost interest in locating any more of us."

"The only time we'll truly need critical mass," I noted, "is when we converge on Washington. That's the time we draw our line in the sand and let humans know they cross it at their own risk, although I had another idea."

"Instead of or in addition to?" Conan woofed.

"Probably in addition to, but they'd work best if they happened at close to the same time. I was considering disseminating information about the secret task force via the Internet. I'm damned certain the original group had no idea they were inviting their own death knell when they mapped out the demise of magic."

"Millions of mortals deserve to know," Nick said.

"Aye, they might turn on the ones who gave fuck-all about them," Clive added. "And make our task simpler."

"I almost put that ball in play," I admitted, "but I wanted everyone to weigh in. It's possible there could be dissenting opinions out there. Reasons to sit on the documents we stole from McMurdy's computer."

"Can I see?" Nick asked.

I snagged a laptop, booted up, and moved the manifesto from an email attachment to my screen. While Nick, Clive, and Conan huddled around the screen reading, I made us more tea and downloaded my other emailed documents to a tablet.

"You say there's a quick-and-dirty way to make this public?" Clive asked when I returned with steaming mugs and the mead bottle.

"Yup. Sure is," I replied.

"Do it," he urged.

I grinned. "Not until the all-mage group knows about it. Democratic process and all. We'll vote later tonight at *Ascent*. Speaking of which, it's time to get moving." I powered down the laptop and tablet and put both back on my desk.

"Where are we going?" Conan asked.

"South of Portland. I have an address, and we'll plan it so we come out maybe a mile away. With a passel of mages in that house, I don't want to risk starting out too close."

"I have a better idea," Conan said.

I furled my brows his way. "Shoot."

"We'll use the lines."

"They'll fry everything electronic in the place," I told him. "The whole purpose is for me to sit in on that call. By now, they'll know the Vegas warehouse went up in smoke. I want to determine if it was the only manufacturing location. Basically, I want to learn as much as I can."

"You didn't let me finish." Conan sounded aggravated.

"Correct. I didn't. I'm sorry."

"I can use the lines to find the others on the multiway

phone meeting. Once you're winding down, I'll take care of them."

"I want a couple," Nick said and shot an engaging grin Conan's way. "Please."

I couldn't resist. "Save some for me."

"And me," Clive joined in.

Conan woofed laughter. "The bunch of you are incorrigible. I only signed up for one Vampire."

"You know you love us," Clive joked.

"The best laid plans." I smirked. "Let's get moving. I'll take us."

"I'll handle warding," Conan said.

Magic rose, guardian power blending with my own in a familiar mix. If Conan returned to his people, I'd miss him, but it had to be his choice. I wouldn't attempt to influence it one way or the other.

"Who are you impersonating?" Nickolas asked as the walls of my house dissolved.

"A Witch named Solaria. Not that I feel sorry for her, but part of the master plan is to wipe out all of the mage allies as soon as they're no longer needed."

"Start there." Conan's tone was abrupt.

"Huh? What do you mean?" I asked him.

"Tell her and see where her loyalties lie," the wolf clarified.

"Sounds good to me," Nick said. "We can always end her."

I wasn't so certain about that. The prudent course was to snuff her and the others in her house and not worry if they'd get cold feet about their human masters.

Nick must have sensed my ambivalence because he said, "It's five extra minutes," next to my ear.

I gripped his hand; he squeezed back. Vampires aren't exactly champs at group process, but this was exactly why I'd chosen to pitch the question of manifesto exposure to the all-mage group. Occasionally, I have solid instincts. If we went that way, though, we'd have to hurry. After the Internet went down, that avenue would be closed.

Conan had jumped on the idea of offering information to the turncoat mages. Nick too. I trusted them, so if Solaria was in a listening mood—and I'd have to judge very carefully —I'd pony up documentation to back up my claims and see what she wanted to do.

CHAPTER NINE, NICKOLAS

I wasn't exactly at my best after the Clan Ravnos Vamps lied to me. It took a lot to hang onto my temper and present a smooth veneer after reading that wretched piece of tripe on Ariana's computer. The nerve of those rotters. How dare they plot and plan to annihilate us—and behind our backs to boot. I itched to teach them a lesson they'd never forget. One underwritten with their own blood.

We were fortunate the various mage groups had let go of grudges and preconceived notions about one another. Otherwise, we'd be in far worse shape squaring off against mortals since every type of magic-wielder would be working independently.

Or some would be doing nothing.

Kind of like the Clan Ravnos Vampires. Their attitude was unconscionable on one hand, but typically vampiric on the other. Despite knowing how they thought, I couldn't excuse their behavior. If Clan Giovanni were still intact, we'd have done our part.

Maybe. Probably. Some things were impossible to know for certain. I was a different Vampire than the one who'd left Italy at the front end of the 1900s. For one thing, I was better at paying attention to emotions. I'd sensed Ariana's uneasiness when Conan added a step to her plans.

And I understood why she was reluctant to go along with his idea.

We'd only have the element of surprise once. It would be so much easier to go in swinging and not deal with anything else. But Conan had a good point. This Solaria person was clearly well-positioned. The mortals she reported to trusted her, and presumably she was on a first-name basis with many of the other mages in the operation. In aggregate, it made her ideal to launch an insurrection from within.

The most effective rebellions happened from the inside. Kind of like the interference that had spelled the end of my clan house...

Better not to go there. I'd avoided perseverating about what had happened in Castelrotto. Easier to concentrate on Ariana, on her hand in mine. She could have told Conan and me to stuff it, that this was her baby and she'd made up her mind how to approach things.

Instead, she'd pivoted to include our suggestion.

I was grateful for Conan's concealing magic as a busy neighborhood took shape around us. Large homes, mostly with two and three stories, lined both sides of a tree-shrouded street. Children raced up and down it on bicycles.

Cars pulled into and out of driveways. Whatever I'd imagined as a hideaway for mages, this certainly wasn't it.

And then I remembered our objective wasn't all that close.

Ariana set off at a reasonable pace for a Vampire, which would have been impossible for most mortals to match. The fancy homes gave way to shoddier ones, and then to a country lane with bleating goats and chickens squawking and foraging behind chain-link fences. The sun was mostly down, the last of its rays flirting with the western horizon.

"How are you doing?" I asked Clive.

"I'll live. It's getting easier."

A quick glance at the backs of his hands was reassuring. They were red but hadn't yet blistered. Ariana stopped abruptly and angled her head at a surprisingly well-appointed cottage. Crafted of mortar and stones, it was surrounded by a white-picket fence and a broad wraparound porch. The architecture didn't match anything we'd seen nearby. Curtains covered all the windows on the side of the place facing us.

"Only two inside," Conan said.

"Maybe the others who live here aren't back from work yet," Ariana speculated.

"They could show up any time," I cautioned everyone.

"I'll watch for them," Clive offered. *"Both traveling in cars or a flare of magic that says they'll arrive another way."*

I clapped him across the back and gave a thumbs-up sign.

"Shall we teleport in or use the door?" Ariana looked from Conan to me.

"Door." Conan started toward it.

We flanked him. Magic shouldn't give us away—we weren't using any outside of the wolf's ward. I was proud of us, we covered the ground to the front steps without making a sound. Vampires walk softly, but so do wolves.

Some of the old legends credit us with flying. We can't, of course, but Ariana's leap that positioned her in front of the door was impressive. Conan and I landed on either side. A quick shot of magic made quick work of the lock, and we rushed through the door.

My fangs were down, in full attack mode. I was willing to give Solaria a couple of minutes to decide which pony she was going to back. Any hesitation, and I'd be on her in a trice.

The downstairs was one large open room. And it was empty. I'd sensed Witches within. Where were they? Conan raised his muzzle and howled. So much for stealth. Compulsion streamed from him. At least we wouldn't have to search the rest of the house.

The patter of feet on stairs produced a diminutive woman with short black hair, angular features, and hooded dark eyes. A colorful peasant skirt and white tunic swathed her slight form, and her feet were bare.

"Guardian?" Her softly accented voice mirrored surprise and suggested her first language was Spanish.

"Where is the other?" Conan asked in a tone that didn't leave space for her not to reply.

The Witch's eyes widened. "*Si*, of course you would know. My aunt is upstairs. She is ill."

"Witches don't get sick," Ariana snapped.

"This one did." Solaria looked from me to Ariana, and

her eyes widened. "Vampires. Since when do guardians keep such shoddy company?"

Conan growled; hackles raised the length of his back. Solaria stumbled through part of an apology before Ariana cut her off. "I know what you're part of," she said without preamble. "Are you aware your human masters will rid themselves of you once they've established dominion over the majority of the rest of us?"

The Witch drew herself up tall, which brought her to mid-chest level on me. "I do not have human masters," she hissed. "And I have no idea what you're talking about."

Conan's transition to his human form was shockingly quick. He closed the distance to the Witch until he towered over her. "Do. Not. Lie. To. Us." Short pauses between words punctuated them.

Power surged around the Witch. "Don't let her leave," I shouted, but Conan was clearly on top of the situation. A silver and gold weave settled around the woman, vibrating until her power guttered and died.

Ariana stomped to the Witch. "The others"—she pointed at Conan and me—"convinced me to give you a chance to recant your sins. What I told you is true. I have the original manifesto the mortals in charge of the anti-magic campaign constructed. The last couple of articles leave zero doubt as to your fate."

Without pausing since she had no need to breathe, Ariana forged ahead. "Do you honestly believe mortals would admit to an association with magical anythings? They've spent the last decade on a crusade to stomp out anyone and anything magical. Do you comprehend what that means?"

Solaria's eyes had rounded into dark moons. She nodded mutely.

"Say something," Ariana pressed. "It's your kind who cuts out tongues. Vampires have other tricks up our sleeves."

"They told us they'd stop." The Witch's accent had grown much more pronounced.

"They will," Conan said dryly. "Once they have magic on the run, and all of us are forced to leave. The ones who are left, that is."

"Why?" I asked.

Her gaze darted my way. "Why, what?"

"Why'd you shackle yourself into such a hideous partnership?"

Her dark eyes sheened with tears. "My aunt. She was set upon by Sorcerers. She hovers at the edge of the abyss, not alive, but not dead, either. They promised me a cure."

"Who's they? And how long ago?" I pressed.

Solaria tossed her hands in the air. "What does it matter? I figured out they had no intention of following through a couple of years back. But if I tell them that, confront them and demand action, they might finally kill her."

"What if I cured her?" Conan's question was silky smooth.

The Witch shook her head. "I'd only be trading who I report to."

"Not the way we roll," Ariana told her. "We're part of an all-mage group. We have one objective. Do enough damage to mortals to make them back off. I'm here because I plan to sit in on your teleconference. My original idea was to take your place, but my associates talked me into offering you a choice."

"How'd you even find out about it?" she sputtered.

"We have our ways," I answered.

"Same way we got hold of the disgusting declaration that lays out mortals' plans for us," Ariana said.

"Decide now," Conan ordered.

"Before she does," I cut in, "when are the other two due back here? And where is your coven?"

"I have no coven affiliation. Not all Witches do. It was one of the reasons I was attractive to...them."

"And the other?" I pressed. "When will your housemates return?"

"Not sure. They're not here all the time."

Something about her words didn't sit right. "It's not the whole story." I took a step closer, fangs on full display. "Don't make me drag this out of you."

"We have about ten minutes before the teleconference," Ariana noted.

Solaria made a sour face and spat on the floor, hooking two fingers into the sigil against evil.

"You will not do that to Ariana," I said in my harshest voice, the one that made mortal blood run cold.

In her first show of spirit, anger flickered around the Witch. "It wasn't for the Vampire," she growled. "The others you asked after are Sidhe. They're not roommates, but my jailers. I have no idea why they're not here. They pretend to help with Auntie, but they go through my things, check my computer."

"We'll take care of them," Conan said, followed by, "Decide."

"Or?" Solaria rolled her shoulders back.

"We go back to my original plan." Ariana shrugged.

"I don't like you." The Witch bared her teeth.

"Yeah, the feeling is mutual. What will you choose?"

"Are you certain you can cure my aunt?" The Witch addressed Conan, still in his human form.

"No, but I am willing to try. Most magics are within my ken, but if she has been treading through Purgatory for too long, no one will be able to call her back."

A muted moan from the Witch betrayed how much she loved her kinswoman. Breath whistled through her teeth. "All right."

"All right, what?" I sought clarification.

"I'll work for you. It's not much worse than what I've been doing."

Conan grabbed her shoulder and shook her. "Apologize, now. Or I won't lift a claw to help your aunt. We've offered you freedom, woman. Freedom and an opportunity to make a difference."

"Why are you even bothering?" Ariana shook her head.

"I'm nearly done." Conan's deep voice buzzed with irritation.

"All right. I'm sorry." The Witch ground out the words. "It's hard to know who to believe. For the first time since I was a girl, I've wished for a coven mistress, someone to talk with. I always had my aunt, but..."

Conan shimmered back to his preferred body and vanished up the stairs.

"It's almost time," Ariana said. "Where's your teleconference set up?"

Solaria walked to the far side of the room where a computer monitor sat atop a cheap pine desk. I dragged another chair over for Ariana, but she pushed it aside, explaining, "I have to stay out of camera range."

The Witch engaged a few keys, and her monitor flared to life. Ariana snatched up a pad and a pen from the desk. I positioned myself off to one side where I had a clear path to everywhere in the room.

"Clive?"

"All quiet out here, mate."

"There are more of you outside?" Solaria's face had taken on a drawn expression. Her voice was high and thin, and sweat beaded across her forehead.

I nodded without offering details. Better if she thought a legion of Vampires circled her house. The computer beeped and chimed. "We're about to begin," the Witch cautioned. "If you talk, they'll hear."

Ariana probably knew that, but it was news to me. Although, if I'd taken the time to think things through, I'd have determined as much. If people in far-flung locales could hear Solaria, they could pick up other voices as well.

Sure enough, after another series of chimes, a man's voice called the Witch's name.

"I'm here, Ben," she said.

"Stand by. Once everyone has signed in, I'll open the meeting."

Moments later, the man's voice was back. "We have

unfortunate news. Someone betrayed the location of our scanner plant to the enemy."

Color drained from Solaria's face. His words meant something to her that I didn't totally understand.

Ben went on, sounding like a rattlesnake with a tongue. "This group comprises the only ones who knew its location."

"What about everyone who worked there?" a man with a Middle Eastern accent asked.

"Their lips were sealed with spells," Ben said. "Since you asked, Emil, you will be the first to welcome my agents."

Solaria's eyes widened until white showed all around the pupils; she'd begun to pant. Apparently, she'd had a run in or two with Ben's agents.

"Of course," Ben went on, "whoever betrayed us could simply admit what they did. I'd be quite appreciative, and your death will be quick rather than prolonged."

Ariana exchanged a glance with me and spun her hand in a circle. Whoever this Ben was, he was playing at being a badass. True savages struck quick and hard without a bunch of extraneous chatter.

"Solaria. What was that?" Ben demanded.

"What was what?" the Witch asked in a surprisingly strong voice.

Ariana edged farther from the computer. It must have picked up the movement from her hand.

"I saw something flutter at the edge of your screen."

Solaria shrugged. "I have no idea. You're upset and seeing things. We help you. All of us."

"Only because we allow it," Ben snarled. "Don't any of you ever forget it."

"Are all of them mages?" I asked Ariana.

She shook her head.

I waited for Ben to dig deeper into what he thought he'd seen. Instead, he moved on. "The plant isn't salvageable. We will have to rebuild. Until we do, this group is disbanded."

"What about distribution?" another man asked. "We were assisting with set up."

"If we require your services, you'll be contacted privately. Today's meeting is over." The screen turned black.

Solaria shook her head slightly and turned off her computer before swiping a sleeve across her forehead. "No wonder you're here," she said. "Are you who hexed the factory?"

"What difference does it make?" Ariana asked. "Who are these agents?"

"Aye and what do they do?" I chimed in. "Torture you?"

The Witch set her trembling mouth in a tight line. "It's what happened to Auntie. Sorcerers tormented her until she lost her mind. She was innocent, knew nothing. It was how I ended up slotted into her place."

"What did they even need this teleconference for?" Ariana demanded. "Seemed inconsequential, at least today."

"They practiced on us with their prototypes," Solaria said. "And we filled in at the factory when the regular workers weren't available." She licked at dry lips. "Some of us—not me—helped set up the scanners and taught humans how to use them. They were complicated and required a lot of maintenance."

"Grab a few things," Ariana said. "You can't remain here,

but I know a guild mistress who might welcome you. Depends how you behave."

"I'm not leaving without my aunt." She glanced at the stairs.

"You need to get moving. Conan will let us know as soon as he can," I told her.

Solaria jumped to her feet. After dragging a duffel bag out of a closet, she started tossing things into it. I noticed she left the computer. "This is enough," she said after a few minutes. "If I run, they'll assume I'm guilty."

"None of you are guilty," Ariana told her. "We had other methods."

Noise in the stairwell was followed by Conan back in mortal form carrying an unconscious woman in his arms.

"Niona. Auntie." Solaria ran to them. "Will she be all right?"

"I don't know," Conan said. "We have to get out of here. Trouble's coming."

"Clive! Get in here." I didn't bother with telepathy. Vampires have exceptional hearing.

He burst through the door moments later. "Aye. I felt it too. Magic is rolling this way. Lots of it."

Guardian enchantment prickled as it expanded, encompassing us in its scents of fur and rain-wet rocks. Solaria grabbed up the valise she'd packed, surprisingly calm after her earlier bout of hysteria.

The cottage dissolved, but not before I heard angry shouts and power words. Nothing they slung our way could touch Conan's magic. We didn't go far, or perhaps we did.

Regardless, it didn't take long before the rounded tunnels housing ley-lines formed around us.

Conan placed Niona near them before taking his preferred form. He must have put out a call for his mother because Moonglow danced deftly along the lines. She bent over Niona, but Solaria jumped between them. "Don't hurt her."

Moonglow turned her amber gaze on the Witch. "My son called for me. I will heal your blood kin if I can."

Niona is in good hands," Ariana told the Witch. "Even though she's not fond of my kind, she saved my life."

Moonglow chuckled. "Will you never leave off reminding me of that day? You could have simply said I saved you and stopped there."

"It could be arranged." Ariana returned her smile.

Moonglow morphed into her human form, white hair cascading to the rocky ground, and gathered Niona into her arms.

"Take me with you," Solaria demanded.

"She cannot," Conan said. "Your aunt has been marked. We must remove the beacons, or those who seek you will always be able to find you."

The Witch's face crumpled. Tears welled. "So that's how they did it. I never knew, and couldn't figure it out no matter how many spells I cast."

"No wonder they kept your aunt alive," I muttered.

"Where will you be?" Moonglow asked.

"Dahlia's coven," Ariana told her, "but I bet you could find me any old time."

"It's a bet you'd win," Moonglow said and walked through a rent in the air.

"Perhaps I should go to the flat," Clive said.

"Is Dahlia still annoyed with you?" Ariana asked.

He managed a sheepish look. "Not sure. I'd love to see Dee, but..."

"I have things to do," Conan said. Jumping onto the ley-lines, he ran along their length until he vanished from sight.

"What kind of things?" Solaria asked.

"We never question him," Ariana replied and readied a transport spell. She exchanged a quick glance with me that told me to keep my mouth shut. I remembered well enough. Conan had planned to home in on locations for some of the other conference call participants with an eye to destroying them. I hoped to hell he started with Ben.

"What do you want to do?" I asked Clive as Ariana readied her casting.

He shrugged. "In for a penny, in for a pound. I'll ride along. Dahlia can always boot me if she's still peeved."

Solaria picked up her bag once again. I was decent at assessing moods, and much of her earlier distrust had dissipated. If anyone could bring her around, it would be Dahlia and her Witches. Did all the treasonous mages end up dealing with mortals like Ben? His sharp tongue and patronizing attitude made me want to hunt him down and rip his throat out.

Why in the fuck would any magic-wielder put up with that kind of treatment unless they had a sick aunt or an ailing child or some other brick balanced over their heads? When it came down to it, we all had weak spots.

Ariana brought us out in the guild house's main room. Dee looked up from a couch where she'd been nose-deep in scrolls. The smile that bloomed on her face was genuine. Jumping to her feet, she ran to Clive and threw her arms around him.

"I've missed you too, darling," he crooned and hugged her back.

"Christ on a two-pronged crutch, what in the fuck are you doing here?" Dahlia inquired caustically.

"Delivering a Witch who needs a home," Ariana said, sidestepping the fact that Dahlia's inquiry had been aimed right at Clive.

More Than Never launched herself from Dahlia's shoulder and flew circles around Solaria. The Witch crooned to the bird, held out an arm, and waited while the raven settled on it.

The harsh lines of Dahlia's gaunt face softened. "My bird approves," she said, "which is more than I can say about the pair of you." She jerked her chin at Clive and Dee, still locked in one another's arms.

"Tough to stand in the way of love," Ariana commented *sotto voce*.

I walked to her side and wrapped an arm around her. "It is, indeed, *Cara*."

Dahlia focused her keen gaze on Solaria. "Before I puke from all the saccharine in here, tell me your story. How'd you get here, and why should my coven take you in?"

"Ready to go?" Ariana whispered in my ear.

I didn't bother answering, just crafted a spell to take us to her house. We'd done a good day's work today, even if we had bushels of unanswered questions. "Do you think Conan needs us?" I asked before we touched down in her living room.

"If he does, he'll let us know. You and I never get any time together."

"We have some now. Maybe not much, so let's not waste a second," I told her and crushed my mouth over hers. I'd been planning to rehash the last few hours and craft our next moves, but her plaintive statement about our lack of alone time brought me to my senses. Clarified my priorities.

The world wouldn't end if we took ten minutes—or even thirty. Sexual heat enveloped me, and I welcomed the weight of Ariana in my arms, her body plastered against mine. Musk, whiskey, and flowers wafted around us as pheromones swirled, thickening the air with our hunger.

I hadn't meant to give voice to that whiney little bit about feeling deprived. If Nick had offered one of his knock-'em-dead smiles and listed all the things we should be doing, I'd have accepted his redirection. Maybe. Our last attempt at intimacy had been snatched away by Kelpies. It added urgency to right now. We had to hurry before something else reared its ugly head and forced us to teleport in like masked crusaders.

Eh, maybe not masked, but you get the idea.

I melted into his embrace, glorying in the feel of his arms around me and his mouth on mine, but the sense we were fucking on borrowed time wouldn't leave me. Which meant we had to get the actual fucking part well in hand. My nipples had turned into pebbled marbles, shooting hot sparks through the rest of me. My crotch wasn't far behind. Slick with heat and need, I mounted Nick's thigh while I grappled with his zipper, frantic to free the inviting, rock-hard length of him trapped in his trousers.

It was nip and tuck before I curled my hand around his cock. Times like now I missed being human. Missed my heartbeat accelerating and my breath coming quick. Missed a man's scorching breath painting my body.

But we had blood. It was better than breathing. The coppery tickle of Nick's in my nostrils told me he'd opened a vein. I tore my mouth from his and glommed onto his wrist, slurping like a mad thing.

Each swallow of the rich liquid tossed me higher until every part of my body was on fire with needing him. I squeezed and caressed his errant member, rewarded with fluid seeping from the velvety tip. My own pants were a problem. So were my boots. I wanted to hang onto Nick forever, but I had to let go to open a path for him to slam into me.

Oh how I longed for those lust-filled thrusts, stretching me to the max as I dissolved around him in a flood of sensual perversion only another Vampire could truly appreciate.

"Sorry. Can't wait, *Cara*." Nick's voice brushed my ear right before he angled a hand and ripped out the crotch of my jeans.

I'd been part of the "can't-wait" party forever. No one needed to draw me a roadmap for what would happen next. Mewling with desire, I climbed up his body and wrapped my legs around his slender hips and my arms around his shoulders. He gripped my waist with one arm, still feeding me with the other, and drove himself to the hilt, buried in my body. Shock waves ratcheted through me.

Connected. We were finally connected. Fang and cock. It didn't get any better than that. Ever.

"You feel ambrosial." He withdrew a bit and slammed into me again. Stretching to accommodate his girth moved from pain, which added its own spice, to pleasure.

My eyes had been shut. I opened them in time to fall into his green gaze, drowning in the totality of Nick. Of everything he was. Intensity streamed from him. His neck was corded with passion, and his pale skin blotchy with streaks of his blood. Letting go of his wrist, licking to seal the wound, I cleaned up the rusty stripes, savoring every atom of Vampire blood. And then I opened a new wound in the wrist I'd abandoned.

I rocked in his arms. My clit was so distended, it could have passed for a puny dick. Each thrust made me hotter, wetter until a climax hit terminal velocity, ripping through me and nearly tearing the top off my head off with its power.

And I just kept coming; wave after wave of delight coursed through me. I wanted to laugh and shriek and yell, "We did it," to every obstacle fate had tossed in our path.

Inside me, Nick's cock swelled still more. I felt the tension build and crest just before he juddered and came. The hand that had been squeezing my butt, added nails to the equation. I cried out, and my ongoing climax ratcheted up another notch.

We stood like that, shuddering and grinding our bodies together for long moments. At some point, Nick had dug his fangs into my neck. I could almost picture our blood circling, traveling from me to him and back again in an endless circle of commitment and desire.

"This is how it's supposed to be," I murmured when I finally let go of his wrist.

"It's amazing. You're amazing." He removed his mouth from my jugular and lifted me off his still-erect cock. It was so beautiful, splashed with our secretions, I fell to my knees and took him into my mouth, licking him clean. I could have stopped there, but I didn't. I swirled my tongue around the head of his member and took him as deep as I could, which was maybe half his length.

He groaned and pressed into my mouth. I had my hands on his ass, so I felt the muscles clench beneath my fingertips. I extended my fangs, grazing his cock with each pass. Vampire jism tastes like nectar. It's nothing like the shit men carry in their balls.

He tangled his hands in my snarled hair, holding my head in place while I teased and licked and sucked and bit. Heat seared me, and I traded holding onto his shaft with both hands to shoving one between my legs. Damn. I was wetter than wet.

I moved my mouth faster, up and down his cock, mirroring the motion with the hand between my legs. The hotter he got, the more aroused I was until I knew I could make both of us come together. Close. We were so close. I felt his approach in the rigidity of his cock, in its swelling in my mouth. All I needed was a little more rubbing, fast, hard, and sure. Another squeeze or two and I crested, ecstasy washing through me as semen burst into my hungry mouth.

He was still holding my head against his belly, cradling me as he fucked my mouth. Savoring the moment, I milked the last strands of jism from his balls.

"*Cara.* When you started to touch yourself, it was icing on the cake. It made me so high, I couldn't think about anything but you and me and us doing this forever."

After a final suck, I let go of his penis. "Forever sounds good to me," I managed before I rolled back onto my ass, grabbed a pillow off a nearby chair, and collapsed on the floor.

Nick positioned himself next to me and held me close. "Apologies for your trousers."

"Eh, I can sew them back up if I feel like it, but I have a lot of clothes. Sacrificing ten pairs of pants would have been worth it."

He cupped the side of my face. Blood seeped from his wrist, and I turned to lick it up. "I love you, Ariana. I can't describe how good it feels. How right. I haven't loved anyone since before I was turned. I told myself the Vampire life was worth sacrifices, and for a long time I believed it."

"It is," I agreed. "Except I never got the memo about not loving. I started my tenure among the Undead in love with Mistral. It never went away."

Nick's gaze bored into me. "Even after you killed him?"

"That made it worse. Even with all the perspective years have added, it doesn't take much to drop me right back into the same impossible situation. I loved him. He lusted after me. He wanted my body, but not all of me."

"Then he was a fool." Nick smoothed strands of hair back from my face.

I shook my head. "Nope. He was just being who he was born to be. A master Vampire. I was the one with a problem.

Guess the whole absolute power thing never went to your head."

Nick winced. "Oh, but it did. A time or two. I came to my senses quick enough. I ended up with the seethe by default, not by armed combat. The master before me did a few ill-advised things, outed himself, and ended up the star of a very public drawing and quartering."

"Ewww. Ouch. I remember those."

"Aye, me as well. In any event, during the time he was imprisoned, he reached out to several of us telepathically, emphatic I was to succeed him."

"What aren't you saying?" I asked.

He held me tighter. "Many things. It wouldn't have been my first choice, but you know how a clan house is structured."

I did, indeed. Normally, a new master only comes into play after the old one is challenged to armed combat—and loses. I nestled my head into the hollow of his shoulder. "The past doesn't matter. For either of us. Only what we do now and in the future."

"Agreed, darling. My darling. That's probably a good place to stop for now. We need to bathe and get ready for whatever happens next." Nick brushed his fangs over my forehead and cheeks and nuzzled my neck. His words were a potent reminder we'd snatched a few stolen moments and weren't entitled to much more.

Not with the world crashing down around us.

I kissed him again, my lips still swollen from our lovemaking, before I disentangled myself and went to work unlacing my boots. Once they were off, the rest of my clothes followed. Nick had been quicker than me, and I heard the splash of water cascading into my copper bathtub. I eyed the ripped-out seam in my pants. I had a sewing machine, and I could repair the damage. Who knew when I'd work my way down to something so relatively unimportant? Regardless, I tossed the pants in my sewing hamper. They smelled of Nick and sex and blood. I wasn't in a hurry to wash them.

By the time I walked into the bathroom, he was already in the tub, back against its rim, knees bent, and water almost covering his thighs. He patted the spot between his legs. After dropping a cake of scented soap into his hand, I settled against him, luxuriating as water rose to breast level before I turned it off.

It would have been the simplest thing in the world to turn to face him and settle myself over his cock, but I didn't. We took turns washing each other, and I finally moved to the shower to shampoo my hair. It needed oodles of conditioner if I was going to have a prayer of getting the knots out of it.

"We deserve a medal," Nick called over the rush of the shower.

I didn't have to ask what he meant. We did, indeed, deserve something for not retreating to my bed and fucking the next week away. By the time I came out of the bathroom, he was dressed in the garments he'd left before we went to rescue Clive and Dee from the Kelpies. Amazingly, we still had quite a bit of night left. I hustled into clothes and braided my wet hair.

"Quick snack?" Nick looked up from where he'd been sitting on a sofa examining a scroll.

"Man after my own heart. All our extracurricular

activity made me hungry." I grabbed my phone, hunting for messages but not finding any. "That's odd." I slid the phone into a back pocket.

"What?" Nick rose to his feet.

I shrugged. "Not sure. I'd have thought I'd have heard from someone. Percy or Dahlia or someone."

"Didn't you say phones weren't especially secure?"

"Yeah, I did, but they haven't tried to raise us telepathically, either. And it's been hours since Conan left."

"I was thinking about him," Nick said. "It's what I was hunting for in your lore collection. Information about guardians."

"Find anything?"

He shook his shaggy head, copper curls framing his arresting face. "Not much."

"They like it that way," I said. "Traveling incognito and all that. I knew almost nothing about them until Conan revealed himself, and I still don't know a whole hell of a lot."

Nick mimed a low bow. "After you, *Cara*. Once we've eaten, we can track everyone down."

I was partway through my third rodent carcass when I realized we'd missed tonight's meeting at *Ascent*. I tossed the vole aside and sprang to my feet. "We have to go. Right now."

Nick looked up from his own pile of small animals. "Did you hear from someone? It didn't register on my end."

"Nope. Everyone was meeting tonight. We may have missed the whole fucking thing, but..."

"It's not all that late. They may still be there." Power

shimmered around Nick as he crafted a teleport spell. Moments later, we were on our way.

I started to say we shouldn't have indulged ourselves, but it had been my idea. How could I have spaced out something as critical as the daily check-in to move our agenda forward?

"It's all right," Nick said.

"Except it's not. Not really." I squeezed my eyes shut for a moment. "The pathetic part is if I had it to do over again, I'd choose you."

"Music to my Vampire ears, darling. Here we go."

Ascent's main room shaped up around us. It teemed with mages. Whew. We hadn't skipped the whole thing. A few people waved; no one asked where we'd been. Percy was talking. Clearly, we'd missed a whole lot, but his words were encouraging.

"We have the bones in place to blow up their communications network. Unfortunately, we'll be in the same boat since there's so much overlap between ISPs."

"We have telepathy," someone shouted.

"It is an advantage." Percy tossed a rare smile toward the speaker.

"Timeframe?" Nick called.

"It depends," Percy rumbled in his deep voice. "How'd your task go tonight?"

His words were addressed to me, so I trotted to his side and gave a concise encapsulation of what we'd found at Solaria's house. Hisses and snarls met my words. I wasn't the only one outraged by Ben's snarky attitude, and how he talked down to mages.

"That's unbelievable," Percy said. "They blamed the task force for what Conan did?"

"About the size of it," I confirmed. "Guess it never occurred to them they have chinks in their organization big enough to drive a tank through."

"Sounds as if there was only the one factory." Ruby glided closer. "If they disbanded the teleconference group, it argues production screeched to a halt."

"Rob came up with a way for us to protect ourselves from discovery," Percy told everyone. The hisses turned to cheers. It was good news indeed since it meant we didn't have to seek out and smash all of the existing machines. Hell, there could be thousands of them.

"We want to know," echoed through the club, interrupted by pounding on the front door. It was just past midnight, well within the realm of our normal operating hours.

Percy strode to the door and yanked it open. "We're closed for another few days," he told whoever stood outside.

"But you're here. I recognize you. And we hear people. Why can't we come in and have a drink?"

"This is a private party." Percy added a tinge of a "go-away" casting to his words. "Keep an eye on the door. We'll post when we plan to reopen." Before whoever was outside could argue further, Percy slammed and latched the entrance. At least my would-be patrons didn't start pounding on it again.

Nick had taken advantage of the break to sidle next to me. "Ask Percy when he's going to take down the communication structure. If he's ready to roll, we should do it right away."

I nodded. Nick had already asked after a timeframe, and Percy had deferred to me. Once the Sorcerer was closer, I said, "Those ISPs could come down anytime. Sooner the better."

Percy heaved his bulk onto his usual stool. "I'll get that ball rolling in a couple of hours. It appears whoever's leading the charge on their side is rattled their little scanner project was disrupted."

A little ping of satisfaction warmed me. I wanted them a hell of a lot more than rattled. I wanted them running so scared they were shitting themselves.

"What about the scanners?" Ruby asked.

"Rob will be here soon with instructions. They're a bit different depending on your type of magic, so you might have to experiment, but I have that prototype machine. Won't take long to map out a master strategy for each of us."

I examined the crowd, picking out Dahlia and her Witches handily. Solaria sat in their midst. I was glad she'd found a home after all this time. If anyone could pull Niona through, it was Moonglow, but I wasn't hopeful. The only magical beings who could endure sustained time in stasis were Vampires.

Clive loped toward us, looking relaxed and his usual, charming self. "Things went well with Dee?" Nick asked.

"Better than good. We're, um, engaged, I guess."

"Dahlia offered her blessings?" I batted my incredulity aside.

"Not exactly, but she said she wouldn't stand in our way." Clive was still grinning from ear to ear.

His joy was infectious, and I smiled too. Good to have a spot of pleasant news in the midst of everything else.

Rob crossed the club from the direction of the bar. Either he'd teleported in or entered the stocking area from the alley. The scanner Dee had stolen was tucked under his arm.

"We're ready to go." Percy amplified his voice with magic to stretch through the nightclub. "But first, I need a few tech-savvy volunteers to help me deep-six all the ISPs."

"What would we be doing?" I asked.

"Depends," the Sorcerer replied. "If Conan gets back, we can harness the lines to amplify a surge and take everything down in one fell swoop."

"And if he doesn't?" Ruby asked.

"I've identified ten locations. We will need to position two mages at each, and we'll strike at the exact same time. It will work just as well, but it takes more of us."

The part he didn't have to say was the additional exposure opened us to discovery. Not that we couldn't kill whoever tried to stop us, but probably not before they took pictures that uploaded to some privately-maintained cloud server and meant we'd be stuck wearing glamours for the foreseeable future.

Glamours that would eat up precious magic stores we needed to fight with.

"Do you want to look for Conan?" Nick asked quietly.

"Wouldn't do any good," I said. "He can always find me, but the reverse isn't true. I can try telepathy, though."

Before I raised my mind voice, the prick of guardian

magic washed over me. Either impeccable timing, or Conan had been keeping tabs on us. My vote was for the latter. Except it wasn't Conan who glided through a spot in the ether, but Moonglow.

The air around her shimmered in a pulsating iridescent glow accentuating the strength of her magic. Solaria ran to her, face drawn into an expression of hope pebbled with despair. Moonglow placed a hand on the Witch's shoulder. "I am sorry," she said, "but Niona is at peace. Her last words were to make certain I let you know. I gave her my word."

Tears welled, running down Solaria's face. "There was never any hope, was there?"

"Nay, child. She trod the paths bordering life for far too long to return. I was successful removing the beacons, though. No one will find her any longer."

Dahlia had moved to Solaria's side. She inclined her head. "Guardian. Thank you for your efforts. May we know where the body is so we can commit her to the goddess?"

"Of course," Moonglow replied. "I shall take you there myself."

"You don't have to—" Solaria began, aiming her words at Dahlia.

"I know, but I want to. You've been through enough. It's the least I can do to help."

"Shall we?" The glimmer around Moonglow deepened as she prepared to sweep the Witches into a spell.

"Wait," I called. "Do you know where Conan is?"

Moonglow smiled softly. "Aye. He will be in your midst soon." The glow deepened, taking on violet hues. When it cleared, she and the two Witches were gone.

Rob had begun his tutorial. I moved nearer to listen with Nick and Clive on either side of me. While I wasn't sure quite what Moonglow's definition of soon was, I was willing to give it an hour or two for Conan to return. By then, everyone should be relatively immune to the risk of discovery the scanner devices hung over our heads.

I whistled to get everyone's attention. "Sorry, Rob," I said, "but this will only take a moment." After the crowd quieted, I mapped out my idea about sharing the manifesto with mortals via the Internet. If we were going to do it, we had to move now.

People exchanged glances. Ruby took a few steps toward me. "While it would be satisfying," the Fae said, "I see problems. It will tip our hand, let the enemy know we've cracked their secrets. They'll be running scared, and they'll add fortifications that will make our job harder."

A Shifter nodded agreement. "If we're successful taking the Net down, no one will have anything to refer to. So we'd only hit those who happened to be online when you distributed the document. And then the whole thing will vanish. Poof."

I held up both hands. "This is why I waited to toss out the question for discussion," I told everyone. "I admit revenge is a powerful motivator, but this wasn't one of my better ideas. Carry on."

Nick draped an arm around my shoulders and gave me a quick squeeze. I leaned into him, appreciating his support.

Rob cupped both hands around his mouth. "Back to the scanners, people."

"How can we tell when we're close to one of those bastardized contraptions?" Dee asked him.

The Sorcerer looked in her direction. "Nothing is perfect. That's the weak link in my design, and I agree it's major. You'll feel a low-key buzz, but by the time you sense it, the thing will have registered you and your location. And sent a picture to a cloud server, although those won't exist at this time tomorrow."

"So, if I launch my ward after I feel the buzz, it's too late?" Dee was clearly hunting for clarification.

"Yes and no," Rob answered her. "What it means is you need to hightail it away from your current location."

"Not sure I like that," Ruby spoke up. "It means we'll always be on the run."

"Wiping out the cloud and all the ISPs will help a lot," Percy jumped into the conversation. "We're flying by the seat of our pants here. Some parts will shape up as we go."

"Want to practice with the scanner next?" Rob pointed at the three of us.

"Take us last," I told him. Despite Moonglow's assurance, I still felt driven to locate Conan. It shouldn't have taken him anywhere near this long to do away with a few mortals.

I moved off to one side with Nick and Clive pacing me. Gathering magic, I infused my telepathy with more oomph than usual. *"Where are you?"*

"Close."

I hadn't expected a reply, and certainly not one on the heels of my question.

"That's a relief," Nick said.

I nodded but wasn't so sure. Something about Conan's tone suggested all was far from well. I told myself it had only been one word, that I was reading far too much into it, but even I recognized a boatload of crap when I tried to smooth over choppy waters.

Ariana was tense. I chalked it up to her being worried about Conan. It did seem odd he'd been gone for so long. With power like his, mowing through a handful of mortals shouldn't have taken nearly this amount of time. But maybe he'd had other tasks to take care of. Fairclaw was sleazy, not trustworthy at all.

Aye, none of my affair, I reminded myself.

A few meters away, Rob was teaching another group of mages how to defeat the scanner. The current circle ranged around him was comprised of Shifters. I'd been surprised when he'd mentioned a rather serious shortcoming: our inability to know when one of the machines was nearby until it was too late to totally hide from it, but maybe we could take advantage of that part.

Rob seemed to be closing on being done with the Shifters. I waited until they began to disperse then raised my voice to make certain I'd be heard. "What about deactivating the machines? Once we know one is close. Instead of tucking our tails between our legs and running for the hills, maybe we could attack and do away with it."

"This one"—Rob pointed at the unit everyone had been practicing with—"has had its outer metal jacket removed."

"Yeah. I did that," Dee called. "Metal isn't as hard on us as it is on you, but it didn't seem to do anything other than make the unit weatherproof."

"Metal is unpleasant, but we can deal with it long enough to crush something," I said. A murmur of assent told me others had been listening to our conversation.

"There you are," Ariana murmured about the same time I scented fur and wet rocks.

I turned expecting a wolf, but Conan was in his human body. His long black hair had been braided in many small rows against his head, and his chest and arms bore tattoos that hadn't been there before. Swirls and runes in blue, violet, and black. Or maybe they were all runes. I didn't know the guardians' language.

I had lots of questions, but they died unspoken. Conan didn't owe answers to me or any of us. Conversations faded as everyone focused on the guardian.

He glanced around the room before he said, "I tracked everyone who was part of the call earlier today. Most of them are dead. All the mortals and mages who chose poorly."

I waited to see what would come next.

Ariana kept her gaze trained on Conan but offered him space. Out of all of us, she was the one who had a relationship with him, and she knew him well enough to remain silent.

The Conan who stood among us had a vastly different feel from the mage I'd become familiar with. Something significant had changed, or maybe it was just now showing. It would be impertinent to question him, though.

Percy walked toward Conan until he stood a meter away facing him. He bowed low. "It's good to see you. We were growing concerned."

Conan drew black brows into a thick line over his amber eyes. Even though he wore a man's body, he didn't resemble anything human. Not really. The planes of his face held an otherworldly aspect as he straightened to his full height.

"I had business to attend to. I am not pleased with the consequences, but I have accepted my rightful place among my kinsmen. It happened a while back. Ariana knew, but she also understood it was my news to impart."

"What does that mean?" Percy asked.

"I am prince to my people," Conan said. "Most have welcomed me, but one faction was...troublesome. They have come to their senses so we can function with a single voice once again."

I exchanged a look with Ariana. Did it mean Fairclaw wouldn't be a problem any longer?

"Guardians will fight alongside every other mage in the war against mortals," Conan went on. "It was our primary point of disagreement, and it no longer exists."

Cheers raced through the nightclub. I felt like whooping myself. Between guardians and Kelpies, we scarcely needed the Clan Ravnos Vampires who'd thought to sucker Clive and me. But then I mulled over how the guardians' newfound arrangement had come to pass. Part of me was certain it hadn't been easily won.

A recent meeting had included Fairclaw and a couple of seers, Future and Past, warning us to step aside and let guardians handle every aspect of the war with humans. It turned out their plan was mass annihilation, leaving Earth littered with millions of rotting corpses. They'd dressed it up with some tripe about Yggdrasil, the One Tree, dying. That part had been true enough, except Yggdrasil has been on its way out for several centuries.

Nothing new there.

"Are congratulations in order?" Ariana's question was carefully worded, otherwise she'd have simply offered Conan her best wishes.

"No." Conan's outline developed a liquid aspect. When it stopped shimmering, he was a wolf again. If I looked carefully through my third eye, the same runic markings swirled through his black-and-silver fur.

"This might not be a good time for you—" Percy began.

Conan woofed once sharply.

"Does that mean you want me to shut up or get on with it?" Percy asked in his usual no-nonsense manner.

"The latter. I already said we'd help."

"We have a Plan B for this campaign," the Sorcerer told him and proceeded to outline the two possibilities to destroy all Internet-based communications. Many of his descriptions may as well have been in some foreign tongue—one I wasn't familiar with—for all the light they shone on what he'd cobbled together.

"I will bend the lines to your purpose," Conan said.

"We appreciate it," Ariana told her longtime companion. "It's safer and accomplishes the same goal."

"Mortals got along without a digitized world for millennia," Ruby spoke up.

"The operative term there is past tense." Dee smirked. "Bet this sends them into quite the tizzy."

"No time like right now to find out," Conan said. "I need six or seven of you. Mages with complementary powers."

"Tell us who." Percy stood quietly, watchful and waiting.

Not surprisingly, Conan rattled off names of mages he knew: Ruby, Dee, Christa, Percy, Ariana, and Selene. He didn't mention me. Could I crash the party anyway?

Ariana saved me from asking by hooking a hand around my arm. "Nick's coming too."

Conan clacked his jaws shut before asking, "Are we ready to leave?"

"Soon," Percy said. "Rob's just finishing up here, and I need to run a couple of short tests to make certain my calculations pan out."

"An hour?" Conan asked.

"Should be perfect," Percy told him and hurried toward the stockroom.

The wolf morphed into a motorcycle complete with muted engine noises. "Let me get the helmets," Ariana told him.

While she was dredging them out of the back room, I furled my brows. "Where are we going?"

"Away from here."

I'd already figured that part out, but I wasn't complaining. The wind buffeting me felt delightful. So did

Ariana's lithe frame balanced between my legs on the narrow seat. Every bump in the road sent waves of heat blasting into my cock. Whoever had designed this form of transportation must have had a rich imagination and a healthy sex drive.

Conan drove us to the same deserted park where we'd first seen the rift some of the guardians clung to as proof the One Tree was dying. After tossing our helmets under a bush, we hustled after the wolf as he loped from the parking area to the beach.

"You didn't bring us here to watch the moon set," Ariana said. "Spill it."

"Fairclaw didn't suddenly come to his senses," Conan said. "Courtesy of my magic, he's locked on another world along with the few rebels who supported him rather than me."

"Seems like good news," I ventured.

"It is, unless he drills a hole through my casting," Conan agreed.

"What are the odds of that happening?" Ariana asked.

"Pretty damned high." Conan punctuated his words with a spate of howling. Answering yowls told me coyotes lurked nearby.

"That's right." Ariana muffled a snort. "Get the local wildlife riled up."

"Maybe a better question is how long we can count on him staying out of the way," I said.

"Any idea what he'll do if he breaks free?" Ariana asked.

"I don't know the answer to either question," Conan

admitted. "It's critical that we hurry. Move up timetables sitting a week or more in the future."

"You left something out." Ariana narrowed her eyes.

"Yes, I did. Darksword is in the wind."

It took a minute before I remembered he was the guardian who'd been at McMurdy's house. One of about twenty mages, he'd been part of a group who'd provided security for the crooked head of San Francisco's paranormal task force.

"Why didn't Fairclaw end him?" I asked.

"It is the question of the hour, isn't it?" Conan returned my query with one of his own.

"But that means Darksword could join forces with Fairclaw," Ariana muttered.

"It might have already happened," Conan said. "Mother believes so."

"Fuck." My fangs wanted out. I didn't see any reason to hold them in place.

"Maybe we can skip the middle objective," Ariana said in a thoughtful tone.

"Which middle objective?" Conan asked.

"The original plan was to take out communications first, financials second, and then descend on Washington en masse. When we wipe out the Internet and the cloud, it will drive a huge hole in banks since virtually all of them have switched to digital deposits and statements. Credit cards will be impacted too. Absent a digitized network, most financial transactions will grind to a halt. It will mean people have to actually go inside a bank, but even that won't do them any good. The banks will only have access to their local servers and won't be able to communicate with any other branches."

She'd been talking faster as she outlined what sounded like chaos with ensuing panic.

"After whatever we do with what's left of tonight," Conan said, "we can converge on Washington and cut a swathe of destruction."

"Might take another day to pull everything together," Ariana cautioned. "No one was thinking it would be quite so soon." She glanced my way. "We'll need platoons or companies or however military shit is organized."

"I'll help with that," I told her. My phone chimed. It startled me, and I had to hunt for which pocket I'd dropped it into.

"Ha! You turned it on," Ariana commented.

I finally found the damned thing. The screen announced Ravnos. I could have ignored it since I was still feeling raw and used, but I punched Accept Call. "What?" I demanded.

"Not sounding overly friendly, Giovanni," a male voice drawled. I didn't give a fuck which of them it was.

"After the shit you pulled, I considered not answering at all," I retorted.

"We offered you a great honor—" he began.

"Stuff it," Ariana said loud enough for him to hear.

"We'd welcome you too," the Clan Ravnos Vampire purred.

"Not on my dance card. Maybe when pigs fly, but not before."

"What do you want?" I sputtered.

"After much discussion and consideration, we've decided to join your little war."

"Put it on speaker," Ariana said. I fumbled around, so she did it for me. "Why'd you change your minds?" she asked.

"It wasn't that we were opposed," the man replied. "But we had a different goal in mind. They weren't mutually exclusive."

Conan growled, followed by, "How do we know we can trust you?"

"Who are you?" the Vampire asked.

"A guardian."

It clearly hadn't been an answer the Vampire expected. After a short pause, he stammered, "You have Kelpies and a guardian as allies?"

"More than one guardian," I told him.

"How is that possible? They hate us?"

"It's a long story," Ariana cut in, "and not relevant right this moment. We will march on Washington DC quite soon. Is this a good number to firm up details?"

"Aye. Looking forward to meeting you, sweetheart."

If the phone had scent capabilities, I'd have smelled pheromones, and it infuriated me. "She is mine," I told him.

"Certainly, for now, but these things never last."

"This thing will," Ariana said. "We'll make good use of your offer of aid, though."

Before I could tell him that if he so much as looked cross-eyed at Ariana, I'd slice his dick off, she'd disconnected.

"I take it that was unexpected," Conan woofed softly.

"Very." I pocketed the phone.

"Wonder what changed their minds," Ariana mused. "It wasn't you and Clive leaving, that's for sure."

"They follow the news," I said. "Maybe they looked up a few things and decided to sign on with the winning side."

Ariana nodded. "It's very much something a Vampire would do. Plentiful blood is another powerful incentive. Damn it."

I angled a worried look her way. "What?"

"His phone number, the one I asked about, won't work after we dismantle the communications networks."

Conan lifted his shoulders slightly. Before dropping them into place, he said, "So? A quick teleport is probably preferable, anyway."

"True enough. We should go back," I said, still annoyed by the impudence of the Ravnos Vampire. After trying to manipulate me, he'd decided he wanted Ariana to grace his bed. It would never happen. Not now. Not ever. She and I had both said as much, but it wouldn't necessarily dissuade him. Sex is a game for us. One heartily worth playing. And a diversion...

"Or have the others come here," Conan suggested, cutting into my sour thoughts. "It's a straight shot to an impressive conjunction of lines that would be just right for what Percy wants to do."

I opened my mind voice, listed names, and said, *"Join us."*

"Timing couldn't have been better," Percy rumbled in his deep voice as he walked through a portal followed by Ruby, Dee, Christa, and Selene.

"I'm more than ready to kiss my cell phone bye-bye." Ruby grinned.

"Yeah, I've always hated the damned thing," Dee said.

"Och, it's because we're old and remember how charming life was without electronics." Christa nodded knowingly.

"Nay, it's because we have magic as a fallback." Percy eyed Conan. "Let's make this happen."

I thought about the motorcycle helmets, but they were reasonably well concealed. We could pick them up later if the day was overcast, or the following night. We'd damned near run this one into dawn, but where we were going it didn't matter.

The unique feel of guardian enchantment filled my nose with rich scents and reminded me how strong Conan was. Transporting all of us didn't faze him as we traded the stretch of deserted lakeshore for curved tunnels lit by the ley-lines' golden glow.

He hadn't been kidding about a conjunction. I counted ten lines jutting out like spokes on a wheel. The place they came together hummed noisily, vibrating with potential. The fine hairs on the back of my neck stood on end, and it felt like I was walking through an electrical storm.

Conan arranged us so we each stood in the vee between two lines. It left two spots unoccupied, but the wolf didn't appear concerned. "Can we absorb the electronic hubs through the lines?" Percy asked. "Or do we need to destroy them individually where they stand?"

"How many?" Conan asked.

"Ten."

He'd mentioned that number before. I was surprised there weren't more, but then maybe smaller operations were dependent on the primary ones.

"We can unmake them with the lines, but it will have to be in two batches," Conan said.

"How long in between?" the Sorcerer asked.

"Maybe an hour. Taking something down to an atomic level doesn't happen quickly. Remember your clan house?"

"Unfortunately, yes," Percy replied, followed by, "An hour is too long. Can we take out half of them the old-fashioned way and then unmake the remaining ones?"

"Aye. We can do that from here as well," Conan said. "No need to expose yourselves needlessly. Do you have placcments for the targets?"

"Of course." Percy rattled off numbers that could have been longitude and latitude, or something else entirely.

Conan jumped onto the lines and walked in a circle, touching each in turn with his nose. The humming intensified; so did the eerie glow throwing gold-orange light on the tunnel walls. "Open your magic to me," he commanded.

The rope-like ley-lines thickened, growing twice the size of my arm. They took on an incandescent glow, reflecting every shade in a color palette. The display was weird and beautiful, a visual representation of our combined enchantments.

Percy read off the numeric coordinates once more, stopping after five of them this time. A loud whooshing filled the tunnel and bounced off the walls. Power shot along some of the lines, followed by silence so total it shocked me.

"That's it?" Percy asked.

"It should be," Conan told him. "Let me see if we're ready for part two?" He nosed the lines again, maybe checking their integrity.

I'd grown better at reading the wolf, and I already knew the news wasn't good before he lifted his head. "What happened?" I asked. So far, this had been too easy. Lobbing off shots from a protected location hadn't worked during my years as a knight. Effective encounters required getting your hands dirty.

The reek of the sea rolled through the cavern, salty but with overtones of rotting kelp. I'd smelled it before, and not all that long ago.

"Balor," Ariana yelled. "How in the fuck are you even breathing?"

He shrugged and grew progressively more visible through a thinning mist. "No one took the time to end me, ergo I'm still here." The Celtic demon god of death smiled, displaying rows of pointy yellow teeth. He towered over Percy's better than two-meter height. Patchy green hair that looked like seaweed fell past his shoulders. He had one enormous leg and one dark eye centered below his forehead.

Conan jumped down from the lines and stood growling in front of the god. "I banished you."

"It didn't stick. The other part did, though, where you removed the Fomori from my oversight. They're running free, killing willy-nilly. Just a passel of pesky mortals, though. Nothing to be concerned with."

"Who are you working for now?" Conan draped a truth weave over Balor and added compulsion to his question.

"Why, one just like you, guardian. Guess your kin aren't picky about whom they hobnob with these days." He batted at the net and whined, "It burns. Remove it."

"You do not command me," Conan told him. "We're not done. Why are you here?"

"To check up on you. Why else?"

"Who is your master?"

Balor opened his mouth, but it twisted at a strange angle. The demon grappled with his throat as if he couldn't breathe.

"He's under a geas that forces his silence," Dee said. "I see it hovering around him."

Balor was panting now. His pale, greenish-skin was turning white, and his lips blue. Conan barked a few words, shimmered into human form, and uttered a few more. Power words, harsh and horrible, they made my head ache.

Balor had been swaying alarmingly on his single leg, but he stabilized and gasped, "Thank you."

Conan narrowed his eyes to slits. "Tell Darksword his days are numbered."

Balor shook his head. "I'll pass. It will only piss him off."

Closing a hand over the demon god's shoulder, Conan squeezed until I heard the crunch of bones breaking. "If I ever see you again, you will suffer. Do we understand one another?"

"He said much the same. About suffering if I failed," Balor mumbled.

"Pick your poison." Conan spat the words. "Now get out of here."

Balor didn't waste any time. The only thing left of him

was the reek of decaying kelp. "Why'd you let him go?" Ariana demanded.

"We have other priorities," Percy said. "Conan chose well."

"And did a wonderfully sneaky job defeating the geas," Dee added.

Conan was a wolf once more. "Let's finish what we came here to do," he snarled. "We'll repeat what we already did, and then I'm going to find my fallen kinsman. Before he aligns himself with Fairclaw and his contingent and turns my existence into a living hell."

My money was on the two already having forged an alliance, but I kept it to myself.

"Do you want help?" I asked, but Conan didn't answer. The same power that had filled the cavern swelled once more. My magical ability was definitely on the wane, but it was daytime. I'm never at my best when the sun is up.

"We will go with him." Ariana's mind voice slammed into me. *"This is one fight he's not taking on alone."*

I met her gaze across the swollen lines and nodded. I was in, and not just because she was the one doing the asking. I respected the hell out of Conan. If there was something she and I could do to turn the Darksword hunt into a slam-dunk, I was all for it.

CHAPTER TWELVE, ARIANA

Seeing Balor waltz through a portal had been a shock. I'd figured we were done with the demon god who reeked of death even worse than Vampires did. Apparently not done after all, but he'd left once Conan lit a fire under him. I wouldn't want to be stuck between competing guardian priorities, but Balor didn't exactly engender sympathy.

If I were him, I'd pick Conan over Darksword any day of the week.

Because this was our second go-round, the next set of ISPs ceded to Conan's spell even quicker than the first ones had. It was hard for me to believe we'd managed to take the whole shebang down from our remote location. We may not have used the ley-lines in a true "reduction to individual atoms" maneuver, but their reach and their magic had enabled Percy's Plan B and allowed us to strike from a protected distance.

I snuck a peek at my phone, but it wouldn't have worked down here anyway. The specter of an Internet-less world was appealing as hell. Dee had moved off to one side and stood in the middle of a herd of shades. Since their bodies all blended together, it was tough to tell how many had mobbed her. She must be comforting them after the ley-lines' burst of power. Or perhaps Balor had stirred them up.

He was enough to give anybody, magical or otherwise, a lifetime of nightmares. Speaking of bad dreams, I still didn't trust Clan Ravnos. Yeah, they'd reached out to Nick, but their motivation remained murky. Did they genuinely want to get in a few licks—in exchange for all the blood they could slurp down? Or did their objectives run deeper?

"If they turn into a problem," Nick murmured, "we can always feed them to the Kelpies."

I snorted. "You were in my thoughts."

"Always, *Cara*."

Evidence of his fascination with me was heady, but now wasn't the time to get lost in fantasies of a life with him.

"Shall we test our work?" Percy asked.

The feel of guardian magic, replete with its characteristic scents wafted around me. It meant Conan was leaving. I executed a forward leap and landed dead in front of him. "Nick and I are coming with you."

"The rest of us could too." Ruby joined me. "More bang for your buck, wolfie-boy. We work well together."

Hackles lifted along Conan's shoulders; his eyes gleamed bright gold in their centers. "Too many," he said.

"You're stuck with Nick and me." I held firm, not willing to be brushed aside. Whoever this Darksword fucker was, we'd make mincemeat out of him. Assuming we could find the scoundrel.

"Lucky me," Conan rumbled around a growl.

"You are lucky," I told him tartly. "Not many non-Vampires are graced with our strength, speed, and bloodthirsty ways."

Percy had gathered Christa, Dee, and Selene next to him. "We will do as you wish," he told Conan. "We stand ready to aid your search."

"If Ariana can claim sovereignty, I can too," Ruby said.

I elbowed her. "Not exactly what I'm doing," I retorted. "I just think it will go faster with help. We're far from done with everything else. This is an unexpected wrinkle."

"Wars are full of those." Nick sent a too-bright smile my way.

"Fine," Conan said. "The three of you may accompany me, but no more. We're leaving now."

"I'll be working with Rob, snipping any loose ends," Percy said. "Ping me when you're back."

I snapped off a mock salute about the time Conan's power sashayed through the tunnel and moved us out of there as if we'd been shot from a cannon. I considered asking where we were going, but I'd find out soon enough.

"Why does Moonglow believe Darksword and Fairglow are in cahoots?" Nick asked.

"She didn't tell me," Conan replied. "We haven't had much time to talk about anything. She was tied up with the damaged Witch, and I had my hands full imprisoning Fairclaw and his allies."

"How many?" I inquired.

"Six including him," Conan snarled.

I ran my tongue over my fangs. They'd come out to play. It happened when I was keyed up. Including Darksword—if he was aligned with the others—we faced seven. It was a lot of guardians, but we'd figure things out. I'd been thinking maybe only two or three had believed in Fairclaw enough to give up their freedom to make a point.

"Are you certain it wouldn't be wise to include a few more of us?" Ruby asked in an unusual burst of diplomacy. The Fae had dispensed with her glamour. Red wings were folded behind her back. The points of her ears stuck up through a fall of violet hair; her golden eyes opened wider for emphasis revealing vertical slit pupils. She must have ten pairs of dark slacks and an equal number of white blouses because the combination was all she ever wore. Her battered leather vest sat atop everything. As usual, her feet were bare.

"Quite certain," Conan answered Ruby. "Each mage adds power but requires oversight. This is a task I would have preferred to handle alone. Particularly if things go badly. Fairclaw will swear allegiance to me if it's the last thing I do."

I winced at his oversight comment. I'd been pushy, but if the wolf had truly wished to fly solo, he'd have left without us. "Fairclaw and allegiance don't belong in the same sentence," I mumbled and left it there. Conan would understand what I was getting at.

"He was their leader for a long while," Conan explained.

"So was Mistral," I shot back, "but tenure doesn't equate to loyalty. I wasn't the only one who resented him, just the only one to turn my bitterness into action."

Conan barked before he said, "Try not to take this wrong, but Vampires and guardians don't have much in common."

Except I did take umbrage. Because it was Conan, I kept hot words from spewing out. Guardians weren't better than us, only different. Or maybe I was reading too much into his statement. Perhaps he'd merely been expressing a fact.

"Ariana?" Conan's gaze drilled into me.

"Yeah, what?"

"Name one element guardians and Vampires share."

"Point taken, but both of us can be manipulative sons of bitches." I suppressed my ire. I've always had a quick fuse, even when I was human.

Conan woofed laughter. The tone of his journey spell changed, which meant we had to be close to wherever he was taking us. Ruby's nostrils flared. "Off world somewhere," she murmured.

I'd figured that part out when it took us more than a few minutes to reach our destination, but then she probably had too. An empty beach with green sand stretched before us. Puny, twisted trees with black leaves grew at intervals, but singly, almost as if their toxicity could spread to their own kind. Pockets of yellow sap formed pustules along their trunks. Some had burst, steaking the scabby bark. A quick sniff told me retreating to my breathing-optional status was in order.

"What is this place?" Ruby asked quietly.

"Where I left Fairclaw," Conan told her. "He's still here. I'm going to pound some answers out of him."

"Maybe you won't need to," Nick said.

"It's the quickest way." Conan argued.

"If Darksword was behind Balor hunting us down," Nick went on, "my guess is he's already here either reporting in or generating new plans. Perhaps both."

I opened what I hoped was a subtle channel and scanned the area around us, not finding anything akin to a guardian except for Conan. "How do you know Fairclaw is here?" I demanded. "I can't find him."

Conan turned a wolfish grin my way, jaws open, tongue lolling. "I hid him well. Not much point dumping him someplace if anyone stopping by could locate him."

A ward chockfull of Fae enchantment snapped into place around us. Ruby said, "Look," and pointed to the incoming tide. A misshapen black lump floated about fifty yards offshore. It looked like a fish at first, except no fish that large would be so close to shore.

Damn it. My magic hadn't registered that, either. "What is it?" I looked at Ruby.

"Feels like Balor to me." She narrowed her odd eyes. "If he's on Darksword's payroll, it means—"

"The whole rotten bunch are already here," Conan cut in. "Makes things simpler."

I wasn't sure about that. My fangs were still down; whatever passes for Vampire adrenaline surged. Conan's wolf form exploded, leaving him in his human body, naked and furious. I'd only caught a quick glimpse of Darksword in McMurdy's home, but if I had to choose whose side to curry favor with, it would be Conan's.

He ground out a few words in the guardian's language; something altered a few yards away. A structure made of stones and mortar came into view. As soon as I could see it, guardian magic plowed into me. Unlike Conan's power, which had a clean, fresh aspect, this enchantment felt dark, perverted. Maybe Conan had done something to force Fairclaw's true nature into the open.

Behind us, the stentorian notes of a monstrous creature breathing suggested Balor had traded sea for shore. I didn't bother turning around. "You're like a bad penny." I aimed my words at him.

"I've told you, Vampire, we could have a lot of fun. I remember you from a very long while back. You were newly turned, wallowing in hubris and bloodlust. Damn but you were a gorgeous sight. My Fomori talked of little else for the next year."

I did look over a shoulder then. "I left," I reminded him.

"I'd have come after you, but Mistral always had quite the possessive streak."

"We all do." Nickolas spaced out his words. "Stay away from her."

"I'm a patient demon." Balor's thick lips spread in a mockery of a smile. "Eventually, I'll hit the front of the line."

"Don't count on it," I told him and returned my attention to the rock building. How in the hell had Conan constructed it? I didn't see anything reassembling those stones anywhere in the vicinity. Eh, maybe they were illusion, but an unimaginably strong one if they imprisoned several guardians.

Nick performed a leap that deposited him in front of Balor, facing him. Vampires are exceptional athletes, but we rarely get to use that side of our talent. "Whose side are you on?" Nick demanded. "Choose now."

"More fun to keep you guessing." Balor leered.

Ruby glided next to Nick and shaded her eyes as she tilted her head to look up at the demon. "What would happen if I cast magic to banish you from this place?"

"Wouldn't work." Balor laughed, spraying her and Nick with salty water.

"Let's see, shall we?" White light arced from Ruby's raised hands. She's one of the strongest Fae I've ever known. Bands of glowing luminescence circled Balor, growing closer as she cinched in her casting.

Balor's hulking form started shrinking; I remembered when we'd first run into him, he'd looked like a gnome. Was he like guardians? Capable of infinite forms?

"Don't let him divert you," Conan shouted.

My attention was split between the stone cottage and Ruby's spell. So far, the demon hadn't eluded Ruby. He was shifting through forms like a riverboat gambler shuffling cards. Conan had labeled it a diversion.

It suggested he knew more about what was going on that I did.

Conan still faced the structure. An eerie glow surrounded him; nacre and pale-green, it reminded me of the inside of abalone shells. I joined him and opened my magic, offering it. The pull was instantaneous, and so strong it nearly yanked me off me feet.

Power built, pummeling me as it expanded. I recognized my own and Conan's, but other elements were mixed in. Earth and water suggested Conan had harnessed the innate power of this world in his spell to secure the other guardians.

A whoop from Ruby suggested she was winning, but I couldn't divide my focus, not with Conan drawing juice from me like a madman. "Let's end them and be done with it," I ground out.

"Looking appealing," he agreed.

A rending, wrenching noise brought my head snapping around, but it wasn't Balor, who was now the size of a housecat. Stones shot into the air; in their place thick vines grew where the cottage had stood. Unlike the stones, I could see through them.

Nick materialized next to me, fangs out. "What's happening here?"

"I'm happening, Vampire," an unfamiliar voice snarled from behind us.

I didn't give a fuck what we faced. I was done standing around. Vampires were never ones to sit behind a blind tracking prey. I laced my fingers in with Nick's and said, "Blood and magic."

He understood I meant it as a battle cry. "Sorry," I told Conan and slammed the gate shut on my power. Letting go of Nick's hand, I executed a midair leap. Once I was faced the right way, a guardian with long black hair came into view.

Darksword.

Nick jumped him from the right; I took the left. We drove him to the ground, but by the time he got there he wasn't human any longer. A hissing, spitting cobra writhed in our combined grip. Eh, bad guess on his part. Snake venom doesn't faze us. Nick had his dirk in hand. It reminded me of the Gerber Ghoststrike blade I'd tucked into an ankle holster a while back. It had been a part of my wardrobe ever since.

I joined Nick carving slashes through the snake's thick, rubbery hide. The acrid stench of poison thickened in the still air of this world. And then our enemy wasn't a snake any longer but something large and scaly with wings. Sheesh. It looked like a winged dinosaur with a bunch of scales missing.

"Don't let it get away," Nick shouted and stabbed one of its eyes. It roared with pain—or maybe fury. First sound it had made.

I drew my arm back again and again, stabbing any part of the thing I could reach. Some spots, its scales were the size of dinner plates and maybe an inch thick. I avoided them but found vulnerabilities at the junctions where the scales fitted together. Darksword was bellowing nonstop now.

My next thrust was in the vicinity of his throat. If I could shut him up, we'd all benefit. I missed his larynx but hit a major vessel. Black blood geysered, coating me and Nick and everything else nearby.

"Wahoo! Looks fun." Ruby hurled herself next to me. She'd sliced the ball of her thumb open. Blood oozed from her, forming daggers that arrowed into the beast's weak spots. Mouth. Eyes. Nose. Neck.

A spider the size of a wolf clattered close. Each foot was tipped in a long, red claw. What the hell? Except it wasn't as if there were a shit ton of choices. "Balor?"

"Who else?" The spider's mouth opened and closed, displaying miniature fangs.

"We made a deal," Ruby panted, still directing her blood at critical junctures.

"I have an idea," Nick yelled over the howling guardian. Vampires can move quickly when we want to. One minute he stood on my other side, the next he sat astride the base of the thing's long neck like an arcane dragon rider. "Kiss it goodbye, guardian," he shouted and sliced his blade, glistening with magic, along the monster's neck.

Mostly severed, the head hung by strips of skin; the reek of blood increased by a factor of ten. I had no idea if we could drink it, but swallowing guardian blood felt wrong, somehow. Maybe it had something to do with my long tenure living with Conan, but it would be akin to killing and draining a fellow Vampire. Not that it didn't happen, but it had always felt perverse to me when Mistral ended one of our own. I'd feed later.

The spider climbed up Darksword's front leg. I hadn't exactly forgotten about Balor, but I'd been focused on Nick and working in synchrony to take down our prey. Between its claws and the uneven scales, the arachnid moved quickly. "What kind of deal?" I asked Ruby.

"He choose freedom." The Fae hooted sharp laughter. "But he waited to see which way the wind was blowing."

"Conan offered him freedom once before," I reminded her.

She nodded. "I made it abundantly clear if he fucks up again, I will personally turn the Fomori loose on him."

"You can do that?"

"You bet I can."

I quit there, cleaned blood off my blade, and tucked it

away. I didn't want to know more about how she and the water demons had developed such a cozy relationship. All magical creatures in the British Isles knew about one another, but my one and only go round with the Fomori, we'd all been rolling around in dead and almost dead bodies, hooting and hollering and having a fine old time. Last I checked, Fae weren't into killing mortals for sport.

Ruby was old though. Incredibly old. My bet was she was chockful of secrets that reeked of blood and death and destruction.

Nick jumped down from his perch, sheathed his knife, and dusted bloody hands together. "The guardian isn't dead, but Balor will finish him off. From the inside."

I craned my neck, looking up. Sure enough, the spider was nowhere in sight, but the gaping neck wound, still spewing blood, was more than big enough to accommodate him. I didn't trust Balor as far as I could see him, but I had faith he'd make a speedy end to the guardian who'd used him as a spy and lord only knew what else.

"Where's Conan?" Nick asked.

The question crashed down on me. I'd slammed the gates on my magic to fight another battle. Conan hadn't lodged a protest, so I'd assumed he didn't need me. After all, he'd wanted to come here alone. The way I read things, we were down one guardian, and Ruby had effectively diverted Balor.

For now.

That demon was more annoying than one of those pop-up clowns that leered at you from a million directions. We were winning, goddammit. It wasn't like Conan to just leave. Not without saying something.

I scanned the place the vines had been. It looked like every other spot on this creepy beach. When my eyes didn't yield data, I turned in a full circle and sent a seeking spell outward. "I can't find him," I admitted. "Or anything that remotely feels like a guardian other than that hunk of wilting protoplasm that used to be Darksword."

Ruby was similarly engaged, nostrils flaring as she searched. "I don't believe they're here," she said. "Any of them."

It stuck in my craw, but I did my best to project sweetness and light when I crooned, "Balor. We could use you for a moment."

I wasn't certain what I expected, but it wasn't instant results. Apparently, I was a bigger draw than the dying guardian because a weird little creature with a huge, bloody mouth and double sets of eyes shot from what was left of Darksword's neck.

Between the sprawled carcass and where I stood, the demon regained his usual, one-legged form. "Sweetheart! Does this mean my number came up?"

I forced a smile. "We need your magic, demon. Where are Conan and the other guardians?"

"One's right there." Balor laughed uproariously and jabbed a finger at Darksword's shuddering bulk.

"The other ones," Nick pressed.

"Why should I tell you anything." Balor pouted. "You're hogging up the lady's time."

"Because I will give my friends, the Fomori, your scent

and a fat purse to run you to ruin," Ruby purred, her tone diametrically opposed to her words.

Balor angled his head back, his nostrils twitching. Apparently, his efforts didn't yield data because power pooled around him. After a few minutes had dribbled past, he shook his head. "Not here. No longer. I can see the place they left, but I have no idea where they went."

The wreck of Darksword's body thrashed weakly from side to side. "Fuck!" Balor rolled his single eye. "Bastard's regenerating."

"Have at it," Ruby suggested silkily. "We'll not interrupt again."

Lights flickered and flashed as Balor adopted his previous form, the one that was mostly teeth, and jumped back into the headless not-quite-corpse.

I shook my head. "I feel like a total shit," I said.

"Why?" Nick asked.

"Conan was sucking magic out of me like there was no tomorrow when I decided my ability would be better spent attacking Darksword."

"You can't blame yourself." Ruby shrugged pragmatically. "No one ever fought anyone else's war."

"Yeah, but where did they go?" My voice had developed a shrill aspect. If something happened to Conan because I'd been a selfish twit, I'd have one hell of a hard time coming to terms with it.

The whisky and wildflower scent of Fae magic wafted around us as Ruby built a transport spell.

"Where are we going?" Nick asked.

"Ley-lines," Ruby told him. "And then we're going to

find Moonglow or Earthtime or one of them so they can track Conan."

It was as good a plan as we were likely to come up with. I was sunk so deep in guilt, I'd quit thinking.

Pull your head out of your ass, my inner maven snarled.

I did my best. The moment I felt the ley-lines' thrum, I kicked my mind voice open and shrieked for Moonglow. Conan shared her blood. If anyone could find him, it would be his mother.

I'd been shocked when I gazed around the beach and didn't find Conan. But I trusted the guardian to take care of himself. I'd started to suggest Ariana do the same—assume the wolf knew what he was about—but she'd never quite moved past her protective role. The one she'd assumed the day she found him when he was a scrawny puppy.

I'd had a hell of a good time slicing and dicing Darksword and fighting alongside Ariana. We had to close off this side trip, though. It wasn't part of our master game plan. While the renegade guardians were annoying and a threat to Conan, dealing them out wouldn't have any impact on our primary objective, which was terrorizing humans enough to force them to back down and leave us alone.

Ruby took the words out of my mouth—or the thoughts out of my mind—when she grabbed the point and teleported us to the nearest ley-line. Not that the concepts of near and far actually fit for ley-lines. They occupy their own universe, wrapping around all worlds in a complex pattern.

We stood in the fey half-light of the rounded tunnel. The lines looked healthy enough, glowing golden and casting shadows on the walls. Ariana was calling Moonglow, so there was no need for me to do anything but wait and admire her lithe form as she paced from one spot to another.

What if Moonglow didn't come?

We needed an alternative approach, and I was fresh out of them. Where would Fairclaw have gone? Surely not back to a guardian stronghold. Or maybe it would be his first stop. If his objective was to wrest power away from Conan, he'd have to plead his case with his kinsmen. For that, he'd require access to other guardians.

The lines pulsed brighter. Breath would have whooshed from me if I'd been the breathing type. Must mean Moonglow's arrival was imminent. Good. The urgency I'd felt earlier had done nothing but grow more insistent. The reality of what it meant punched me in the gut. We'd been snared in a diversion. Something to keep us from decimating mortals.

It had to mean Fairclaw was somehow associated with the humans who were intent on destroying us. Except it made zero sense. His last master plan had called for murdering everything human on Earth.

It might have been a ruse to throw us off track. Or maybe one of the two seers had come up with it, and Fairclaw had acted as their mouthpiece with no intention of ever following through. Conan had said the seers couldn't lie. Did that prohibition extend to Fairclaw?

Damn it. I had questions, but answers weren't likely to be forthcoming.

The lines glowed brighter still. Ariana took off at a dead run in the direction guardian power burned strongest. Worried it might not be Moonglow, I ran after her, shouting, "Wait."

By the time I caught up, she was firing questions at a white wolf. Moonglow jumped down from the lines, shifting to her human form. I grabbed Ariana's upper arm. "That was risky."

She shook me off. "Don't go all Neanderthal on me. Moonglow and I have had a link ever since she saved me from silver poisoning, and—"

"What's wrong?" Moonglow skewered Ariana and me with her amber eyes. Her white hair was done up in braids, and the blue gemstone she always wore was suspended from a golden chain around her neck.

"Conan's gone," Ariana told her.

Moonglow added a pointed aspect to her stare. "He's often gone."

"Yeah, but you can find him," Ariana pressed.

Ruby ran lightly to where we stood. "We went after Fairclaw and his contingent. Found 'em right where Conan left them. Balor was there too, and Darksword—"

A strident hiss puffed from Moonglow. "Damn that treasonous scum."

I considered reminding her Fairclaw fit the bill too, but wisely kept my mouth shut. Moonglow had spent a whole lot of years with him and might still have a soft spot for the other guardian. If Fairclaw wanted to sidetrack us, I'd be damned if I'd fall headlong into whatever trap he'd baited by forcing his kinsmen to line up on one side or the other.

For him or against him. Five had chosen him. Probably others had struggled with whom to support…

"We made short work of Darksword." Ruby's words resonated with pride. "Balor isn't a threat any longer—and least not today. Probably not tomorrow, either."

"When we surfaced from destroying Darksword," I spoke up, "Conan, Fairclaw, and his minions were gone."

"Guardians don't have minions," she corrected me. Twin lines formed between her eyebrows as she considered what I'd said.

"Not the point," I said somewhat stiffly.

Moonglow nodded slowly. "No, it's not. You want me to find Conan, right?"

"Yes," Ariana screeched, and then added, "Please. He was borrowing magic from me until I needed it to fight Darksword, and then when I looked for him, he was gone."

"Let me see what I can do." Moonglow's form took on a shadowy aspect.

"We want to come." Ariana must have recognized the guardian was leaving.

"Not possible. You'll only slow me down." Moonglow tilted her head back as if she were looking at something above her.

"But—" Ariana sputtered.

The guardian turned to her and dropped a hand onto her shoulder. "No. I will figure this out, but it requires more guardians, not a mix of magics. Collecting a few kinsmen is my first stop."

After a brief internal tussle, mostly because I didn't want to look stupid or like a conspiracy theorist, I said, "Wait a moment. It's possible Fairclaw somehow joined forces with the mortals who've underwritten our destruction." I held up a hand. "Before you say it's preposterous, consider all the mages who've been coopted in this war."

Moonglow crooked two fingers my way. "And you believe this why?"

Her question was encouraging. It meant she wasn't discounting my theory and was willing to listen—for a short while. "He's been throwing roadblocks out from the beginning. The first was his gambit to keep everyone except guardians out of the picture."

"Mmph. You may be onto something," Moonglow muttered.

Before I could keep going, she turned and walked away. Ariana ran after her. I could have listened in as they talked. Instead, I waited until she came back to where Ruby and I stood. "Well?" I asked.

"She said for us to return to the others, that she'd alert me when she knows something."

"Not good enough," Ruby said firmly.

"If you have an idea, let's hear it," Ariana told the Fae.

"I do. It involves returning to my guild house. We'll get Christa to look in her pool or toss bones or tea leaves. She's good at finding those who don't wish to be found."

"If Conan's in trouble, he'll welcome aid," Ariana said firmly.

"Maybe," Ruby replied. "He has a lot of pride."

"How long will this take?" I asked.

"I already told Christa we're coming." Ruby showed me a mouthful of teeth. It was a good reminder to sheathe my fangs.

"You've have made a good Vampire," I told her.

"There was a time, I'd have locked you away in a vault for impertinence." Ruby's wings fluttered.

"And now?" Ariana's question held interesting undernotes.

"Now, I take it as quite the compliment." Ruby chuckled. "Shall we?" The scent of her magic thickened, and the tunnel vanished replaced by a large room paneled in dark wood. Shelves overflowing with books, and scrolls lined three of four walls. The fourth contained a floor-to-ceiling fireplace with an enormous cauldron suspended from a swinging-arm affair.

I'd have smiled if our situation weren't so dire. Vintage Celt, complete with a spell pot that would have made Ceridwen proud. I'd always wondered about the relationship between the Celts, the Fae, and the Sidhe.

Christa strode into the room, her silver wings folded tightly across her back. Curly black hair fell past her shoulders, and her milk-white eyes held a worried cast. An unusual pallor marked her dusky skin. "Found him," she said without preamble.

"Where?" Ariana leapt across the room to the Fae seer.

"Remember our seek-and-destroy project where we took down prisons?"

"Aw shit. He's in one of them? Which one?" Ariana raked curved fingers through her dark hair.

Christa nodded. "The nuclear storage site in northern Nevada."

Ariana shut her eyes for a moment. "Is he by himself?"

"Best I can tell," the seer replied. "It appears the others overpowered and incarcerated him."

"Not bad news," Ruby said in her best no-nonsense voice. The same one she'd used when she'd first met me and said something like, "Crap, not another one."

"Maybe not, but we have to hurry." Power surged around Ariana as she patched a teleport spell together.

"Hold up," I said.

She rounded on me. "Why? We can wing this."

"Can we?" I arched a brow. "Conan is apparently stuck in there."

"They must have hobbled his magic," Ariana said. "Doesn't mean their snare will bother us."

"We'll all go," Ruby announced.

"Yes. Me too," Christa said. "I'll control the journey spell since I have the coordinates freshly to hand."

"Fine by me. If we hurry"—Ariana reeled in her magic—"maybe we can get in and out before Fairclaw and them return."

"Or worse," Ruby said darkly. "Balor killed Darksword. Fairclaw could have other monsters on tap."

"Balor ended up working for us," Ariana reminded her.

"Only because I threatened something he fears," Ruby retorted.

I winced and wished she hadn't said any of that. Ariana was worried enough. I had to get over shielding her, though. She didn't need it or appreciate me playing knight errant.

"Tell me about where we're going," I urged as Christa's spell caught us up.

"It's part of an extensive underground complex that was originally constructed to contain nuclear missiles and waste," Ruby told me. "Don't worry about exactly what they are. Nuclear power came into being while you were asleep, but it's hell on the atmosphere and toxic as shit to mortals."

"So they invented something that ended up killing them?" I sought clarification.

"Pretty much," Ariana said.

"Hell, they're even dumber than I thought," I mumbled.

"Says a whole hell of a lot," Christa chimed in. "Alrighty, folks, we're almost there."

There turned out to be an expanse of desert peppered with stunted bushes bent in the direction of the prevailing wind. When I didn't see anything else, I employed my psychic view. Still nothing. "Is this the right spot?" I asked.

"Nope. Everything is down there." Christa pointed at the dirt we stood on. "I picked the surface to avoid walking into a trap."

"This place must have some kind of guards," Ariana concurred. "Even if they're electronic."

"Would they still work?" I asked, aware I was treading uncertain waters.

Ruby narrowed her golden eyes. "Maybe not. Depends if it's a direct hookup or runs through the web."

I almost understood. The Internet was relatively new. Electronic devices predated it as did communications networks. The ones that weren't linked to the ISPs we'd hopefully knocked out would still be operational.

Ariana had broken a stick off one of the bushes and was drawing something in the dirt. "General layout," she said. "Unless they changed something since we mapped this location."

"We should aim for here." Ruby tapped her toe over a particular spot. "It was the office with all the controls."

"Are there still people here?" I didn't see how there could be with no visible entrance and no cars.

Christa shook her head. "Mortals abandoned this spot after they'd isolated nuclear weaponry and waste underground. They've created many bunkers like this one. When they're full, they seal them off and walk away."

Seemed like a stupid system, but I kept my thoughts to myself. "Where did the prison part come into play?"

"They built a few cells when they were still collecting nuclear material," Ariana said. "Because this place was on the smallish side, we didn't prioritize dismantling it."

"Your memory is full of holes," Ruby said.

"Oh yeah?" Ariana bristled.

"In this case, yeah," the Fae replied. "We skipped this one because we were worried magic might inadvertently activate nuclear fission."

"Fuck. You're right." Ariana shook her head. "We need to be careful."

The desert disappeared, replaced by a concrete-block room. Blinking consoles suggested some kind of activity. Christa bent and took a closer look at the panel of red, green, and yellow lights. "Oh-oh."

"Oh-oh what?" Ruby peered over her shoulder.

"One of the cells has been compromised. It's no longer stable."

Maybe the expression on my face screamed confusion because Ariana said, "This complex had thirty containers, for want of a better word. Each was filled with potentially volatile nuclear material. The working assumption behind bunkers like this one was that if problems arose, the sheer weight of thousands of tons of dirt on top of everything would minimize blast damage."

"The people who built installations like this," Ruby went on, "installed fail safes to alert them to any problems, but they were a joke. If things go wrong with nuclear products, there's a point of no return where no one can do anything to halt the process."

"It's all right." I flapped a hand her way. "I don't have to understand. Is the compromised cell where Conan is?"

"That would be my guess," Ariana said and looked from Ruby to Christa. "Does radioactive fallout impact Fae?"

"Eventually," Ruby gritted out the word.

"But not right away," Christa added. "Let's get this over with."

"Does it affect us?" I asked Ariana.

"The short answer is no." She sliced an arm downward. A heavy door at one end of the room creaked and swung inward as the lock shattered.

We ran down a hallway lit by red bulbs recessed into the ceiling. The entire building appeared to be constructed of concrete. Maybe it would fare better if one of those atomic things got loose.

"I can feel him." Ariana sounded jubilant. "He's alive."

I hunted too; the faint pulse of guardian enchantment pinged back at me. We pelted down several flights of stairs, Conan's magical signature growing stronger by the moment. At the bottom of the stairwell, we headed along a corridor identical to the one above. Wooden doors constructed of thick, overlapping planks were inset along both sides of the hall. On closer inspection, the doors had been built into the walls. They wouldn't open without taking them apart.

Ariana stood in front of a door at the very end of the hall, hands raised to decimate the thing with magic.

"Wait!" Ruby shouted.

"What for?" Ariana didn't even look her way. "No one else is in there."

The Fae closed a hand around Ariana's forearm. "The door would be the first thing I'd boobytrap." Power streamed from her as she inspected it.

"Forget the door," Ariana said. "We can teleport through it."

"Probably a safer bet," I agreed.

Ruby didn't let go of Ariana. She extended her other hand. Christa grasped it. I got the picture and took hold of Ariana's free hand. "Join your magic with mine," Ruby instructed. "No matter what happens, do not disengage."

"What do you sense?" Ariana asked.

"Not sure. It doesn't matter. We're stronger together."

The hallway yielded to a room so large I couldn't see the end of it. Things were stacked along two walls from floor to ceiling. We hugged the middle of the aisle between them. I felt Conan's presence, but couldn't locate him.

"Conan!" Ariana projected her voice with magic.

"Nooooo. Go away."

Conan's reply was so weak, I rushed forward, intent on finding him and getting out of this place before he sank even further into whatever fresh hell had trapped him. Something stopped me, tossed me backward.

"Shit. Are you all right?" Ariana offered me a hand up, but I was already on my feet.

"There's a wall, but it's invisible until you run into it," I told everyone.

Power flared from Ruby's hands; blue-white, it arced from her fingertips and was joined by magic from Christa. The thing I'd smacked into, an interlaced bunch of iron staves, became visible. The air crackled as guardian enchantment ran headlong against Fae power.

"I know that casting," Christa cried. "Hang on." The pitch and timbre of her magic changed, developing reddish overtones; the slats fell against each other like a stack of dominoes. In their wake the head of a spiral staircase became visible.

"Just a little cleanup," Christa muttered as she cleared a path through the staves with short jabs of magic, taking care to avoid direct contact.

I didn't wait but pelted down the metal stairs with Ariana right behind me. The iron stung, but I could tolerate it for a while. The door at the bottom was locked.

"Got it," Ariana ground out.

Sure enough, tumblers clicked and clacked, unnaturally loud in this odd place. I felt different energies, almost as if we stood at a juncture between worlds, but mortals didn't command that kind of power—or any at all.

One more piece of validation how deeply humans had their claws in our realm, a place they weren't welcome and would never belong.

I gave the door a kick, ran inside, and stopped dead. Conan stood a few meters away in his human body, strapped to something I'd never seen the like of. Wires spread every which way, and some kind of vest wound around his torso. Lights flashed in various colors, not remaining on for long.

"There is no way to defuse it. Go away, Ariana." He tried to imbue command into his voice but ended up sounding sad and defeated.

"Bullshit," Ariana said and hustled forward, bending as she took a close look at whatever surrounded Conan's body.

"If it blows," Conan told her, "this whole installation will go with it. Enough atomic destruction to wipe out the entire West Coast."

"What's in your hand?" I asked.

"Dead man's switch."

"Tells me less than nothing."

"So long as I hold it in place," the guardian explained, "nothing happens. If I let go, the bomb attached to me detonates."

"Hence, dead man's switch," Ariana snarled. "But you are not going to die. I will not let it happen."

"I can't magic my way out of this," Conan said. "Too much power will ignite everything too."

"Then we'll have to do things the old-fashioned way," Ruby said, sounding determined. I'd been so fixated on Conan, I hadn't heard her and Christa come into the room.

"I'll run back to the office and see if I can find some

tools." Christa raced up the stairs and returned so fast, she must have changed her mind and teleported. "Thank the goddess these were right on top of a cabinet." She dropped a black plastic box onto the floor. It clanked when it landed.

"You have to get out of here," Conan insisted. "They'll return."

"Not leaving without you," Ariana told him. "Get used to it."

"How can I help?" I knelt next to her.

She shut her eyes for a moment. "Wish I knew. We have to dismantle the bomb part, but it can't be as simple as snipping through wires."

Christa pushed between us with a screwdriver and something I didn't recognize clasped in one hand. "Don't move," she told Conan and proceeded to unscrew a plate on the front of the vest that circled him. Moving carefully, she pulled the plate off and set it aside. More blinking lights were beneath it.

Reaching forward, she clipped something to two spots. "Putting in a shunt between relays," she explained. "This is a standard suicide vest. I've seen them before."

"Hurry," Conan said, suggesting he'd moved past his initial stance of telling us all to get lost.

"This is the delicate part," the Fae muttered. "If it doesn't work, I'll see all of you in the *Dreaming*."

"Not us," Ariana said.

"Details." Christa had a snipping tool in one hand. "Now would be a good time to ask the goddess for grace," she said and clipped a wire. Nothing happened, but a few of the blinking lights went out.

"Later, once we're out of here," Ariana said, "I want to know what you're doing."

"If there is a later," Christa replied, "I'll tell you. One more." Her gaze flitted from one spot to another. Finally, she blew out a tight breath and clipped another wire. Sweat beaded on her forehead. I heard her counting, "Five. Four. Three. Two. One. Whew. Guessed right."

The rest of the lights gradually stopped flashing.

Can I cut it off him?" Ariana asked.

"Aye. Do it now," Ruby's gruff tone revealed how rattled she'd been.

Ariana snagged the clippers from Christa, who'd rocked back on her heels breathing as if she'd just run a race. A few judicious snips, and the vest fell to the floor.

Conan dropped to his knees. His long hair fanned around him as he struggled to stand.

"What's wrong?" Ariana asked him, followed by, "Find your wolf form."

"Can't," he rasped.

"Never mind that," Ruby said. "We're out of here."

I poured magic into her spell. Even with all of us working as a team—except Conan who was weak as a newborn colt—it took far longer than I would have liked before the walls of this underground crypt developed the insubstantial aspect that meant we'd soon be gone.

A low ominous rumble pummeled me as the chamber vanished, replaced by the blackness of most teleport enchantments. "We're going to *Ascent*," Ariana said in a voice that didn't sound much like her.

"Works for me," Ruby said.

"Ditto," Christa chimed in.

I had an arm around one side of Conan. Ariana supported the other. He sagged between us. The familiar stockroom formed, and we lowered him to the wooden floor. "What's wrong?" I asked.

"Don't know"—Ariana looked at me with stricken eyes—"but we didn't come this far to lose him now."

I considered calling Moonglow, but I'd already defied direct orders from her. Besides, if she was hunting for her son, she'd find out I'd thumbed my nose at her instructions soon enough. Not that she'd hold my insurrection against Conan, but surely she was a last resort.

"You have healers," I said to Ruby and Christa.

"Aye, so do the Witches, and much as I hate to admit it, they're better than we are with their charms and potions," Ruby murmured.

"What was that noise as we were leaving?" Nick asked.

"Good question." Ruby snatched her phone from a pocket and tapped its display a few times. A slow smile formed. "One bit of welcome news. No more Verizon—or WiFi. I was going to see if I could find information about a nuclear blast near Elko."

"Is that what you think it was?" Nick persisted.

The Fae shrugged. "A bomb is the most likely

explanation. We didn't use any magic getting Conan out of that vest, but we didn't return to our entry point to leave, either."

I'd been kneeling over Conan, poking and prodding. My head snapped around. "Couldn't have been that bad an explosion. It didn't reach us here in Kirkland."

"Not yet," Ruby said. "Atomic fallout requires—"

"Skip the lecture," I told her. "Besides, we don't know what we loosed. It's possible it was just a cave-in, and it's not important. He's my first priority." I turned back around and gazed at Conan, sprawled on the floor. At least he was breathing, but his skin had taken on an ashen hue.

"Dahlia!"

Maybe something about my mind voice relayed how frantic I was feeling because her reply was instantaneous. *"What is it?"*

"Send your best healers to Ascent. Please. Conan's in a bad way."

I'll hand it to the coven mistress, she was fast. In less than five minutes, two Witches hustled through a portal and knelt next to Conan. "What happened to him?" one asked as she let her hands hover over his inert form.

"We don't know. Not really," I told her.

"He fought other guardians," Ruby said. "They might have hobbled his power somehow. We found him in a nuclear storage bunker with a suicide vest on."

"Goddess be damned," one of the Witches mumbled. "A suicide vest."

"I thought those were only on television and in the

Middle East," the other one tossed out as she continued her examination.

Dahlia strode through a portal. More Than Never squawked up a storm from her perch on the Witch's shoulder. "I heard that last. A suicide vest? How primitive."

Christa snickered. "That would be me. Archaic. It's the reason I knew how to deactivate it."

"Why didn't he teleport out of there?" Dahlia asked me.

"He was afraid a big blast of power would activate the vest and blow the whole installation to kingdom-come." As soon as the words were out, I remembered the low rumble. "Erm, it's possible we detonated something when we teleported out of there. We weren't gentle about it."

Dahlia made a grab for her phone, but she set it on my desk without looking at it. "Amazing how dependent we've become on everything being instant," she mumbled. "I was going to look up the news, but then I remembered it's no longer at my fingertips."

"But that's good, right?" Nick looked up from where he'd established a vigil near Conan's head. "Means our earlier efforts bore fruit."

"It does, indeed," Dahlia concurred. "Unfortunately, it also means we'll have no idea what happened in Nevada until it shows up in a newspaper, and that won't happen anytime soon. Transitioning back to a pre-digitized world won't occur overnight."

A long, low moan bubbled from Conan.

"Aw shit. Is he in pain?" I bent over him again, smoothing dark hair back from his forehead.

"I don't believe so." One of the healer Witches met my

gaze with very blue eyes. Honey-colored hair had been gathered in a bun low on her neck, and she wore faded jeans and a cream-colored sweater.

"Have you figured out what's wrong?" Ruby asked.

"Maybe," the other Witch said.

Ruby spun one hand in a circle. "Out with it."

"I don't answer to you," she bristled. Close-cropped dark curls framed her face, and her eyes were hazel.

"For fuck's sake, don't get into one of those mage-against-mage tussles," I sputtered.

The blonde healer narrowed her eyes. "Someone created a wedge all the way around his magical center. So far, it's been intransigent, as in I can't get it to budge."

"It's guardian magic, isn't it?" Dahlia stepped closer.

"Yeah, best I can tell," the dark-haired Witch said.

"Conan said the reason he couldn't escape was because he'd set off an atomic explosion," I explained. "He didn't say word one about magic not being available to him."

"Humph. So maybe all guardians look like this?" the blonde muttered.

"We need to wake him up," Nick said. "Either that or call Moonglow."

The door to the nightclub swooshed open, clattering against its stops. "You are back," Percy exclaimed. "It worked. Slam. Bang. No more Internet, and— What the hell happened to Conan?"

"Long story. Can you help us wake him?"

"Eh, not sure." Percy clumped closer. Visible bands of bluish power pulsed from his hands, wrapping around Conan. The Witches wove enchantment in with Percy's efforts. Something about the combination reached the guardian because he stirred, thrashing weakly from side to side.

"Keep it up," Nick urged.

I moved Conan's head into my lap, keeping hold of him. *"Wake up, Conan."* I spoke into his mind. *"Help us help you."*

The body stretched between us glistened. At first I thought it was an artifact of the magics wrapping around him, but then I felt the first flutters of guardian power with its scents of fur and damp granite.

"That's it." I loosed my grip on his head. "You can do this."

The Witches had begun to chant; the blonde tucked a glowing bit of something in Conan's hand. It turned the flesh luminous. When I looked up, I met Nick's gaze across the expanse of Conan's body. He offered a thumbs-up. I returned the gesture.

Maybe, just maybe, we'd win this one.

Not calling for Moonglow or another guardian had been a huge gamble. If anyone would understand what had gone wrong, it would be one of Conan's kin. I'd been well aware of that when I'd opted for Witch support. My day of reckoning would come.

Moonglow would be furious once she found out. And she would. Find out, that is. Not only that I'd gone after Conan when she'd told me to stand down, but also that I hadn't alerted her when he'd hovered near a critical juncture, one which might have spelled his doom.

The skin beneath my fingers didn't feel the same.

Prickles of transformative power poked me. "Let go of him," I cried. "He's shifting."

Sure enough, the mortal yielded to Conan's-black-and-silver wolf, with the Witchy talisman still gripped in a front paw. Vampires don't cry, but the unmistakable bite of tears made my eyes hot and gritty. Slowly, jerkily, Conan got his feet under him and shook his body out, one leg at a time.

Percy and the Witches reeled in their power.

"Do you know what was wrong?" Nick asked.

"Not really," Percy said. "He was a long way from us, but then he moved closer. It might have been our combined efforts that drew him. Or it might have happened anyway, given time."

"I know." Conan's voice was garbled. He woofed a few times. I bounded upright and dragged his water bucket close enough for him to drink.

"You need food and water," I told him. "Explanations can wait."

He shook his shaggy head. "No. They can't." This time, his voice was stronger. "Fairclaw set a trap. He's known me all my life; he recognized I'd return. I should have been warded. I wasn't. I assumed my spell would hold him and the others. It did to some extent, but they were still able to spring a trap they'd built just for me. Once I was unconscious, the spell holding them dissipated, and they took me to that place in Nevada."

"But where would they have gotten hold of a suicide vest?" Ruby asked the same question hovering at the forefront of my mind.

"Fairclaw has human associates. He must have asked

them for something that would stop me in my tracks." Conan drank more water. Once he raised his head, water sluiced off his muzzle and he kept talking. "I woke after they had the vest attached, and I struggled. A Sorcerer materialized out of nowhere and told me if I didn't tone it down, the whole place would blow. And then, he described where I was."

"In the center of an atomic playground," I growled.

The wolf nodded. "I admit, taking those bastards out was downright appealing, but they said the whole West Coast could blow up. I didn't know if they were telling the truth, but they traipsed up the stairs and left. I'd just settled in to think about what to do when you showed up."

"Who were they?" Nick asked.

"Aye, I want to know too," Percy chimed in.

"Fairclaw, the Sorcerer, a couple of mortals, and two of Fairclaw's followers."

I screwed my mouth into a grimace. "Full disclosure here. We blew through scads of power teleporting out of there."

"And heard something like an explosion just as we were leaving," Ruby tacked on.

Dahlia shrugged and held her forearm out for her bird to settle on. "I suppose we'll find out eventually if you detonated anything."

Christa exhaled noisily. "The reason they put those places so deep underground is in case something explodes all those tons of dirt act as a barrier and hold the fallout in place. As long as we didn't blow up every bomb in the place, we should be all right."

A harsh blast of guardian magic gave me a whopping

two seconds' warning before Moonglow leapt through a gash in the air and somersaulted to the ground shaking her finger at me. "Goddess damn your eyes, Vampire. I told you—"

Conan walked between us. "Stand down, Mother. She and Nick and the Fae saved me. With modern knowledge. You wouldn't have fared as well. This wasn't a place magic would have made any difference."

I was still relieved the flare of guardian power hadn't produced Fairclaw and his contingent of rebels. I stepped in front of Moonglow and held up both hands, palms out. "I'd apologize, but if the situation rose again—"

"You'd do the same thing," she growled.

I nodded slowly. "Yup. I would. Conan is dear to me. There was a time you thanked me for standing in when you couldn't be his mother." It was a low blow, that reminder, but she needed to hear it.

"The important thing," Conan said, "is finding Fairclaw and ending him. Without him leading them, the others will return to the fold."

Moonglow skinned her lips back from her teeth. Her wolf form hovered in the background. "Nay. I am done with all of them. We have crossed their entries out of the Book of Names—in blood. Their lives are forfeit. Our tribunal has spoken."

"Pushing forward is imperative," Percy said. "Our battle plan is well underway. If the bunch of you set off a bomb or two in Nevada, it will aid our cause. At this point, any and everything that can be bent to our favor will be."

"We're going to the guild house," Dahlia announced.

"We'll return around nine tonight to finalize what happens next."

I had no idea what time it was, but a sliver of light from beneath the curtain covering the one window in the stockroom suggested midday. "Thank you so much for dropping everything when I called you," I told the Witch.

Dahlia smiled. "I've never heard you sound so rattled. Figured it was really important, and then when you said Conan had fallen—" Her smile faded. "Any magic strong enough to fell a guardian is serious."

"Glad we could help." The blonde Witch stuck out a hand. I shook it, and then the other healer Witch's as well.

"I'm going to see if I can dredge up any information about Nevada," Percy said. "Rob set up his old Citizen's Band radio. It's been running off the rails with people talking ever since we demolished all the ISPs."

Nick cleared his throat, but didn't ask what they were. Today must have been overwhelming in some respects between atomic power, suicide vests, and now CB radios. Instead, he said, "We need to feed. Conan too."

"Mind if I join you?" Moonglow's question caught me off-guard.

"Not at all," Nick replied with a touch of gallantry. It comes easy to male Vampires, not so much to us females. We can be charming, sexy as hell, but never particularly gallant.

"I'll take us," I said and opened a teleport spell to my usual hunting grounds not far from my house. Did Moonglow have ulterior motives? Was she waiting until we had a spot of privacy to read me the riot act for disobedience? If so, she'd have a surprise on her hands. I didn't report to her. The only place she would have had a justified beef was if I'd dragged my heels calling her in to help Conan until it was too late.

Hadn't happened. I've never been one to comb through might-have-beens.

Recognizing unwarranted defensiveness, I put a lid on it. I could always bring out my fangs, but not until I needed them.

The sky suggested it was midafternoon. Mesmerism sheeted from Nick and me; small animals flocked to our call. We went to work draining them, leaving Conan and Moonglow to hunt. They'd get our leavings too, but this way they wouldn't have to wait.

I figured out quick enough Moonglow had suggested riding shotgun because she wanted time with Conan. By the time the clearing in the forest shaped up around us, she'd morphed into her white wolf's body, and she and Conan loped away through the trees. All my fussing and conjecturing had been for nothing, but that's often the case.

Nick looked up from the raccoon he'd been intent on draining. His fangs were streaked with blood. So was his chin, and he was the most beautiful thing I'd ever seen. After looking at me for a moment, his gaze skittered away. "I'm sorry," he mumbled.

Picking up the rat I'd been working on, I stood and walked over to sit next to him. "For what?"

He shook his head. "I know so little, I'm almost a liability. You have to waste time explaining things to me, and even after you have I'm still clueless sometimes."

I laid the rat aside. The worst of my hunger had been

slaked, and this was more important. I curled a hand around his wrist. "Not the way I see things at all."

"You're being kind."

"Ha! Vampires are never kind. I have my rare moments of consideration, but I wouldn't have said that if it weren't true."

Nickolas twisted to face me. "Then how do you view my lack of knowledge—about everything."

"First off, it's not about everything," I pointed out. "You ran into a few puzzles in a row, but that doesn't mean you're a liability." I chewed my lower lip, feeling the prick of fangs. "Something happened this last century. People lost a lot of their ability to think things through, to reason, to persevere in the face of adversity. You have all those elements, and they're worth way more than knowing what an atomic bomb is, or a suicide vest."

"I wanted to help, though. I knew how desperate you were over Conan's plight."

"You did help," I told him. "It's not as if anything I did made a difference. It was Witch and Sorcerer enchantments that did the trick." I squeezed my eyes shut for a moment. When I opened them, I said, "I took a huge chance. A gamble, and it wasn't rooted in knowing jack shit. Conan's surest bet to survive would have been Moonglow."

"I wondered about that." Nick nodded.

"I didn't loop her in because—"

"I understand. She told us to go away, and we didn't. She'd have had ample reason to be furious."

I slid my hand down and laced my fingers with his. "All's well that ends well. In this case, Conan admitted a few mistakes of his own. The important thing is we're all still here." It would have been a good spot to blow out a breath—except I don't breathe.

"Six months from now," I went on, "you'll have most everything you need to know down pat."

"Eh, you're giving me too much credit, *Cara*. Maybe a year."

I shrugged. "What difference does it make? We live forever."

"Most of the time," he said. "This atomic whatever would have ended us."

"We're not sensitive to radioactive fallout, but the blast would have killed us and everything else in a many-mile radius. Wiping out the whole West Coast isn't that far off the mark if every warhead in that bunker detonated."

Leaves rustled, branches crackled, and the two guardians trotted near where we sat. "These up for grabs?" Conan snatched a marmot without waiting for an answer.

"They sure are," Nick told him.

For the next hour, we drank and they ate until Moonglow lifted her rust-streaked muzzle and said, "I'd love to remain, but I can't. I will come to your meeting tonight and bring others with me."

"I must leave with her," Conan said, "but I shall return as well."

I hooked an arm around his neck and hugged him before turning to Moonglow. "Thanks. For everything." It was only three words, but they had many implications. The biggest one was relief she wasn't going to hold my sins against me.

The wolf padded to me and laid her muzzle against my

thigh. "Thank you for intervening and getting Conan away from that horrible place. If it weren't so volatile, I'd destroy it."

"Might have already happened," I told her.

"No loss." Her tail plumed. "I don't completely understand radioactivity, but it doesn't harm us and is fatal to mortals."

"It doesn't hurt Vampires, either," I told her, "but I'm not certain of its effect on our fellow mages."

"We can ask them later tonight." Ears pricked forward, tails held proudly, both wolves turned away from me and walked through a gateway that formed and vanished in seconds.

"Someone needs to let the Kelpies know about tonight," Nick said.

"Mmph." I'd picked up another rat and was midway through draining it. Once I was done, I furrowed my brow, thinking. "Clive holds the secret decoder ring on that one. Or in this case, the magic stone."

Nick laughed. "One more mystery reference, but that one's simple to figure out."

"Let's stop by my house and clean up. Then you can alert Clive to make sure our water horse allies at least know there's a war council."

"Certainly," Nick replied. "What do you want to do about the Clan Ravnos Vamps?"

I sucked in a worthless breath because I wanted air to hiss through my fangs. "Well, crap. You did tell them you'd let them know when we were moving out."

"I did," Nick agreed, "but it doesn't mean I have to

follow through. It's not as if they're going to hunt me down and drain me."

I thought about it. I didn't trust them, but neither did I trust the Kelpies. "The more the merrier," I said at last and got to my feet. "But it won't be simple. We'll have to teleport there since cell phones don't work any longer."

"Easily doable." Nick sprang upright and extended a hand. We covered the short distance to my house fast. Nothing like a few rays of sunlight to make Vampires hustle. "Wish we could just hunker down and never leave here," I murmured.

"Soon, *Cara*. A few more hurdles, and we'll be able to retire from the world until we're tired of fucking each other."

A laugh bubbled from whatever passed for my soul. "That would be never, sweetheart."

Instead of answering, he crushed his mouth down on mine. Our fangs clanked together. We tasted of blood and lust and Vampire magic, and I hugged him close. A stolen moment if ever there was one, and all the sweeter for it being a very bad idea.

"Five minutes," Nick murmured between kisses.

"We have to clean up anyway," I said and, grinning like a reincarnation of Aphrodite, I sprinted inside, shedding clothing as I went.

CHAPTER FIFTEEN, NICKOLAS

We might have taken a little more than five minutes, but not much. Stopping after such a brief, sweet, lusty interlude hadn't been easy. Ariana's amazing musky scent was thick in my nostrils and clung to my damp hair. My cock was still hard and bent at an uncomfortable angle inside my trousers.

"Focus," I muttered and put out a telepathic call to Clive. Again. I hadn't heard from him yet, and I'd told him to alert the Kelpies before Ariana snugged her arms and legs around me, wiping everything else from my mind.

"What was that?" Ariana breezed into the living room garbed in black work clothes crafted of some heavy material. Her dark hair had been braided out of the way and tucked beneath the collar of her jacket. It wasn't a bad idea.

"Nothing," I said. "Do you have some extra bits of leather?"

She drew her brows together and swept her gaze over

me. It added heat to my already aroused state. "I'd love for you to tie me up, sweetie, but we don't have time."

Laughter rolled from my belly. "How about a raincheck? The leather cords are for my hair. The same things you use."

Ariana was laughing too. "We've come a long way baby since leather and hair ribbons." Turning, she detoured into her bedroom and returned with a colorful assortment of circular bands. Slipping one over her thumb and index finger, she said, "See? They're elastic. They stretch."

"Thanks." Opting for expediency, I gathered my hair into a bundle at the base of my neck and secured it with one of her elastic things. "I hate to leave, but we have to."

"Yeah. We probably should have been gone fifteen minutes ago. Have you heard from Clive?"

I shook my head. "We'll see him soon enough."

"Hope so. It's not like him not to answer you."

I'd thought the same but was trying not to worry about it. The Kelpies had captured him and Dee once. If it happened again, Dahlia would probably have something less than encouraging to say about a Vampire mating with one of her Witches.

"Do we have everything we'll need?" I glanced around what had become a familiar place.

She patted her ankle. "I have my knife. Carrying a weapon is a good idea. Not much else I can think of. No reason to cart my phone or tablet around any longer."

Ariana turned in a full circle, surveying her domain. When she was facing me again, she said, "Uh, there's no easy way to say this, but if something happens to me, you're welcome to my home. My mail comes to the club. Just make sure to pay the bills as they show up, and—"

Alarm washed through me. I closed the distance between us and wrapped my arms around her. "Ssht. Nothing will happen to you. Nothing. Don't even say such a thing."

Her full mouth formed a soft smile. "Didn't you leave superstition behind after you were turned? Vampires don't believe in bad luck. Speaking of which, how do you want to handle the Ravnos bunch?"

"I'd planned on sending Clive."

"Okay. On a scale of one to ten, they're the least of our worries."

I agreed with her assessment and readied a teleport spell to take us to *Ascent*.

Ariana held up a hand. "Just a second. If we have time, I'd rather drive. Sometimes having a car comes in handy. Remember when we had to borrow Dee's?" She raised her mind voice. *"Ruby?"*

"Present and accounted for," the Fae's voice rustled like dry leaves.

"Is everyone there?"

"Nah. Only about five of us. Why?"

"Settles it. I'm driving. See you in about half an hour."

Ariana trotted toward the door with me right behind her. So long as Ruby was readily available, I asked, *"Is Clive there?"*

"No, honey, he isn't. Haven't seen him or Dee now that you mention it."

"Thanks," I told her and cut the connection.

Ariana sealed her home with a spell I was familiar with, and we got into her car. The sun had long since set, leaving soft velvety darkness. A quick tap and the motor hummed to life.

"I never did learn to drive," I mused.

"We'll prioritize it after we get through the next little while."

I clipped the seatbelt and leaned into the soft upholstery, enjoying its simple comfort. Conveyances had come a long way since people traveled in carriages and railroad cars, or on horseback. Ariana had been humming softly, but she broke off when I said, "We'll wait to see what the world looks like once we're done with whatever happens next."

"You said that for a reason. What was it?"

I sank deeper into the seat. "I wasn't a knight for very long. Maybe ten years, but one lesson that sank in was to not make plans for after anything. Even if we won a campaign, the result rarely looked like I'd envisioned it. The same is true here. For all we know, I may not need to learn how to drive."

"Or it might become even more important," she replied thoughtfully before adding, "The only wars I've fought have been personal ones. Mages who hated Vampires. Mortals who were a pain in the ass. Turning *Ascent* into a profitable venture was the most challenging struggle I've ever dealt with, and it was scarcely a war."

We'd turned off back roads onto surprisingly deserted streets. Perhaps losing the Internet had scared people into staying home. "The principles are the same, though," I told her. "You have checkpoints where you determine something isn't working the way you need it to and institute changes to modify your outcomes in a more promising direction."

"Sorry for the silence," Clive's voice pummeled into my mind.

"It's all right." My response was gruffer than I meant it to be as I masked the relief running through me.

"Nay. Not really. After your first message, I teleported to the nearest beach. It was still light out, so I was covered up pretty good. Still got burned, but it's not important. Anyway, the Kelpies are on their way to the pub. Their magic was too strong to drill through to answer you the second time you tried to raise me."

"Where are you now?" Ariana jumped into the conversation.

"With Dee. She and a couple of Witches are patching me up."

I ground my teeth together. I'd sent him on an assignment. In broad daylight. If I still had master Vampire status, someone should strip it from me. *"I'm really sorry—"* I began.

"Stuff it, mate. I really am all right. I was the logical one to send. I could have waited until later in the day, so this one is on me." After a pause, Clive added, *"Sorry. Stuff it wasn't very respectful."*

"Don't worry. We'll be at Ascent in maybe fifteen minutes. See you there."

"That you will, mate." He closed off the connection.

"Sooner than that." Ariana flapped a hand at the windshield. "No traffic. The streets are so empty, it looks like three in the morning, except it's barely eight o'clock. I'm glad we heard from Clive."

"Makes two of us." Hearing him say the Kelpies would be there reminded me of a story. "Care to hear a bit of history?" I asked.

"Of course. Fire away."

"Back when I was still mortal but well into my knighthood, we teamed up with a bunch of Vikings," I began, culling through memories I'd gone to a lot of trouble to bury. "They were an unknown quantity, but we needed their ships for a particular project."

"Oh-oh. I have a feeling this didn't end well." Ariana turned the wheel and guided us onto the freeway.

"It didn't. They had ulterior motives and turned on us once we'd overpowered our enemies, thinking to grab the spoils for themselves."

"And?" Ariana cast a glance my way.

"We'd feared such an event, so we were ready for them. Regardless, it was bloody and unpleasant. We lost another twenty men, but we killed every last one of those unholy bastards. And sold their boats for a tidy sum at auction."

She let go of the steering wheel long enough to dust her hands together. "Good for you. You told me that story because of the Kelpies, right?"

"Aye, and the Ravnos Vamps."

"Oh yeah. Them. Are you still going to send Clive?"

I thought about it. "Don't know. I want to see what kind of shape he's in. Maybe I'll go myself. I can make it quick. Maybe an hour portal to portal."

Ariana's fangs had dropped. "Or I could go. Just let them

fuck with me. I'm the Vampire who didn't get the memo about not killing our makers."

Protectiveness surged, hot and feral. Rather than telling her hell would freeze over before I'd let her go, which made me sound like some kind of caveman, I murmured, "Let's figure it out once we see how our plans shape up."

"Diplomatic." She grinned.

"You have no idea how much it cost me," I retorted, remembering the Ravnos vamp who'd been eager to hustle her into his bed.

"Erm yeah, I do. Remember, we come from common roots, you and me."

The sign for our exit flashed past. This trip had gone surprisingly quickly. Even in the middle of Kirkland, we still hadn't encountered any traffic. "The lack of that Internet-thing did all this? Sent people into their homes to grieve?"

"More likely to panic. Only explanation I can think of. Sheesh. If I'd known it was this easy to drive mortals to ground, I'd have suggested it long ago."

"But they're your primary customers at the club," I reminded her.

"Only because I designed it that way," she countered. "I could just as easily have set *Ascent* up to only serve immortals. And it might come to that." She pulled down the alley behind the club and parked in one of her usual spots.

I got out and waited for her as she draped the car in illusion to hide it from mortals. "Not sure why I did that," she said as she walked past me and opened the club's back door. "But it's the only car in this whole section of Kirkland, and it sticks out like a sore thumb."

"Are you expecting cops to be on the prowl?"

She turned toward me, forehead furrowed into a welter of fine lines. "Not sure. Their com network's gone down, but they can still use two-way radios. They don't have much range, though."

"Define what that means." I followed her into the stockroom.

"Five miles, line of sight. So conceivably a cop at one end of town could communicate with one at the other, so long as there weren't any big buildings in between them."

The buzz of conversation wafted through the door that led into the nightclub's main room. "Sounds like a lot of folk have shown up since you talked with Ruby," I said.

Ariana nodded. "This will be our last get-together. Democratic process. We'll vote and go with the plan most of us want."

"I can't see Kelpies participating unless they agree with the consensus," I muttered.

"Ditto for guardians," Ariana said, "but they'll at least try to work with everyone. Kelpies are more a 'my way or the highway' bunch. Not much we can do about it." She hooked an arm through mine, and we walked into the bar.

Mages sat at tables and stood in small groups. A cursory glance suggested people were sticking with their kin, but a few cross-magic groups had sprung up. Kelpies weren't here yet. Neither were guardians. Was there any point in moving forward before they showed up?

Clive loped toward me. One side of his face was blistered, but other than that, he seemed to have escaped major damage. "Good to see you, mate."

"You as well." I shook his hand. It wasn't a Vampire custom, but we were adapting to our new circumstances. "Did Dee go with you to find the Kelpies?"

"Ha! Same thing I was about to ask," Ariana chimed in.

Clive snorted. "Oh hell, no. She wanted to, but after last time I wouldn't have brought her for anything." He lowered his voice. "Luckily, Dahlia overheard us arguing about it and stepped in. I'm not sure Dee would have acquiesced, otherwise."

"I bet she was worried," Ariana said.

"Och, she clucked and fussed over me something fierce after I got back." Clive grinned, apparently having enjoyed all the attention.

"I'm going to get this show on the road," Ariana said. After walking briskly away from me, she leapt on top of the bar and clapped her hands smartly together. "Welcome, everyone."

A barrage of greetings rolled through the room. The distinctive smell of the North Sea, brackish and tinged with salt and copper wafted through the bar and wrapped around it like a shroud. The Kelpies had somehow moved our gathering beyond easy reach of discovery. I hoped everyone was here. I wasn't at all certain I could have punched through the water horses' concealment casting.

Guardians had yet to show up, but I had faith they could see through any illusion crafted with all types of power. Rather than a herd of Kelpies, two shimmered into being. They had the oddest way of showing up—and leaving. One minute they were visible, the next gone.

"We do not plan to remain," one of the Kelpies said and pawed the wooden floor with an enormous hoof.

"We have our own plans," Kelpie Number Two added.

"Are you going to tell us what they are?" Ariana called from her perch atop the bar.

"Why would you need to know?" he replied with a question of his own.

"So we're not at cross-purposes," she told him. "You can scrimp on details, but where are you planning to be? And when?"

"'Tis the when that's still open," the first Kelpie said.

"And the only reason we are here," the other one piped up. "When will you march on Washington?"

Ariana scanned the group. "Does tomorrow night work for everyone? We can launch at dusk, or you could begin earlier."

"Where's Conan? Have you spoken with him?" Percy called from his usual spot near the door.

"Good point. The answer is no, not about timing." Ariana turned to the Kelpies. "We should wait for the guardians. They said they'd be here tonight."

"Guardians, eh?" one of the Kelpies said. "We like them, especially that Conan fellow."

"Aye, should be interesting," the other added just before they opened a discussion in their language of clicks, clacks, and whinnies. Before they were done, a silvery portal punched through the mist that had taken up residence in the bar. The edge sizzled alarmingly, and strands of it caught fire. Like all magefire, it burned while awaiting instructions for what to consume. I stared at the rectangle, expecting Conan, Moonglow, and who knew how many others.

A minute ticked by, followed by another. Ariana vaulted through the air and landed in front of the portal, calling, "Conan."

The wolf catapulted through, followed by ten guardians. The only other one I recognized was Moonglow. They were all in their wolf bodies, but not for long.

Conan was mostly human when he turned to the Kelpies, the planes and angles of his face radiating suppressed anger. "Was it your intent to block us from this place?" He crossed his arms over his chest, waiting.

What happened next surprised the hell out of me. Both Kelpies bowed. Not for long or particularly deeply, but they did incline their heads in Conan's direction. "Nay, princeling. We merely meant to shield this spot from prying eyes and ears."

"We had no idea you were coming until the Vampire said as much a few moments ago," the other said, followed by, "We apologize."

Conan narrowed his eyes. Power flickered around him as he tested the Kelpies' words—or perhaps he was looking deeper, into their non-existent souls. So far as I know, us and them are the only varieties of mage who lack them.

"Accepted." Conan barked the word.

Moonglow and the other guardians had positioned themselves next to and behind Conan, almost like an honor guard. My fangs had dropped, anticipating a squabble between guardians and Kelpies; I pulled them back and took a good look at the guardians.

It appeared they'd been fighting. Long red welts ran down Conan's sides, but they were healing quickly. The other guardians bore similar evidence of injury. I wanted to ask if they'd run Fairclaw and his stooges to ground—permanently—but it could wait.

"All we require is a timeframe," one of the Kelpies said.

"And then we shall be on our way," the other one reiterated.

"Does tomorrow night work for you?" Ariana asked the guardians.

"It does," Conan said.

"Tonight works too." Moonglow bared her teeth. They had blood on them. Good for her.

"We need tonight to plan," Percy said. "By the time we have everything tacked down, we'll have lost valuable evening time when our Vampire allies are strongest."

My eyes widened; I might have fallen back a pace. It was the first time I'd ever heard another mage refer to us as allies. It felt terrific. Finally, someone appreciated us, and a Sorcerer no less.

"You have the time nailed down; now tell us what you'll be doing?" Ariana's gaze bored into the Kelpies.

"Simple enough," one said.

"We shall swim up the river that borders the city. Groups of us will exit at many points and kill whatever crosses our path. When we weary of killing, we will take to the river once more and leave."

"Will you be horses or men?" Ruby asked.

One of the Kelpies grinned, revealing his equine teeth. "A little of both, Fae. Why? Fancy a ride?"

"Nay. Been there." She grinned back, but it looked more threatening than anything happier.

Tonight was chockful of surprises. I'd have to ask Ruby about her skirmish with the Kelpies someday. And about the Fomori. As quickly as they'd drifted in, the water horses departed, hauling their mists and their spells behind them.

"Did you find Fairclaw?" Ariana asked Conan.

"Yes, and it's the last I shall say about it. He and his followers will trouble us no more."

I wanted details, but my questions died unspoken after Ariana prodded for specifics. "But you're hurt"—she crooked two fingers his way—"What happened?"

A long, low growl issued from Conan's throat, sounding far more menacing than when his wolf did the same thing. Ariana held up a hand. "All right. I get the picture. Glad you made it through."

"I am still here." Dignity rode beneath Conan's words. "But I shall never be the same."

I looked away, offering what privacy I could. I understood how it felt to kill a Vampire. The ones we'd ended had deserved to suffer far more than they did, but raising my fangs against my own kind had been hard. Sometimes that night still haunted me. I'd told myself it was because they'd joined forces with mortals, but it was far more than that.

I'd been the instrument of their destruction. It wasn't the same as ending a newly made Vampire who'd run amok. I'd been forced into doing that a handful of times, and while not pleasant, it was necessary. Rather like cleaning up a mess of my own making.

Ending the Clan Ravnos Vampires—Undead who should have known better—was an entirely different story.

Killing our own carried a steep price. Ariana knew it well. I'd seen the torment in her eyes. Killing Mistral had changed her life, marked her in ways she'd have had no way of predicting...

"Places, people," Percy shouted to break through the din of many side conversations that had started up. "We have a war to plan and very little time."

"Before we begin," I projected my voice with magic to make certain everyone heard me, "we have a choice to make. Another Vampire clan is willing to aid us. They aren't trustworthy, but then neither are the Kelpies. Should I go to New Orleans and tell them to show up tomorrow night?"

"How many?" Ruby called.

I didn't know, but Clive cupped his hands around his mouth and yelled, "At least fifty."

"I say we include them," Moonglow spoke up. Any similarity to a mortal had departed long since. She was beautiful with her gobs of white hair and her amber eyes. Beautiful, yes. But no one would ever mistake that alien face for a human's.

"It could be a major win," Conan tossed out. "All those Vamps draining people right and left. Between them and the Kelpies, I bet no one who lives there will ever sleep easy again."

The thought made me smile. In that moment, I understood how much I loathed mortals. The guardians' plan—one of them—that would have wiped out mortals and left lots of room for us to roam was sounding better by the day.

"Want me to come along?" Clive asked from where he stood next to me.

"Sure. This will be a quick trip. In and out. If they give us any shit, we're not going to hang around begging."

"Got it." He gave me a thumbs up. Vampire power rose as he built a travel spell.

Ariana ran to my side and hugged me once, quick and hard. "See you soon. By the time you get back, we'll have our strategy mapped out."

I wanted to be part of that too. Maybe there'd still be some decisions to be made after Clive and I returned. "Ready?" he asked.

"Never readier," I told him.

"I'm aiming for that spot at the end of Marvel Lane where we last saw them," he told me as his casting swept us away.

"Not the swamp?" I joked.

"What? Are you missing a pet alligator?"

"Nay, but the dead ones were good to sit on. It's off topic, but things are going well with Dee, then?"

Clive looked my way, blue eyes glowing with enthusiasm. "Better than good. I'm smitten, and it's amazing... But then, so is she, and..."

Happy for him, I let him blither on as I built a ward. If the Ravnos vamps thought to snare us a second time, I'd be ready for them.

CHAPTER SIXTEEN, ARIANA

Everyone remained until around three in the morning forming battalions and finalizing details. Maryland had its own paranormal task force, but it was much smaller than Seattle's and not especially active. We included it in our raid sites in case our intel was wrong, not because we viewed them as a serious threat. As we adopted and discarded approaches, I kicked myself for not getting more details nailed down before we demolished the Internet.

Absent hard data, we were limited to people's memories and a ratty old copy of the Encyclopedia Britannica Percy came up with from somewhere. Reference books had mostly gone the way of the Dodo bird. For all I knew, he'd lifted it from the public library. Ruby provided maps. Dogeared and well-used, they were crisscrossed with notes scrawled in black ink.

"Had these for a while, haven't you?" I tapped a spot where writing obliterated map details.

"I like to travel. So shoot me." She waggled her dark brows my way.

Nick and Clive returned well before midnight with news that the Clan Ravnos Vampires would show up the following evening and do their own thing. Rather like the Kelpies. No one seemed too worried about the lack of a coordinated approach, but I was. Vampires aren't known for good manners or holding back when something pisses us off. Neither are Kelpies. I could see the two mage groups getting into a tussle that would undermine our efforts.

Nothing I could do about it. Communicating telepathically required some degree of geographic proximity. We'd be able to talk with everyone once we got there, but reaching the other Vampires—or the Kelpies—wouldn't be possible until then. Clive had that stone thing, but it wasn't a vehicle for two-way chatter.

Not much point in going home. I'd waited out many a day at my club, and I expected various mage groups to come and go as the hours marched forward and edged into the following evening. Everyone was keyed up. And well they should be. This was it. Our final salvo. If it didn't work, nothing would.

I was worried about Conan, but he brushed off attempts to talk with him. After the third try, I gave up. He wasn't the little wolfling I'd stumbled across centuries ago. He hadn't actually been that even then, except I hadn't known what he was. I'd made a lot of assumptions, and he hadn't contradicted me because they worked in his favor.

To avoid pacing and moving from group to group like an imitation of a mother hen, I sat at my desk typing up lists of who was on which team, which teams provided backup, and a general flow chart. Part of me knew it was pure busy work, that what we found on the ground would vary enough my plans would like as not crumble to dust. Our assignment was the Pentagon. Though not exactly in Washington DC, it sat right across the Potomac in Arlington, Virginia. I wondered if we'd run into Kelpies in the river. A chance meeting with the Scottish water horses—our presumed allies—did not make me any more comfortable. So much for my attempts to tack down loose ends.

Our other targets were the Supreme Court, the U.S. Capitol, the House and Senate buildings, Library of Congress, the Smithsonian, the State Department, the Treasury Department, and FBI Headquarters. We'd crossed the White House off our list. Not enough people to bother with there.

Nick and Clive sat at a card table I'd dragged out from behind the bar. Clive's blisters were mostly healed. Where I was typing, Nick was writing things out. I got up and walked to where I could look over his shoulder at a welter of slashes and circles. "What's all that?" I tapped the paper with an index finger.

"The Pentagon. I know it doesn't look like any of the pictures, but each part of the drawing serves a purpose for me." Nick pointed at one end. "The primary entrance should be here. If there's not too much metal in the walls and foundation, we should be able to teleport into the lowest level and sweep the place from the bottom up. In and out in less than half an hour by my reckoning."

"We have to teleport in, no matter what," I told him.

"There's far too much surveillance and security to waltz through any door."

"Is there some way we could get more information about the building?" Clive asked.

I rubbed my eyes and refocused on Nick's schematic. "This won't make a hell of a lot of sense to you, but there's still a satellite communications system. Not all programs run off satellites, but some mapping ones can."

I returned to my computer, clicked on a topographic program, and waited to see if it still yielded data. The theory was it would switch to satellites if it couldn't find anything else. My screen flickered; a box popped up that said: Access Forbidden. Beneath it were a few lines in legalese, but the gist was the government had hijacked the satellites for their use during what they perceived to be a worldwide crisis.

"At least they're taking this seriously," I mumbled.

"Can we get rid of those satellite things?" Nick asked.

"Not sure. Let me see if Conan's still here." Pushing out of my chair, I ran lightly into the bar searching for guardian energy. A surprising number of mages were still in the nightclub hunkered in their assigned groups. I located Conan, Moonglow, and a few other guardians easily. Their magic is like none other.

"We missed something," I said as I reached where they stood in a tight circle wearing their human forms.

"What would that be?" Conan sounded tired, which wasn't like him. I wondered if he'd fully recovered from his episode in the atomic bunker.

"We missed part of the communications network. Satellites are still transmitting data."

"Aren't there lots of them?" Moonglow asked.

"I believe so," Conan told her and focused his amber eyes on me.

I bit my tongue to make certain I didn't ask how he was doing. Again. Instead, I synopsized how I'd discovered the sat network had been hijacked by the government. "It may be important," I concluded. "Important enough to undermine the rest of our efforts since there's still a mechanism for them to talk with one another."

"Show me your display," Conan said. "I have an idea."

"Do you need more firepower?" Moonglow asked.

"Not sure yet, but feel free to join me." Without waiting, he strode briskly toward the back room. Not much reason for him to wait for me. He knew the way as well as I did.

Conan sat in my chair and tapped a few keys. The warning box flashed and reformed. Moonglow stood behind him. "We can follow the electronic path," she said.

Conan nodded. "Aye, but that will only net us one satellite. I want to knock out all of them that are near this one."

"Ley-lines?" I guessed, thinking out loud.

Conan cracked the first smile I'd seen since we'd found him with the end-of-days vest strapped to his chest. "What else? They're kind of my baby."

"Can we help?" Nick asked.

Conan shook his head. "Move back a little and give me space to work."

As I watched from my spot not too far from the door, power swirled, digging a hole in my floor. Nothing in Conan's world obeyed the laws of physics. He'd no sooner opened my floorboards than I caught a glimpse of the ley-lines' characteristic golden glow. It rose and formed a shining nimbus around Conan and his mother.

Both guardians began to chant in their language, the only one besides Kelpie I didn't understand. As they urged destructive magic to flow—or whatever they were about—the glow intensified, bouncing off the walls of my office as beams shot every which way.

Conan was on his feet weaving his hands in an arcane pattern. The beams understood his summons and formed a single thick rope with strands wrapped around one another. The air in my office grew heavy with guardian power and thorny possibilities. When he had what he wanted, Conan herded the magical construct to the ethernet cord that attached my computer to a modem. Slowly at first, and then more quickly, the rope vanished into the cable until a muted pop signified it was done. The gaping space in the floor sealed over as if it had never been there.

"Well?" Conan angled a glance at Moonglow, who stood gazing at the screen.

"It went black," she said.

I crossed the room and clicked a few keys, trying to resurrect it. Nothing. "Either you did it," I told Conan, "or the satellite recognized an intruder and blocked us."

"What are the odds of that?" Nick asked.

"I have no idea," I told him. "Probably, I've watched too many daytime soap operas and crime procedurals."

"Whatever they are," he mumbled.

"Is there another computer you can check?" Moonglow asked.

I dug my phone out of the drawer I'd dropped it in and tapped until I brought up Gaia, a common topographic app. After a momentary pause, a message flashed across my screen: Satellite Not Available.

"You did it," I told Conan. "No idea how many are left, but it's a start."

He turned to face me. "And an end. The only reason I had any success was I had a signal to follow. By the time we're done, the remaining satellites will be the least of mortals' problems. Are you ready for tonight?"

"Ready for everything to be over," I said.

"It may not be," he reminded me as he reclaimed his wolf form. Because it was the only way I'd known him for so long, he felt safer, more familiar. I knew I was being ridiculous, but with so many unknowns facing us, I'd take all the familiar I could lay my hands on.

Dee walked into the stockroom. Dark circles scribed beneath her eyes, and she looked worried. Her usually styled black hair hung limply around her face. "Figured I'd find you here," she said to Clive. "I'm heading back to the guild house to get some rest." She craned her neck, nostrils flaring. "I sense magic. Lots of it, and expended quite recently. Are we under attack?"

I hurried to her and gave her a hug, concerned by how wasted she appeared. "No, hon. We're okay. Conan and Moonglow obliterated a few satellites."

Dee rolled her eyes. "Fuck. We forgot all about them, huh?"

"Not a huge oversight," Conan woofed. Something about him made her smile, and she sank a hand into his neck ruff.

Clive had jumped to his feet when Dee walked in. "Would you like company?" he asked.

Her smile widened. "If we sleep, sure."

He tucked an arm protectively around her thin shoulders. "We can do whatever you'd like, darling." He stopped there, but I knew the part he hadn't said. The coming night would be difficult. Some of us would lose our immortal lives. If the next few hours were all he'd have with the Witch he'd fallen in love with, Clive didn't want to squander a moment of it.

They turned and walked out of the room.

"Probably a good idea," Moonglow said. "Not the rest part, but the making certain I haven't left too many loose ends." She knelt and draped an arm around Conan's neck. "Where will you be?"

He leaned into her touch. "I should be with the other guardians, but I shall spend the day with Ariana and Nick. She was my only family for an awfully long time."

"I understand." Moonglow kissed the top of his head before straightening. "See all of you back here around five this afternoon. We'll form our groups and teleport to our targets."

"Been thinking about that," Conan said. "If we have a guardian in each group, and I believe we do, we should use the lines. It's faster, cleaner, uses less magic, and a big blast of power won't alert people on the other end our arrival is imminent."

"Depends who might be lying in wait for us," Moonglow said. "If there are other renegade guardians about, they'll feel a disturbance."

Conan angled his head. "Is anyone else missing? Besides Darksword? I was gone for centuries."

"A few," Moonglow admitted through gritted teeth.

"You should have told me before. Too late to do anything about it now," Conan growled, "except kill them if they cross our path."

An odd expression flitted across Moonglow's peculiar features. Like I've said, no one would ever mistake her for human. If I hadn't been watching her, I'd have missed the play of concern, regret, and possibly shame that took turns marching across her face. Rather than clarify anything, she spun on her heel and walked through a hole in the air.

Daylight filtered through the heavy curtain covering my stockroom's only window. Dawn had come while I wasn't paying attention.

"Feel like going home for a couple of hours?" Conan asked.

"Sure, we can do that," I told him. I'd been planning to stay put, but maybe inserting some space between me and the club for a while was a good idea.

The wolf head-butted me. "You didn't correct me, so it's still my home too."

I sank into a crouch and hugged his shaggy head. "Always."

Clinging to the last bit of normal I was likely to see for a while, I said, "Let's drive. We have the time."

The fur beneath my fingers turned to metal and leather as Conan took to his motorcycle form. I'd retrieved the helmets we'd left near the lakefront park, and snagged them off hooks near the door.

"I meant driving my car," I said as I buckled the helmet into place, "but this is better."

"It is," Nick concurred. His helmet was on, and he opened the back door for Conan to roll through.

Morning light washed over me. It was early yet, but daylight was daylight anyway you sliced and diced it. I went back for gloves and tossed Nick a pair. They'd be snug, but the ride didn't take that long. I settled between Nick's legs and leaned against his muscled frame. For now, for the next little while, I'd pretend this was just another day and dredge every last iota of joy from it.

THE TIME PASSED FAR TOO QUICKLY. We hunted and chatted and spent time like old friends do. Reminiscing about this and that or hauling out old jokes. Toward the end of afternoon, when it was nearly time to go, Conan said, "Thank you for everything, Ariana Hawke. You've enriched my life beyond measure."

His words brought tears remarkably close to the surface. A few even spilled over despite my best efforts to contain them. I stumbled through trying to tell him how much his presence had honed who I was, smoothed my vampiric edges, and made me a candidate for polite company. I didn't do a particularly good job, but at least I tried until the wolf dropped a paw over my hand and said, "I know."

Nick and I had stolen a few hugs, but neither of us wanted to leave Conan for the time it would take to make love. We were a unit, the three of us, and who knew if there would still be three at this time tomorrow.

I tried to rein in my thoughts, told myself I was being unnecessarily morbid, but truth has a nasty way of taking a stand. When assignments were being parceled out, I'd volunteered for the Pentagon building because I had the strongest team. And the largest. Everyone else's consisted of six mages, while we had eight.

Myself. Nick. Conan. Clive. Dee. Ruby. Percy. Dahlia.

A smaller number was more manageable, more maneuverable, but Percy had insisted on joining us. His argument was sound. His power complemented Witch magic. Together they were far stronger than either individually. And I don't think Dahlia quite trusted Dee alone with Clive.

And so, we became eight.

If anyplace in the DC region would be well-guarded, it was the Pentagon. I halfway expected to be blown to smithereens before we even got off a shot of magic, but I buried my pessimism deep. It had no place mucking up the works. The nightclub shimmered into being around me. We'd teleported this time, rather than riding Conan.

A quick look around told me some groups had already left. A sign-out sheet was tacked on a wall in my office with another column for everyone to check back in. I added our first names to the list. Someone had the bright idea of borrowing one of my scheduling forms, so it appeared to be a work calendar rather than a battle blueprint.

Not that anyone would be rummaging through *Ascent* anytime soon. If tonight had even half the impact I hoped for, mortals would be running far too scared to bother with someplace as minor as my club.

Percy strode toward us. He'd traded his usual kilt for leather trousers. A wicked-looking broadsword was strapped across his back. Dee and Clive hurried over too. She carried a blade as well. And a gun. And looked perkier than she had early this morning. It's wise to have backups if magic doesn't cut it. I patted my ankle scabbard, but I trusted my fangs above all else.

Dahlia and Ruby joined us last. More Than Never wasn't on the Witch's shoulder. Leaving her home was a prudent choice, but I was certain the bird had kicked up a fuss.

"Before Moonglow departed, she mentioned we were riding the lines," Percy said.

"That's right." Conan nodded. A vortex gathered momentum around him; we traded the club's familiar walls for the curved tunnels housing the ley-lines. Their magic was stronger, more pervasive. It pummeled me the nearer I came, harsh and relentless. If I didn't know better, I'd have thought the lines were delighted at being employed to defeat evil.

Ruby's words clinched my impressions as she said, "Whoa! You've come a long way, baby," and waved a hand at the pulsating line.

The wolf jumped deftly atop the nearest one; an orange-gold glow enveloped him. "We will emerge inside the building. It's large, and we must be thorough."

I'd been considering how to proceed. The longer I'd rolled it around, the more convinced I was we needed a stronger plan of attack than we had. "Thousands work there," I said. "As many as twenty thousand, or maybe even more, not that anywhere near those numbers will be there during evening hours, but I'm certain they work assigned shifts. Can we hatch up a spell to wipe them out in batches?"

"Aye, it's possible," Percy said, "but a spell to demolish a hundred mortals takes a lot of magic. We'd run out of juice somewhere around the first thousand."

"We could mesmerize them," Nick said. "Maybe."

The words were sour in my mouth when I muttered, "We'd need additional Vampires. A whole lot more."

Nick arched a rakish brow. "We'll have them. The Ravnos master Vamp said to get in touch once we were close."

"Change of plans, then," Conan said. "We'll emerge beneath the building in the cavern housing the lines. It will offer us a sheltered place to locate the other Vampires. And maybe a Kelpie or two."

"Aren't you worried this might turn into a free-for-all?" I asked, curious what he thought. Just because it was in the forefront of my mind didn't mean it was bothering anyone else. Kelpies weren't team players, but then neither were Vampires.

"Ariana." Conan skewered me with his lupine eyes. "It's the only way we have a prayer of winning."

"We don't have raw numbers on our side," Dahlia agreed. "Magic only goes so far."

"Aye, so chaos is our fallback." Eagerness streamed from Percy; he liked the idea. "Mortals may blanche when they see me, but nothing like a set of Vampire fangs or a Scottish water horse to make any man shit his pants."

On that confident note, Conan barked a time or two. The lines enveloped us with their clean, fresh scent, and our surroundings shifted. Nothing looked much different when the lines settled out, but we'd moved into position. Next to me, Nick opened his mind voice and called for the Clan Ravnos Vampires.

Clive dug out the Kelpies' summoning stone and spoke into it.

I buried my antipathy ten feet under and spaded magic over the whole mess. With dicey allies, a positive attitude could be the difference between working as a team or having them turn on us.

If things went sour, it wouldn't be my fault.

"They're not that bad," Nick spoke into my mind. It startled me, and I did a rather thorough job concealing my bleak predictions.

"Appreciate the effort to make me feel better, but I've met them," I told him. *"So I know different, but I'll behave. We won't need them for very long."*

"No," he agreed. *"We shouldn't."*

I'd said won't; his comeback had been shouldn't. Two words with quite different meanings. I took a deep, totally unnecessary breath to center myself, huffed it out, and turned to face a leering herd of Kelpies.

"You rang?" One's sneer deepened. "We knew you'd never be able to resist the allure of our magic." Blood smeared across his stark cheekbones and dripped down his chin. I caught a glimpse of bits of gristle and tissue stuck between his squared-off teeth. They still rocked the bad-boy motorcycle gang motif with leather, tatts, piercings, and long dark hair. Even with that cover, their eerie beauty shone through, wicked and tantalizing.

It might have been the blood scent, or the evidence of Kelpies already having begun the evening's carnage, but the Vampire in me took over. Doubts dropped away as my fangs clicked into place. I was ready, goddammit. More than ready to make every human I saw—and all the traitorous mages too —sorry they'd ever been born.

The blood-musk stench of Vampires on the prowl washed through the tunnel. "Wahoo!" someone yelled.

"Kelpies," Another shouted. "Cool!"

A long, withering whinny shut the Vampire up fast.

Fuckity-fuck, here we go...

"Welcome. Glad you were already here," Nick called, charm streaming from him. If anyone could pull this rabbit out of its murky den, it was him.

A dozen Vamps surged from shadows with other Undead materializing by the moment. "We never welch on a promise," one said.

"Aye, appreciate it." Nick shook hands all around while snorts and neighs and pawing and stamping suggested the Kelpies would just as soon murder the Clan Ravnos Vamps and be done with it.

Ariana may have met the Ravnos crew, but they'd fucked me over pretty good. Or tried to. I'd been smarter than them, but brainpower aside, any Vampire can cast a hypnotic spell. My plan was to get the spell cooking and then turn them loose to feed. It should be an irresistible invitation, and it would do double duty. Enticing them and getting them out of our hair at the same time.

Unless we ended up needing them a second time. And a third.

We didn't have to kill every person in the Pentagon building. But we did need to cull out mages and make certain they'd never draw another breath. Beyond that, humans in command positions needed to go. When we ran out of them, we could retreat and consider this a job well done.

I was shocked how quickly the Ravnos Vampires responded to my mind voice. I'd expected them to dick with me, drag their heels. Unfortunately, the Kelpies showed up first. Smoothing the waters kept me busy. On the good news front, everyone appeared to have already begun killing. Nothing like fresh blood to perk up the spirits and nurture a positive mood. Somewhere along the way, my fangs had dropped.

Conan growled, not loud, but it effectively shut everyone up including the Kelpies who'd been mimicking an entire stable of restless racehorses hyped up on drugs.

"We'll ride the lines to the lower of two basement levels," Conan said. "The Vampires will push a mesmerism spell as far as they can. Once it takes, we'll mow through the herd and move upward."

"Killing as we go," a Kelpie snarled, showing stained teeth.

"And eating." Another Kelpie sounded jubilant.

"If it doesn't slow you down," Conan told him.

"What's your plan, guardian? Not that we're under any obligation to follow it." The Kelpie pushed in front of where the wolf stood.

Conan's big paws balanced on a vibrating ley-line; he stared back at the Kelpie. "Once we've swept through the whole building, you can remain here eating for the next hundred years if you want. We have a job to do. If you hunker over every corpse you create, we'll never get to the end."

"Goes for us as well," I told the other Vampires.

"We'll do our best." A woman who looked about twenty with short purple hair grinned, showing me her fangs. "We might require, erm, sustenance. To keep going. You know?"

Conan's growl deepened. "Mortals and mages will be fighting back," he reminded everyone.

"Why would they?" a Kelpie countered around a snort.

"Aye, they'll be flat on their backs from the Vampires' enchantment," another said.

It was time to clarify a few things. I did a quick nose count and came up with fifty-two Ravnos Vamps, Ariana, and me. "Even with all of us," I told the group, "we won't come close to dropping everyone up there"—I jerked my chin upward—"in their tracks. We will have to move from floor to floor, and our magic won't be as robust after a while."

"Eh, we'll wing it," a Kelpie said.

"Aye," another chimed in. "It's what we always do."

Conan didn't say another word. The glow around him deepened, developing reddish overtones. I raised my voice to make certain the Vampires heard me. "Let's try the mesmerism casting with ten of us," I suggested. "If it works, we can stagger our magic as we seize the building, floor by floor."

If we did it that way, maybe our combined skills would last through the entire structure. It was supposed to have seven floors; two below ground and five above. Regardless, Conan had been correct about it being huge. I felt it above us, daunting in its stolid presence. I'd read a little about it before we axed the communications channels, and it was the heart of America's defenses against enemies.

We hadn't been adversaries, mortals and mages. Not really. We could have coexisted side-by-side forever. The blame for what was to come sat squarely on the mortals' shoulders. Their insatiable need to control everything would be their downfall.

I hoped.

I'd gotten a little bit ahead of the game. We had some serious fighting standing between us and declaring victory.

"Good idea." A Ravnos Vampire apparently liked my plan about not including all of us in every group mesmerism spell. He counted off Undead for our first skirmish.

I tasted musk and copper as they prepared the violet curtain that should buy the rest of us killing time. They did a credible job, but hypnosis is where we live. Any Vampire who can't immobilize potential prey doesn't last long.

"Let's go!" Ruby shouted. For once, her wings were spread. Blood formed daggers in both hands, and she looked like something out of a hell-spawned dream. I was glad she was on our side, but then I reminded myself we could easily face Fae who'd been turned to human minions.

Whatever demons had plagued Ariana appeared to have departed. The twin worry lines between her eyebrows were no longer present, and she was as eager as the rest of us to get moving.

"Want a bit of help managing the lines?" a Kelpie asked Conan.

The wolf swelled to half again his usual size. "Mine," he shouted. "The ley-lines belong to me."

The Kelpie held up a hand. "Just asking, buddy. Just asking."

I exchanged a glance with Ariana. She offered a very slight shoulder shrug. I'd never known Conan to be particularly territorial, but maybe his laissez-faire attitude didn't extend to the seat of his power.

"We're ready," a Clan Ravnos Vampire announced. The bones of their spell bounced between a few of them.

Conan slammed his front paws on the lines. A shower of golden sparks sailed around us, and the tunnel disappeared, replaced by thick concrete walls and scuffed green linoleum floors. We were inside a vast room stuffed with electronic equipment mounted on racks that went from floor to ceiling. Lights flickered red on most of it. I didn't imagine the array of gear was worth much anymore.

A wide purple wave rolled from the Vampires, coating the room from one side to the other. Inert in its current state, it could be activated in seconds. This couldn't be the entire basement. "Reserve some of that spell," I said and tapped one of the Vampires on a shoulder.

"I smell humans." She cast a sidelong glance at me out of dark eyes.

My nostrils flared as I took a moment to breathe, something I should have done sooner. "I do too, but they're not in this room."

Percy was stopping from time to time, clicking keys and moving on. If this computer farm—or whatever it was called —hadn't been in bad shape before, it would be now.

We were bunched up near a double metal door with an intricate locking system. "They know we're here," Percy shouted.

"Open the doors and let them come," I yelled back, and then added, "Ward yourselves so the enchantment doesn't nail you when our Ravnos allies ignite it."

Turned out we didn't have to open anything. The twin doors buzzed and swung open. A klaxon alarm blared, so loud it hurt my ears. About twenty men, pistols raised and ready to fire, roared into the room. Were any of them ready for immortal visitors?

Another sniff yielded a partial answer. I smelled silver. Whether it came from jewelry or ammunition remained to be seen. The violet carpet floating at floor level leapt to life, and the sweetish smells of wildflowers, copper, and musk surrounded me. The men in front had lobbed off a few rounds; they fell facedown. The spell caught some of them with their fingers depressing triggers. Their guns kept on firing. Bullets ricocheted off walls. Computers exploded and caught fire. So far, none of us had been injured.

A nasty, burnt smell oozed through the chamber.

The drone of voices, mostly calling for reinforcements, reminded me we had an entire building to dispatch. We couldn't afford to get stuck down here. I loped to Ariana's side. "Can we take out their internal communication system?"

"Heh. I was just wondering the same thing."

More uniformed men, this group carting rifles, swarmed through the door. The Kelpies must have been growing impatient. They didn't wait for the newcomers to succumb to the purple haze swirling through the room. I'd never seen them fight, which made sense since I'd never seen them at all before Clive conjured them out of the sea.

Some transformed into horses. Those who still looked like men punched and shoved the guards. Once they went down, horses stomped their heads to pulp. It was quick, efficient, and chilling. Even Vampires can't kill quite that fast. My other bit of take-home knowledge was Kelpies were seemingly impervious to bullets.

Gunfire and screams added to the cacophony filling the air. The guards had moved beyond needing two-way radios. Everyone anywhere near would hear the ruckus and come at a run. We surged into the hall; pandemonium reigned. Guns fired from all sides, but bullets hit their companions rather than us. Squeals of pain escalated.

I expected everyone to take off, but they were milling about like a pack of confused sheep. If they had any brains at all, they'd run like hell and get the fuck out of the building. The sound of hoofbeats alerted me the Kelpies were on the move, rampaging down a broad central corridor. No reason for them to remain in the room we'd just vacated. Nothing alive was left in there. Howls of terror told me people had seen the Scottish water horses. Excellent. Maybe it would knock sense into them.

No human who'd ever laid eyes on a Kelpie escaped unscathed. I was still caught between horror and wanting to cheer after watching them dispatch upward of fifty guards with guns. Maybe this would go better than I'd thought.

Ruby ran past me grinning like a fool as she shot daggers made from her own blood from both hands. Her aim was eerily accurate. Some blades doubled back to augur into their targets. Every mortal she stabbed dropped like a stone, presumably dead.

"Like shooting fish in a barrel," she shouted over one shoulder and launched another volley.

"Clear Level B2," a tinny voice blared over some kind of

speaker system. "One minute and counting. Sixty. Fifty-nine..." People flowed out of nooks and crannies running flat out for stairwells.

"Time to move out," Percy shouted. "They're about to flood this whole area with poison gas and seal it off."

How could he possibly know? But I didn't question his assessment. He needed to breathe. I didn't.

"To me!" Conan shouted. Everyone shot to his side except the Kelpies. They were having a grand time munching on body parts. Swift and resourceful, they ate with the same abandon with which they killed.

"I'm moving us one floor up," Conan said. "This one won't be as easy."

"We're ready." A Vampire nodded sharply. From the looks of things, he'd been feeding too. Blood dripped from his fangs; it made me crazy with envy. I wanted some of the free-flowing ruby river for myself.

The chaotic tableau fell away, replaced by a similar corridor with doors opening off both sides. People stood in the hall, wearing worried looks. Unlike the floor below, this group wasn't armed. At least not the ones milling around.

A purple carpet reeking of Vampire enchantment rolled down the hall. Everyone it touched crumpled to their knees. The call of beating carotids was tough to resist. Ariana joined me. I eyed an unconscious woman a meter or so away, but Ariana shook her head. "I'm hungry too, but something isn't right."

I dragged my attention away from dinner. "What are you picking up?"

"Not sure. On the surface, we seem to be doing well, but

this has been too easy. It's almost as if they might have been expecting us."

"Then why are they shooting each other?"

She dragged her fangs over her lower lip. "I don't know. Something feels off to me, though."

A fresh spate of squeals brought my head snapping around. The Kelpies had arrived, clearly working their own timetable. For all I knew whatever substance was circulating one floor down wouldn't hurt them. Adding to their gruesome factor, they munched on freshly severed body parts as they trotted along. Many were in equine form.

Everyone was killing. The Witches were lopping heads off with blades. Clive's fangs were all it took to send mortals screeching toward Dee and Dahlia. Ruby was hooting and hollering, and Percy stood like a tree, dealing death from outstretched hands. People still came, running out of offices or storerooms or wherever the hell they'd been working.

"Clear Level B1," the same tinny voice announced. "You have ninety seconds starting now. Ninety. Eighty-nine..."

"I have a surprise for them," Conan announced in a cheerful voice. "I've redirected the airducts. Poison should blow right back in their faces."

"Nice work, guardian!" A Kelpie patted the wolf as he trotted past.

People grabbed cell phones, and then remembered they no longer worked. The smack and crash of glass and metal hitting linoleum reeked of hopelessness. "Why don't they leave?" I turned to Ariana.

"They'll run soon enough to avoid the toxic gas. These idiots still think they're better than us." She danced nimbly through an open office door and confronted a man who had yet to abandon his workstation. He was typing frantically, and she plopped on his keyboard, legs dangling.

"Any idea what I am?" She flashed her fangs.

"This ain't Halloween, girlie. That's some kind of costume."

Ariana shook her head. "Wrong. You really should have paid more attention when you went to horror movies as a kid. Tell me I'm real. I might leave you alone."

"In a pig's eye, bitch. Get off my keyboard. I have to get out of here. And damned soon. Or haven't you been listening?"

"I've never been much of a direction follower," she said sweetly.

Extending an index finger, the one with an exceptionally long, sharp nail, she casually sliced it across the man's neck. His eyes widened in shock as blood spewed from his severed artery. Leaning close to his other ear, she said. "I'm real as fuck. Welcome to the last eight minutes of your life."

She ducked away from the geysering blood and trotted back to where I stood. "That was juvenile," she admitted, "but if it weren't for dicks like him, we wouldn't be stuck in this cesspit."

Saliva pooled in my mouth; impossible to avoid in the midst of all that sweet, sweet blood. I spit it on the floor. The countdown had continued over the speaker. "Three. Two. One..."

A swooshing noise grew impossibly loud, almost as if an airplane was taking off in the center of the corridor. Conan stood, tail pluming, ears pricked forward, as power flowed from him.

Ariana pointed to a series of grates mounted high on one wall. "Keep your eyes on them," she said.

"What am I looking for?"

"Anything blowing through it. Most toxic gasses are invisible, but they're heavier than air. If you look with your third eye, you'll see a difference."

"We're skipping the next floor." A Kelpie skirted near enough to tell us. "The guardian said to aim for the second above-ground story."

"But we're going to take a peek, anyway. One floor up." Another Kelpie elbowed the first one. "Aren't we?"

"Why?" His companion frowned. "If they die like the ones in Nazi Germany, they won't be any good to eat."

"Where would they get Zyklon B over here?" the other Kelpie countered. "It hasn't been manufactured since the 1970s. Do what you will. I'm not leaving all that meat to rot. We'll never see another feast like this one."

Ariana hadn't quit staring at the grate; her mouth spread in a slow smile. "Damn. Conan did it. If anything was going to percolate through to this floor, it would be here." Her eyes rounded, and she ran toward the wolf, still spewing power and chanting. I knew her well enough to understand she had an idea. I wanted to know what Nazi Germany was and about Zyklon B, but they could wait.

Maybe forever.

I caught up with Ariana in time to hear her saying, "Can you do that to the whole building, Conan? Spread poison through the duct system?"

"Not all at once." The wolf used his mind voice.

Percy, Clive, Ruby, and the rest of our original team formed a circle around us. The Kelpies and Clan Ravnos Vampires were nowhere in sight. I didn't think I'd have to look particularly hard for them, though. They'd be feeding.

"Nice work," Percy told Conan.

"Thanks. We're far from done."

After a final examination of the air vents lining the corridor, he cut off his casting. I felt him redirect his considerable ability into a teleport spell meant to move us two floors up.

Conan barked sharply. Sure enough, the other Vampires surged toward us. Telltale blood smears ran rampant, but the Ravnos Vampires were just being what we were. Undead who preferred human blood above all else. Impossible to fault them for that.

A veritable sea of guardian power, marked by fur and wet rocks, rolled through the spot we stood. I expected Moonglow, but a malevolent growl from Conan suggested otherwise.

"Who are they?" Ariana demanded.

I followed her gaze to three guardians I'd never seen before. All men, they wore their human bodies. Conan faced them as a wolf. "Return to your holes," he bellowed. "I command it."

One of the guardians bawled laughter. Black hair billowed around his tall, spare form. Like all of his ilk, his eyes were amber, and his face starkly carved in planes and angles. A large gold signet ring graced the middle finger of one hand.

"Well met, at last," he said.

"I don't think so," Conan retorted. "I know none of you, which means you were banished. Begone. I have work to do here."

"So do we," another of the guardians said. "Our job is protecting those who work here. Leave before we summon our army of mages to force you out."

A long, low hiss burbled from Ariana. "You're traitors? I thought once we killed Darksword, we'd be done with those like you."

"Think again, Vampire," the guardian who'd voiced the "well met" comment growled.

"Why should I?" Ariana drew herself up tall. "I don't answer to you."

"You may," he countered and faced Conan. "You truly don't recognize me?"

Conan's nostrils twitched as he scented the guardian. A horrified expression twisted his lupine features into a scowl. "No. I don't believe it. Mother said you were gone."

"She spoke true. I have been gone. For many a long year, but it's time, Son, for us to get to know one another. You are the sole reason the lot of you aren't twisting on spits. I have Sorcerers at my beck and call. Witches too, and dark Sidhe."

I stared from him to Conan and back again, disbelieving. I'd wondered about Conan's father. Of course, it had to be another guardian, but for him to be a traitor to his kind? My heart went out to the wolf who'd become my friend.

Ariana rushed to his side and bared her fangs at Conan's father. "Go to hell," she gritted out.

"Leave," Conan said.

"Not on your life," Ariana told him.

Magic bubbled around Conan then, so strong it was a struggle to remain upright. When it cleared, we were in a different place, and Conan had taken his human form. "This is your next objective," he said firmly. "I will catch up to you when I can."

"You are not going back there to fight him by yourself," Ariana sputtered.

Conan shrugged. "No fighting if I can help it." Before she could question him further, he vanished.

People with guns rushed us from all sides. Ariana and I joined forces with the other Vampires and tossed mesmerism all over the place. But there were a lot of adversaries. Mortals may be slow on the uptake, but by now, everyone in this building had figured out they were under attack.

I slashed and bit and stabbed, trying to keep Ariana in my line of sight. She was holding her own, but we'd never fight our way out of this press of humans. Ruby flashed by. "Might be time to exit stage left," she shouted.

"Nay. We're not done here," I shouted back.

In the distance, horse hooves clattered on the hard-surfaced floor. Never thought I'd be glad to see Kelpies, but they carved through the mass of humans like a hot knife through butter. Just seeing them was enough to freeze mortals in place.

Ariana climbed over a small mountain of corpses and jumped down next to me. "We're going to help Conan," she said. "Now."

"All of us are," Percy told her. "And then we may be done here."

"But we have a couple more floors," I reminded everyone. Once we found Conan, we'd be up to our asses in combat. With a mage army, not a bunch of ragtag humans.

"Eh, the Kelpies probably got there first," Ruby said and rolled her golden eyes. "They look happier than pigs rolling in shit."

"Even if they didn't," Dahlia broke in, "we did plenty of damage here. Thousands are dead. It's not a blow they'll recover from soon."

"Or at all," Dee said. Vicious pleasure laced into her words.

"What's up next?" A Clan Ravnos Vampire vaulted over bodies to where we stood.

"Feed as you wish," I told him. "We're nearly done."

He clapped me across the back with a bloody hand. "Thanks, bro. It's been a pleasure. Let us know anytime you need to field an army. We'll drop everything and suit up."

"We just might do that," Ariana told him as power glistened around her. "Next stop. Conan."

"Is he in the same place?" I asked as her spell gathered velocity.

"Nope, but it will be a sorry day when I can't find the wolfling I rescued."

CHAPTER EIGHTEEN, ARIANA

Conan's father, his forever-absent parent, was a traitor. No wonder Moonglow had developed that odd look I hadn't been able to decipher. The mix of concern, regret, and shame when Conan had asked her about other renegades. She'd known about his father—of course, she had—and she damn well should have had the guts to tell him.

Yeah, that was the shame part. Every living, breathing female has spread her legs a time or two for someone she later decided was a huge mistake. Goes for us Undead too. Anyway, no percentage in me being angry. Conan needed all of us to stand by him. No wonder he'd been hesitant about stepping into his true role. Who in their right mind would want to claim sovereignty over such an arrogant group?

Guardians shielded their miscreants by pretending they'd never existed. Damn. Even Vampires had the decency rid the world of our losers.

I wove a tracking spell. It's my second higher power,

right after the skill to hypnotize whoever stands in my way. Being able to hunt anyone under any circumstances has always made Vampires invincible in the field.

Despite my particular talents, the guardians had been crafty. I cursed them roundly and corrected course over and over as I crashed through false markers only to discover I'd lost the trail.

A warm glow kindled in my midsection as Nick wound his power in with mine. He'd sensed I was floundering. I glommed onto his magic and pressed forward.

"Crap," Percy muttered. "Those bastards took him a long way distant."

"The question is whether he went willingly," Dee said.

My guess was he had. Conan would have wanted his black hearted kin as far away from the rest of us as possible. Whoever had tossed red herrings into my path apparently decided they'd provided sufficient diversion. Finally, we were getting closer. Conan's energy pulsed strong and sure. Thank all the gods. I'd been afraid his father would kill him.

It could still happen. Once Daddy-No-Name discovered Conan had less than zero interest in a schmaltzy family reunion, his immortal existence could be either snuffed out or buried under so many layers of spells even I wouldn't be able to locate him.

My casting developed grayish edges. "Nearly there," I told everyone, even though they could easily have figured it out for themselves.

We emerged on a hilly snowfield that stretched in every direction. Something familiar nagged me, and not in a good way.

Percy made a fist and punched the cold, dry air. "I'll be jacked. We're back on Omega Two."

"Either they picked it on purpose because they know it's toxic to Vampires," I said, "or they've been living here."

"This was the guardians' original world, so it could be both," Nick pointed out before adding, "Look, Ariana, I wasn't harmed by the time I spent here. So long as you don't dig and disturb anything, or—"

"I just won't breathe," I told him. "It should solve the problem."

"Is this the place you got silver poisoning?" Clive asked.

"Yup. Better if you don't breathe, either," I told him.

Dee hooked a hand around his arm and said, "You can manage that."

I turned in a full circle. While I sensed Conan, for some reason I couldn't tell which direction to strike out in. Before I had a chance to ask for help, Ruby said, "The silver in this world's core is interrupting your power, even when you're not breathing it in. Conan's that way." She tilted her head and took off at a brisk pace. The snowy surface wasn't easy walking; she slipped and slid before she added magic to enhance her balance.

We marched along as fast as we could for maybe half an hour. It was cold, and while I kept expecting to see a building, nothing broke the unending, undulating white. At least the characteristic slow drain from silver wasn't bothering me.

Not yet.

"This isn't good," Nick muttered from where he trotted next to me.

"What isn't?"

"No one in their right might would build anything above ground here. You told me about the tiny beach far below; it wouldn't provide an adequate site, either. When the guardians lived here, they must have constructed underground arrangements. Maybe ice caves. Maybe dirt and rock ones. Regardless, we can't go down there."

My near-death experience had hazy aspects, but I remembered leading the charge to dig nearer the core of this world, assuming we could tap power from it. The deeper I got, the more overwhelming the urge was to breathe. Once I began sucking silver fumes into my body, I'd signed my own death warrant.

Wretchedly inconvenient that the core of this world included molten silver along with other, more usual elements. Moonglow could have counteracted it, but she wasn't here.

"There has to be a way around it," I muttered as visions of gas masks flitted through my mind. Yeah, like I was about to stumble across something that handy on this remote world. Even finding them on Earth would be a scramble.

I hadn't been paying attention and practically ran into Ruby, Percy, and the others. "Hold," she said.

"Why'd you stop?" Nick asked the Fae.

"Ssht." She narrowed her eyes and leaned forward.

I wasn't using my power to track Conan, so I shaped a subtle seeking spell. My fangs dropped. "We're about to have company," I growled.

"Aye, and not guardians," Percy noted sharply. "They're not taking any chances they might lose their prize."

"Nah, they're a bunch of cowards," I sniped back. "Why get their hands dirty when they can send others to fill the void?"

"I sense Witches and Sorcerers and Sidhe. Must be the mage army Conan's father mentioned," Ruby agreed. "Depending on how many, we might have to leave and return with reinforcements."

"I am not leaving Conan here," I told the Fae.

"You may not have a choice." She shot a piercing look my way. "You won't do him any good if you're dead."

I started to point out I was already dead, but it didn't seem relevant. I could be deader, and I'd be damned if that would happen. I glanced at the vista of endless white surrounding our small group. This was a shit spot to defend ourselves. Nothing to back up against, which left us vulnerable on all sides.

"Remember the beach where we started the first time we were here?" I asked.

The feel of various magics was closing. If we were going to make a move, we had to do it now. It was a gamble. If their only motive was to steer us off the plateau, they might not follow our lead.

"Aye. What about it?" Percy asked.

"It's a better place to make a stand," I told him.

"Depends on the tide," he reminded me.

"Let's wait until we see who we face," Nick suggested. "If we're badly outnumbered, we can jeer at them, call them a bunch of lily-livered cravens, and then teleport to the beach."

It did up the odds of them following.

"Goddess be damned," Dahlia muttered. "How many wicked mages could there possibly be?"

"Lots," Nick said succinctly. "They're what drove Clive and me into stasis."

He didn't mention Lorenzo, another Clan Giovanni Vampire whose poor judgement had cost him his life. We hadn't talked about it much, but Nick still blamed himself for Lorenzo's death at the hands of cops with silver dart guns.

"I was prepared for oodles of treacherous mages in the Pentagon," I told Dahlia.

"They may have been there," she retorted. "We have no idea who the Kelpies wiped out as they rampaged through the building."

Contemplating vast numbers of mages who'd reneged on their loyalty to their kinsmen gave me a creepy feeling. Meanwhile, the feel of Percy's magic, replete with whiskey and wildflowers, surrounded us. Good man. While I'd been scratching my ass, he was preparing to get us the fuck out of here.

I didn't scent guardian power, but it was the only way mages could have popped out in synchrony forming a ragged circle all around us.

"Plan B," Nick suggested silkily as he scanned the growing crowd.

I quit counting after fifty. No magic in the world, beyond guardian or maybe Kelpies, could have evened the odds. Cupping my hands around my mouth, I shouted, "Lackeys. Minions. Brainless twits."

"Ye're no better than pawns and flunkies," Ruby tossed out in Gaelic.

"Aye, where is your pride?" Percy demanded while balancing a teleport spell between his hands.

The circle of mages drew nearer. Power flickered and flared in the still, cold air of this alien world. A Sorcerer about Percy's size kicked back his head and laughed. "Brave words. You're cornered, and you know it."

"Fortune could still smile on you this day," a Sidhe with cropped silver hair and violet eyes advised.

"Fortune already has." I showed a mouthful of fangs.

"Leave now." The Sorcerer ladled compulsion into his words.

"Meh," Dee sneered. "You'll have to do a whole lot better than that to make the slightest difference."

"Your long association as patsies has made you soft," Dahlia pronounced.

Nick took up a chant; we turned it into a round-robin.

"Patsy. Flunky. Minion. Chump. Dickwad. Coward. Sycophant. Toady."

Even I had to admit it had a catchy beat once we got into it.

"Show some respect!" the Sorcerer thundered.

I broke away from the group chant long enough to yell, "Respect has to be earned. So long as you kowtow to mortals —or fallen guardians—you lost the right to anything even close to it."

Nick altered the chant, adding kowtow and losers to the mix. Might have been the proverbial straw. With a collective roar, the crowd leapt toward us, clearly intent on ripping us to shreds.

"Perfect timing," Percy crooned as his spell snapped us

up and dropped us on a narrow strip of sand I remembered all too well. Luck was with us because the tide was out and still retreating. We'd have hours before the sea reclaimed this spot.

"Warm," Ruby squealed, flexing fingers that had turned white. "It's warm down here."

"Warmer," I corrected her and moved until I stood with the seawall to my back. The others formed a line on both sides of me.

"Much better." Clive nodded approvingly.

"The sixty-four-thousand-dollar question," I said, "is if we pissed them off enough to come after us."

"Depends how deferential they are to their guardian masters," Nick replied. "Conan's sire and his cronies only wanted to drive us away from their territory. To their way of thinking, mission accomplished."

"They'll show up." Percy sounded certain.

I started to ask how he knew when the same rush of mixed magics that had alerted me to trouble above pulsed around us. "Yes!" I fist-pumped the air. "Suckers."

"There are still way too many of them," Percy cautioned.

"Don't be so certain of that." Ruby's mouth split into a grisly smile that would have struck fear into anyone's heart. Even mine, and I've known her a long while. Hands raised, she faced the sea and began to chant in a very old form of Gaelic.

"What's she doing?" Nick whispered.

"Summoning something," I told him. Like a shot between the eyes, I remembered her connection with the Fomori. In the lore I'd read, they feasted on mortals just as they'd been doing the one time I came across them, but blood was blood. Maybe getting out from under Balor's thumb had thrown the brakes off their power.

One by one, mages popped out. Fury streamed from them as they leapt through the surf and over rocks to reach our protected position. I yanked the knife from my ankle sheath and reminded myself immortal only went so far. If I dealt out more damage than they could repair with magic, they were goners.

A different, deliciously wicked thought rocked me. If not reporting to Balor had maybe strengthened the Fomori, it was possible being subjugated to magic not of their making would have weakened the ravening pack bearing down on us.

Only one way to find out.

I waited, timing things as best I could until a Witch moved close enough for me to grab. I was faster than him, and far more agile. Ruby's chant had escalated, and the waves had gained at least two feet in height as they rocked and rolled out to sea, but I couldn't pay attention to them.

The Witch was about my height but outweighed me by a good fifty pounds. I turned his bulk to my advantage and forced an arm behind his back, bending it until I heard the shoulder dislocate and one of the bones break. His neck was tantalizingly close, so near I couldn't resist. Unlike Sorcerer blood, Witch blood isn't poison for me.

While I was forcing his neck at a decent feeding angle, he bucked beneath my hold. He couldn't break it, but he pressed a charm against my hand. The flesh beneath it smoked and caught fire. Fury boiled through me, anger that the feeble fucker could touch me at all. Pain followed as my fingers burned.

"Let me go," he rasped, "or your entire disease-riddled, undead corpse will go up like a torch."

A quick glance at my hand suggested he might not be blowing smoke. The back of it had charred until bones showed through, and flames were creeping up my wrist.

No way ever would I let this creep live, but I'd lost any desire to turn him into a meal. A quick downward slice with my good hand broke his neck. Once it hung at an unnatural angle, I sliced my knife through his neck vessels and ran for the sea.

Dousing my hand in sea water didn't slow the flames one whit. Of course, it didn't. These were magical flames, and the carnage extended a couple of inches above my wrist. The charm was long gone. Running on instinct, I raced back to where the Witch twitched in death throes and dug in the wet sand until I found the fucking thing.

Dee plucked it from my hand and shouted a few words. The charm vanished in a puff of noxious smoke that stank of dead things. The second it was gone, the fire plaguing my arm went out. This would have been a good time to be panting with relief, except breathing isn't second nature to me.

Dee closed a hand over my shoulder. "Pull it together. We need you. You cannot check out now."

I shook myself, aimed healing magic at my abraded flesh, and scanned the beach with bleary eyes. Ruby was crooning at the waves, but I couldn't see anyone but her and Dee.

Everyone else was buried beneath piles of mages intent on their destruction.

My mind wasn't nearly as sharp as I would have liked. Pain has that effect. "Ruby!" I shouted.

She didn't even turn around.

"What in the goddess's name is she doing?" Dee demanded. Spinning, she swung the long blade dangling from one hand, getting a two-handed grip on the hilt before she cleaved a Sorcerer's head from his shoulders.

"Nice!" I shouted her way. No reason to speculate on Ruby's endgame. We'd find out soon enough.

The Witch shrugged. "Anyone who's lived long enough learned how to heft a blade."

It reminded me I had no idea how old she or any of my friends from *Ascent* were. Not the kind of question we asked one another.

The restless waves didn't look much like waves any longer. A phalanx of Fomori rolled out of them and onto the beach. About four feet tall, they had troll-like heads, cloven hoofs for feet, a mouthful of sharp teeth, and wispy green hair. Ruby swung an arm wide. "Kill every tainted mage."

One of the demons ran to where Ruby stood. "How will we know which ones they are?"

"They stink of treason."

The demon's head bobbed. "We shall figure it out, Mistress."

Mistress, eh? Ruby didn't owe me anything, but I'd ask for an explanation. Once we got out of this.

"Where's the last place you saw Nick?" I asked Dee.

"Two piles to our right," the necromancer Witch said. "I

was on my way to help Clive when I noticed your plight. Smart of you to figure out you had to destroy the charm."

"I have my moments."

She flashed me a warm grin. "You're one of the smartest women I've ever known."

Her praise ran through me, thick and sweet like warm honey. I sprinted to the pile of mages with Nick beneath them and started tossing bodies right and left. Supernatural strength and speed have their place, and this was it. A group of demons saw what I was doing and pitched in to help. Their version of help was making short work of each body as I kicked it aside. Lethal and efficient, their assistance meant I didn't have to stop to kill anyone.

Once we dispatched this pack of losers, we'd return to where Conan was. I might not be able to breach the surface of this world, but by god I'd figure something out. Maybe Ruby could instruct the Fomori to dig, although I had a feeling their power came from the sea. If that were true, they probably couldn't go far from the beach.

By the time I worked my way down to Nick, he was slugging it out with a Sorcerer. He had a special hatred for dark Sorcerers. They'd been who drove him and his kin into stasis for a hundred years.

He was winning, so I didn't intervene. This was his kill. The others, no doubt victims of too many televised football games, had piled on in case their man lost. The Sorcerer must have been one of the old ones; his magic was strong enough to repair damage as Nick meted it out, but the last slash across his neck was slower to knit together than the previous one had been. He was tiring. No one's magical reservoir was bottomless. Not even guardians.

Thinking about them added urgency to my need to return to Conan. He'd had plenty of time to piss his poor excuse for a father off by now.

"Does he need help?" A Fomori bent over my shoulder showering me with fetid breath that reminded me of mass graves from the rounds of Black Death that used to plague Europe.

I shook my head, but the demon didn't leave. Saliva pooled, dripping down his chin. He was waiting to eat the hapless Sorcerer. It made me grin. "No competition from me," I told him. The Fomori waggled bushy green brows, raising them into a question mark. "Their blood makes me sick," I clarified.

With a mighty heave, Nick tossed the Sorcerer onto his stomach, broke his neck, and slit his throat for the millionth time. Grunting with effort, he rose to his feet. "Bastard. He'll stay dead this time."

"You bet he will." The demon straddled the body and took a huge chunk out of his bleeding neck.

Nick's eyes widened. "Where'd you come from?"

"The sea. Mistress required our services." Not a fan of table manners, the Fomori talked around a mouthful of Sorcerer. The effect was grisly and satisfying by turns.

"Come on," I told Nick. "We can sort everything later. Conan's still up there with that fucker who claims to be his father."

"Unfortunately, the assertion is true enough," Nick said

gently, "but it takes a lot more than lying with a woman to be a father."

In a very weak moment, I longed for my humanity. For the days when Nick and I could have made babies of our own. It was only a moment, though, and then I moved on. Ruby, Dee, Clive, Dahlia, and Percy stood in the surf. A quick perusal of the beach yielded reams of dead mages, most of them with demons firmly attached and chewing them down to nothing but bones.

Nick and I hurried to the others. "Thanks, Ruby." I gave her a high five, which she returned.

"First time I've tested my dominion over them. After Balor was deposed, it left a vacuum, and I jumped in." She shrugged. "Lucky for us today's gambit panned out. Next time, they'll come a whole lot faster because they'll remember this feast."

"Never mind that. We have to get back to Conan," I urged.

"No. You don't." His familiar voice preceded his form as he walked through a gash in the damp, salty air.

I raced to him and threw my arms around his furry black-and-silver bulk. "Aw geez. You're all right. You're all right." Tears flowed down my face in a very unVampirelike display of emotion. I really had to stop doing that.

"Of course, I'm all right." Conan shook free of me and licked my cheeks. "Was there ever any doubt?"

"Of course not," Nick said.

"What happened?" Ruby demanded and sank a hand into the wolf's pelt.

Conan shook her off too and took a step away until he

faced us all. Kicking his muzzle back, he howled, the sound plaintive and tortured. "The guardians who shanghaied me are dead," he said at last. "All dead. Forever. By my hand. It is all you need to know."

Already raw, my heart, or what passed for one, seized in my chest. "Oh. Conan. I'm so sorry. You—"

"We shall never speak of this day again." He shut me up by steamrolling over my words, replacing them with his own. "Never. All of you shall give me your pledge. Neither will you discuss this with anyone else."

"I promise," rose from everyone's lips.

"Good." The wolf nodded solemnly. "Shall we go home?"

"What about us?" A Fomori looked up from where he'd been intent on feeding.

Conan produced the lupine equivalent of a benevolent smile. "Remain here as long as you'd like." His amber eyes settled on Ruby. "You're full of surprises, Madame Fae."

She smiled warmly. "Thank you. Some choices turn out to be diamonds."

All around us, the Fomori broke into hoots, hollers, and cheers as they lauded their new mistress.

Tears still welled as guardian power wrapped all of us— minus the demons—in a comforting layer of enchantment. Because he could, Conan dropped each of us out of the teleport spell at different spots until he, Nick, and I were the only ones left. I expected him to take us to either *Ascent* or my house.

Instead, he brought us out at a juncture just past where we normally exited the freeway for home and transformed into a motorcycle. Night was on our side. We accomplished the transition in thick shadows that effectively blocked us from sight.

"*Humor me,*" he said. "*Get on.*"

So we did.

EPILOGUE, ARIANA

*T*wo *Months Later*

It took more than three weeks after our return to patch a full picture together about our evening rioting through Washington DC and its nearby hotspots. Every group had been successful, demolishing better than half the people at each target location.

We'd gathered at the club the night after our return to compare notes. It seemed like we'd meted out sufficient damage to discourage anyone except a complete and total fool, but humans had dropped a whole lot in my estimation through this whole process.

Despite my view of them as dumb as dirt, they had managed to cobble an emergency communication system together, utilizing the remaining satellites. It wasn't especially secure, and Percy and I had hacked into it to monitor news bulletins. Even they'd taken a while to drift in.

Between our efforts and "collateral damage"—ergo

humans who'd inadvertently killed one another as they panicked—the tally was upward of fifty thousand dead. Layered on top of the obliterated com network, the carnage provided an impressive display of raw magical power.

Mortals recognized who was behind the wholesale destruction, and even they apparently decided it wasn't smart to tangle with us. No one was talking about establishing authority over mages any longer. Once we became inconvenient and too unpredictable to hassle, the mages mortals had drafted as stooges vanished. For a while some of us expected stragglers to petition for clemency, tails between their legs.

It never happened.

My current theory is they're either imprisoned or dead.

After about a month, Nick received a letter from Roseann. As an aside, the loss of digital communications has been a huge shot in the arm for the postal service. In any event, Roseann was jubilant. Fearful of a repeat rebellion on the continent, the humans in charge had dropped any and all efforts to round up mages.

Roseann was certain Nick had played a key role in whatever mayhem had convinced humans to stand down, and she invited him to take over as master of Clan Giovanni again. Not that Vampires can operate openly, but then we never did.

He and I had talked about it. If he'd truly wished to return to Italy, I'd have gone with him, but I'd been relieved when he'd demurred. Far as he was concerned, his life was here with me and Conan and our other assorted friends.

I reopened the club to unprecedented crowds four weeks

from the day I'd closed it. I hadn't realized what a pivotal role *Ascent* played in my patrons' lives, but thousands of them made a point of thanking me for keeping the nightclub open. When its closure had extended long beyond my original seven-day estimate, most of them had been convinced it was down for the count.

Conan hadn't been kidding about wanting to close the books on whatever he'd done to his father and however many other guardians were in exile with him. I never did get a firm count. I'd tried a few times to broach the topic, and been shut down handily. Moonglow had visited a few times, but she and Conan had gone off to points unknown.

I didn't figure grilling her would yield anything more than questioning Conan had done. It was more than raw curiosity on my part. I loved the wolf. He was hurting. I saw it in the downward cast to his gaze and in long periods of silence. But I also recognized some things aren't amenable to sifting through. It had taken me hundreds of years to risk opening up about Mistral.

Maybe, eventually, Conan would want a friend to listen, a shoulder to lean on. If it ever happened, I'd be there. Nick too.

Ah, Nick. Just thinking his name makes me smile and go all warm and gushy inside. He tells me my runaway emotions are a stain on the fabric of Vampire-dom, and we laugh uproariously because he's not your typical Vampire, either.

I dragged my thoughts away from rehashing the past and took a quick peek at a large, ornate freestanding clock. So much had changed, but some things remained the same.

Time marched on whether I read it from a cell phone or my old grandfather clock. I hadn't been certain I could get it running again. In the end, Clive had managed it with a bit of assistance from Rob.

A flutter of Fae power announced Ruby's arrival a scant moment before she morphed into view. Swathed in a beautiful turquoise robe with embroidered runes and holes to accommodate her wings, she clucked at me. "You're not dressed yet? Goddess's tits, Ariana, you'll be late for your own wedding."

A laugh bubbled from my belly. In this instance it was more than just a saying. Nick and I were going to be officially mated in a double ceremony with Clive and Dee about ninety minutes from now.

"Not getting cold feet, are you? Bride's jitters?" Ruby's implacable golden eyes bored into me.

I shook my head, but carefully. I'd spent the better part of an hour arranging my hair into an ornate updo with sparkly beads and a few gemstones.

"Not much to do," I told Ruby and dropped my robe over a chair.

She snatched up the emerald sheathe I'd arranged on my bed and turned it this way and that. "It's beautiful," she said, "but why not something white?"

"Ha! You're damned lucky I didn't opt for black. It's more Vampire-chic." I extended my hand for the dress, Ruby shook her head.

"Step into it. I'll hold it so it doesn't wrinkle."

"You're worse than a fairy godmother," I groused and

placed one leg inside the narrow tube of silk, followed by the other. Ruby tugged it into place and zipped it.

I'd made the gown, and it fit me like a proverbial glove.

"Has Nick seen this yet?" Ruby demanded.

"Of course not." I tilted my chin in mock outrage. "Bad luck for the groom to see the bride—or her dress—before the ceremony."

She licked her lower lip in a lascivious gesture. "You look amazing. And hot as fuck. He's going to come in his pants."

"Not likely," I told her. "He's come so much lately, I'm always blown away when he gets hard again."

"No, you're not," she countered.

"Eh. Busted." I'd have blushed if I had that kind of a circulatory system. "Vampires can keep going forever. It's one of our more endearing traits."

I slid my feet into jeweled sandals and clipped a diamond necklace into place around my neck. The stones had a bluish cast to them that was attractive against my pale skin tones.

"There. See. I'm ready, and we still have an hour to go."

A raucous woof from the living room told me Conan had arrived. I rushed out of the bedroom and bent to hug his furry head. "Are you still going to give me away?" I demanded.

"Who else?" He pulled out of my embrace. "You'll get wolf hair all over that stunning dress."

Ruby bent and riffled her fingers through the wolf's lush pelt. "One of these days, you're going to let me ride you."

He tilted his head to one side and sent an appraising glance her way. "Maybe. I'm getting closer."

"Oooooh," Ruby squealed. "Music to my ears."

Conan lowered his voice to a conspiratorial whisper. "The draw is your new status as mistress of demons."

Fingertips on her forehead, Ruby mimed a swoon. "If I'd only known, I'd have rounded up those little fuckers a whole lot sooner."

"Shall we?" Conan's power filled my living room with its scents of warm fur and wet granite.

"Best chariot, ever," I told him. And meant it.

Ascent's main room shimmered into view around us. I blinked, flabbergasted. Someone, or a whole lot of someones, had decorated it to the nines with flowers and magical light shows flickering like an old-time LSD-powered illusion.

Nick burst from the center of one of the pinwheels, but he stopped before he got to me, mouth opening and closing like a landed fish.

I offered up my best sex-siren smile. "Do you like it?" I turned slowly, displaying the girls and all the rest of my assets.

"Och, Christ, *Cara*. You're the loveliest thing I've ever laid eyes on. Are you certain you want to shackle yourself to a poor sod like me?"

I took him in from head to toe with his masses of copper curls, emerald eyes, broad shoulders, and long, lithe legs. Breath would have caught in my throat, if I'd bothered to breathe. He wore tan trousers that left nothing to the imagination as they hugged his hips and legs. His feet were laced into soft leather boots that hit him mid-calf. A cream-colored linen shirt swathed his torso. Long bell sleeves that cinched at the wrist harkened to an earlier era.

When I located my voice, it came out as a croak. "By every demon who ever walked, you're the gorgeous one. If any mortal so much as looks at you, I'll rip out her throat and drain her."

"How about another Vampire?" he teased.

"Yeah, she wouldn't fare so well, either."

"We're ready," Dee called from across the room.

"Aye, stop fawning over each other and let's get rolling," Clive added.

Conan woofed.

"Small change of plans," I told Nick. "Conan offered to give both me and Dee away. So if you go join Clive and send Dee this way, we'll start the festivities."

"I heard that." Dee ran toward us and knelt in front of Conan. "Thank you so much."

He woofed again, and we took our positions on either side of him.

Music started up from Witches who frequently played at *Ascent*. This time, Dahlia wasn't part of the group because she'd be who bound us as mates. Amid cheers, well wishes, and a bevy of flower petals, we slowly walked the length of the large room to a bower the Witches had been building these past few days. It was midnight of midsummer's eve.

An auspicious time for joinings.

At some point as we walked, Conan took his human form. After delivering us to the altar, he bowed formally. "May the goddess smile on your matings. Now and always."

After he moved off to one side, I noticed he joined Moonglow and a group of other guardians. I hadn't been responsible for anything except showing up, but my friends had done a stellar job organizing our double wedding.

Dahlia bound our hands in leather and sealed our mating in blood. It felt right. Familiar. Everything Vampire was blood-linked in some way. And then we were exchanging the vows Nick and I had written. Promises to seal our fate together through this life and all others to come.

Long before we were done reciting them, tears flowed freely. Dee and Clive's vows were just a beautiful as ours had been. I couldn't stop crying. Damn. I had to do something about that little glitch. If I'd still been part of a seethe, they'd have kicked me out.

Dahlia pronounced us mates and unwound the leather strips from our wrists. Our wounds sealed as quickly as she'd created them. We tossed flowers, and everyone else threw rice and more flower petals.

Nick swept me into his arms and crushed his mouth over mine. His fangs pricked, but I'm sure mine did too. They always surface in the midst of overwhelming emotion.

Ruby grabbed my arm and shook it. "Save something for later," she admonished. "I have a special present for all four of you. Erm. Maybe only three will appreciate it, but—"

"Whatever it is, I'll kiss your toes," Dee said.

Nick lifted his mouth from mine and swiveled to look at the Fae. "This better be good, Fae. I was kissing my woman."

Something about how he said "my woman" made my heart do little flip-flops.

"Oh, you'll like it well enough. Turn around."

We did. Ruby sliced an arm downward and a small herd of Fomori came into view. She'd kept them hidden behind illusion. The demons whooped and squealed before hauling buckets of something red and wet and coppery into view.

"Fresh," one said.

"Aye. We just killed," another chimed in. "Let us toast your nuptials with blood."

I took a tentative look at my guests, expecting the odd grimace or mild disgust, but I didn't find any such thing. "We have food," Dahlia said. "You should too."

A Fomori walked forward with a golden goblet that he sluiced through one of the buckets. He handed it to Nick, and we shared its contents. I licked my lips. "Mmm. Human."

"Best not to ask too many questions," Nick said and accepted a refill from a wandering demon.

I snorted. "Or any at all."

Next to us, Dee and Clive were sharing another goblet. The implications registered, and my eyes widened. "Dee?"

She turned her head and nodded at me with a smile. I saw the telltale tips of her brand-new fangs. If I'd been overcome before, I pretty much lost it when I bolted to her side and hugged her tight.

"You chose to become one of the Undead." I could barely get the words out because it meant Vampires had finally emerged from our status as *persona non grata*. The lines separating us from other mages were well and truly broken, once and for all.

"With my blessing." Dahlia smiled. More Than Never flew high above the throngs of well-wishers, quorking like a mad thing.

Nick stood next to me, goblet in hand. "Did you know?" I demanded.

He nodded. "It was a hard secret to keep, but I helped Clive make her. We tried to talk her out of it, but she was determined."

I brushed the never-ending cavalcade of tears from my cheeks.

Cradled in the midst of friends and family and well-wishers, I'd come home. Or made a home, more like.

I took the goblet from Nick and raised it high. "To friends!"

"To friends," echoed through *Ascent*.

I turned to Nick. "I've never been so happy. I'm almost afraid to believe it's real."

"Believe it, *Cara*. I'll devote the rest of my immortal days to making certain you're—"

I put a hand over his mouth. "We'll take care of each other," I told him. "We'll do the best we can each and every day. It's schmaltzy but our lives truly will be the sweeter for knowing one another."

More Than Never landed on my shoulder in a flurry of feathers and squawks. I reached to stroke her fluffy head, but she dipped her beak in the goblet, intent on its ruby contents.

"That's okay," I told the raven. "You can use me as a feeding pad anytime."

The bird lifted her beak, squawked once, and returned to drinking.

You've reached the end of *Broken Line*, and the Cataclysm

series. I do hope you've enjoyed reading these books as much as I enjoyed writing them. Please take a moment and leave a review for *Broken Line*. Do it now while the story is fresh in your mind. Reviews mean so much to authors, and they're a way to let other readers know what you loved about a book.

If you enjoyed the Cataclysm books, you might like my Gatekeeper series. A sample from *Shadow Reaper* follows.

The dead are restless, and a whole lot less cooperative than they have been. That was true even before I drew the short straw and ended up with Vampire duty.

Since then, Reaping has taken way more time. So much, I'm worried I'll lose all the clients from the career that actually feeds me. I run a small private pilot school. It pays most of the bills and means I don't have to keep regular hours.

Death wants me to remain in one piece. She's bailed me out often enough, she's all but ordered me to find other employment. I just smile and nod after our little talks, and then I climb back into a cockpit.

Our last toe-to-toe didn't go so well. She went and assigned Vampires to me. That's when Reaping turned into a million-hour-a-week job. I can almost hear the Reaper who was stuck with them before, laughing his head off.

I shepherd souls to the other side. Vampires have zero interest in leaving, but I have a quota to fill. Means I have to trick them, but it didn't work for long. They're onto me. Damn Death, anyway. She painted a target on my back, and now the Vamps are out for blood.

In more ways than one.

The screen on my crappy monitor looked blurrier than usual, but it might have been my vision. No sleep these past few nights had to be taking a toll. I rubbed grit out of my eyes and shut them, promising myself it would only be for a couple of seconds. Then I had to get back to last month's books.

They weren't looking good. I'd spent more on mechanic bills and aviation fuel than I'd made. Big surprise. To teach flying, I have to actually be here. Not off chasing Vampires. A sigh started in my chest and burbled out my mouth before I could stop it. Sighing is for wimps.

I'm more of a take-charge type. Or maybe I'm deluding myself.

A pair of ghosts drifted through the far wall, making a beeline right for me. They were on the youngish side, maybe late forties when their lives had been cut out from under them. I'm a Reaper, and souls who have yet to cross are drawn to me like the proverbial moth to a flame. It's a scent thing, kind of like pheromones, except keyed to crossing the veil rather than for sex.

They say hearing is the last sense to go. Nope. It's smell.

I stood and flapped my hands at the approaching pair. "Find another Reaper. I've been reassigned."

"But we're here," the man protested.

"Here," the woman echoed.

They were only a few feet away. A closer look revealed bullet holes in both their foreheads. Crap. Had they been victimized by another mass murderer?

"Please," the man said. "Winnie and me, we—"

"Nope." I turned both hands palms out. "Determining where you end up is above my pay grade. Sorry you're dead, but telling me how it happened is a waste of your time."

At this point, acting as a conduit was simpler than arguing. I covered the remaining distance between us and opened my arms. The duo didn't require further instructions. They walked into my embrace, first one then the other, more than ready to depart this portion of their existence. As I held them, they passed through me.

My Reaper side channeled the dark forever of death, and a chill I knew all too well shot from my toes to my head. If I'd had any hopes of finishing my bookwork, it just went up in smoke. Or ice chips. Reaping is hard work. There are several of us, but never enough to go around.

Fuck it.

I sat back down. Next I pushed the keyboard aside, folded my arms on my dusty desk, and laid my head on top of them. A fifteen-minute nap would do me wonders. Maybe after I finished the books, I'd clean my office. Customers offered pilots latitude when it came to neatness, but I'm not sure I'd climb into an airplane with someone whose workplace looked quite as down-at-the-heels as mine.

Carrick Sky Sports is located in a small Quonset hut right next to the hangar housing my three planes. The hangar was a whole lot cleaner than my digs, but then so were the planes.

I took care of them. They were my babies. Thoughts of airplanes and Vampires and Reaping whirled through my tired brain before I finally nodded off.

A staunch knock startled me so badly, I nearly tumbled out of my chair. It skidded back a few inches, leaving me fighting not to end up on my ass.

"Cait Carrick?" a deep male voice inquired.

I had yet to get a visual on the speaker. At least he wasn't dead. Their voices lacked resonance.

"Yeah. Um, yes. That would be me." I stuffed my feet under my body and stood, turning until I faced the single door into my office. I'm tall, so tall I'm used to looking down at everyone, including men, but the dude who stood there was at least six foot four, topping me by a good two inches.

Faded Levis encased his long legs. Torn trail runners might have been black once, but they'd faded to gray. A battered leather vest and frayed blue-plaid shirt covered his torso. Fair hair was long enough for him to have gathered it behind his head into a ragged braid. He had an interesting face, all planes and angles with a square chin and sharp cheekbones, but his most unusual feature was his eyes. I suppose they were hazel, but in the light streaming through the door behind him, they glowed like burnished copper.

"Sorry to disturb you." He grinned rakishly. "I tried knocking softer, but you were really out of it."

I swallowed back annoyance. I'd be damned if I'd stand here while a total stranger blithely assessed my physical state.

"And you are?" I raised my eyebrows.

"Liam. Liam Hunter." He glided toward me, hand extended.

Something about him bothered me, but I couldn't home in on what it was. I tucked my hands behind my back. "Sorry," I mumbled, "I've got grease all over me. What can I do for you?"

"They say you're the best flight instructor around." His smile, which had slipped a few notches, bloomed again.

"Who's they?" I winced. I should just have said "thank you" and let it be.

"Why all the pilots down at *The Tailwind*."

It was a small bar and grill at the far end of the airstrip I used. Most days, they served breakfast and lunch. Weekends, they served dinner. While I knew all the local pilots, I wasn't aware they ever talked up my skills. Most of them were pretty old-school. Chauvinistic enough to believe women belonged in the kitchen—or the bedroom—rather than in an airplane.

I'd dealt with a lot of flak a decade ago when I opened my business. Once the guys figured out I wasn't a flash in the pan, they dialed back the harassment but never totally accepted me.

What to do about the dude standing three feet away?

He had an expectant look on his face, as if he'd offered up the aeronautical equivalent of "Open Sesame." If I didn't have so many unpaid bills, I'd have chased him out of my office. On the other hand, I didn't want to share a cockpit with someone who started out on the wrong foot by lying to me.

I pushed my shoulders straighter. If I'd gotten any mileage out of my nap, it wasn't readily apparent. "Um, look, Mr. Hunter—if that's even your name—the other pilots would never steer business my way. Either you play this again from the top, or we have nothing to talk about."

His smile developed a definite sheepish cast. "That transparent, huh?"

I nodded and waited, too tired to spar with him. Night would fall soon enough, and then I'd be back to herding Vampires. Death wanted them in Hell, but they were a slimy, sleazy lot with a huge investment in remaining on Earth.

There it was. My problem in a nutshell. Their motivation in staying topside was significantly more pressing than my need to move them across the veil. I'd quit if I could, but Reapers are born into Reaping.

And we live for a very long time.

The thought of chasing down Vampires until the moon fell out of the sky depressed the living fuck out of me.

"Ms. Carrick?"

I started. I hadn't exactly forgotten Mr. False Name, but he'd moved away from dead-center on my radar. He kicked the door shut. A surge of magic flickered around him, turning the air as blurry as my monitor had been.

"You're right about me being tired," I told him. "If you're about to cut the crap and tell me who you are and why you're here, we'll both be money ahead."

The angles in his face grew more pronounced, his fingers more elongated, the copper cast to his eyes deeper, shinier.

I narrowed my eyes. "Sidhe or Fae. Am I right?"

"Aye, Ms. Carrick. I'm Daoine Sidhe. Liam is a modernization of my name, and my family name is Warwick." His accent had shifted from pure American to a lilting Irish brogue, or maybe it was Scottish. Never could tell them apart.

Breath hissed through my teeth. At least he'd offered his true name. The teensy jolt I'd gotten from the other one hadn't bothered me this time. "You scarcely need my airplanes. You can teleport."

The corners of his generous mouth twisted into a wry expression. "You know about us?"

No point dancing around what I was. I was certain he knew, and my soul-herding skills were why he was here. "I went to Reaper school. We have to get passing grades before Death turns us loose."

He furled a blond brow. "Fascinating. I had no idea."

"How about if you tell me why you're here? Then you can leave. I have work to do." A quick glance through my single window told me time was about to betray me. Sunset would be in maybe an hour. With it would come the Vampire horde blood-bent on my destruction.

Or my assimilation, to be more precise.

He frowned. "You're about to have company. I shall return later."

Before I could tell him not to bother coming back, the place he'd stood was empty. I could still feel the beat of his soul, but damn if he hadn't vanished before my eyes.

I stared at the door. I might not know Mr. Warwick, but I trusted his paranormal ability. Sure enough, a knock was followed by a swoosh as the door flew open. Kiko Tanaka strode inside, dark hair billowing around her head like a cloud. She's my closest friend, and another pilot when she's not busy being a pharmacist. Her Japanese heritage is evident in her slight figure and dark, almond-shaped eyes.

"Not late, am I?" She grinned at me. It lightened her features and made her look about sixteen.

I must have appeared blank because she added, "Remember? You promised me an under-the-hood check ride."

Heat rose to my cheeks. "Sorry. I didn't exactly forget. But it's okay. I have time."

"Are you sure?" Kiko asked. "You're looking a little ragged around the edges."

"Yeah. I'm sure. I'm good for a check ride." To avoid more commentary about how trashed I appeared, I strode to the board and snapped up keys for the Cessna 172. Like I said, I have three airplanes, a Cessna 152 trainer, the 172, and a Piper Seneca. The Piper is a twin-engine jobbie. It costs me five hundred bucks an hour to keep it in the air, so I rarely fly the old girl. She's left over from when I used to have a contract for air freight runs. Then she made sense because she has a great payload.

I really should sell her, but I don't have the heart. Like I said, the planes are my babies.

We left the Quonset hut with Kiko chattering a mile a minute about a hunky dude she'd met the night before. I kicked back and let her manage the preflight checklist. She's efficient. No wasted motion. She even remembered to grab the cushion that made up for her short arms and legs.

She took the left seat; I settled into the right as she nosed the Cessna out of the hangar. I love the moment when a plane is barreling down a runway, gaining the momentum it needs for its wings to carry it skyward. Once we were upstairs, Kiko tugged a hood over her head and proceeded to follow my instructions using the instrument panel rather than her eyes.

We're both IFR certified, which means instrument flight rules. It's the step that comes after VFR. All pilots have to be able to manage their planes under visual flight rules, or they don't get to fly anything.

Didn't take long before we were circling to land. Kiko did a great job, flared at just the right time, and the plane settled gently to the tarmac, right on the numbers at its eastern end.

"Do you want her back inside?" Kiko asked. Her hood lay across her lap. She'd removed it on our final approach.

I shook my head. "Think I'll take her back up for a bit."

She taxied the plane off the runway and patted my thigh. "If there's anything I can do, just holler."

"Thank you." What I didn't say was that talking about my particular problem wouldn't solve anything. She offered up her logbook, and I initialed our check ride.

"I'll leave a check on your desk," Kiko told me. Pushing the door open, she climbed down. I handed her pillow outside before I switched sides of the plane. She knows what I am, but not about my Vampire-herding assignment. I'm not about to tell her—or anyone else, either.

Magic came out of the closet about fifty years ago, but the presence of supernaturals makes most mortals really uncomfortable. If it had only been one variety, things might have gone smoother, but when it became apparent the dude next door could be a witch or a shifter or a Druid or one of the Fae, a backlash developed.

Humans still aren't certain Vampires are real. The fuckers are masters at hiding the corpses they've drained. And the newly turned ones are kept on a very short leash.

Over time, the friction between mortals and magic had done nothing but grow worse. Lots of anger and hatred on both sides of the fence. This group, Humans Rule, has been a particular thorn in my side. Mostly, I keep a low profile and stay out of everyone's way, though.

I have enough problems without turning into a crusader for magic wielders and our rights.

I nosed the Cessna back into the air, glorying in the feel of the plane as I put her through her paces. She's a good compromise. Light, reasonably fuel efficient—for an airplane —and responsive. The sky to the west lit with what was shaping up to be a glorious sunset. On a whim, I flew into it, chasing the colors across the Olympic Peninsula.

When I finally turned back to the east and set the three-axis autopilot to take me home, I considered how to spend the coming evening. Really only two choices. I could barricade myself into my houseboat on Lake Union.

A fortunate choice of residences since Vampires hate water.

Or I could go hunting. Problem was, I'm about out of tricks. Vampires are very old. Even older than me, for the most part. With age comes shrewdness. Because they all talk with each other in some perversion of telepathy, I can only use a strategy once. They were onto me. It was either come up with something new or lie low.

By the time my wheels kissed the tarmac, I'd come to a decision. I had to have another sit-down with Death. If she wanted to purge Earth of Vampires, maybe she had some ideas—other than driving the Reaper assigned to them nuts. The guy before me had done pretty much nothing. It's not like Death can fire us.

I considered my options as I taxied off the runway and into my hangar. I could follow the other Reaper's example, but it went against the grain. I'm not lazy. Beyond that, I do not like to lose. At anything.

Right now, I was slightly ahead. Majorly ahead, actually. I'd shunted an even dozen Vamps to their rightful spot, presumably in Hell. The way it works is this. I'm a gateway, a link between Earth and Death's domain. The dead pass through me, but I have no jurisdiction over their destination.

Better if I don't know.

I can't imagine a Vampire ending up in the good spot, though.

I buttoned up the plane and pulled the hangar door shut. It creaked on its rollers, and I added spraying them with silicone to my endless to-do list. Once the hangar was locked, I trotted to the Quonset hut. I was feeling better. Flying always lifted my spirits.

And I had a direction scoped out. My next heart-to-heart with Death had to happen soon. I'd make some notes, to be sure I didn't miss anything, and then I'd reach out to her.

It was full dark when I unlocked my office and walked through the door, clicking on the overheads as I passed the bank of switches. I returned the Cessna's keys to their hook on the board. Kiko's money was dead center on my desk. If I hadn't been so cash-strapped, I'd have told her the check ride was on the house, but av gas wasn't cheap. Last week it topped six bucks a gallon, and we'd burned through seventy dollars' worth before my solo indulgence flight.

My monitor had long since blacked out as my computer went into sleep mode. I considered returning to my bookwork but didn't feel like it. The bad news would hold till tomorrow. Even without hard figures, I had choices to make. Either I freed up enough time to make *Carrick Sky Sports* profitable again, or I'd have to sell my planes. Hangar rent was two thousand dollars a month. Upkeep on the planes another thousand—if I was lucky.

Normally, it was doable. Flight lessons were expensive. And I could always bid to fly freight with the Piper Seneca again. But to do those things, I needed time. And a decent night's sleep every night. Not sleeping because I was on Vampire patrol was the linchpin that was killing me.

I rolled my eyes. What an unfortunate turn of phrase. I was only about six months into Vampire patrol, and I was sick of it.

Maybe thinking about the Undead drew them, but the lights flickered, and the chill of grave dirt descended on my head like a ton of bricks. Thank all the gods I had a moment's warning. It was enough for me to dash to the locker where I keep my street clothes and grab the saber I'd bought for just these occasions.

It had cost me an obscene amount of money, but the blade is a mix of silver and iron. Perfect for unruly Vamps and not quite as personal as impaling them through the heart with silver stakes. This way, the length of the blade is between us. Stakes would have required me to be right up next to the loathsome fuckers.

I swung the blade, ready for damn near anything. I'd taken a few lessons in swordsmanship once I bought the saber. Those were a bitch to find. It's not the Middle Ages anymore. Not too many knights errant wandering about running schools for wanna-be warriors.

My death-sense intensified. The smell of rot pervaded my office. Could they come in without an invitation? The lore suggested otherwise, but I'd run across the occasional Vampire in broad daylight, so the rulebook didn't seem to apply any longer.

Sure enough, one sashayed through a wall. I didn't bother looking at him. They're all hunks. And they all reek of decay. Another followed him. And another, until half a dozen formed a semicircle around me. I'd been savvy enough to place a wall behind me, or I'd have been surrounded.

Smart fuckers. They understood my blade would end them, so they kept just beyond its path. I glared. They glared back. Every time I made a move, they jumped nimbly out of my way. They're fast. Superhuman speed and strength comes along with the blood-spell that turns them.

Dawn might end my predicament, but I did not want to spend the next nine hours staring down the maw of a Vampire horde. More were joining the ones already here. Naturally. A telepathic summons must have gone out. My throat was dry, my breathing shallow. They'd planned this, probably just been waiting for a night when I was stupid enough to be in my office after the sun went down.

I raised my mind voice and shrieked, *"Death!"*

"She can't help you." A blond who could have been a cover model for GQ leered at me.

"You'll like us. Once you're one of us." A woman with long russet hair smiled, displaying her fangs.

Yeah. That is so not going to happen. I can't teleport, though. The floor wasn't about to open up and swallow me. If I charged forward, blade swinging, I might behead a few, but not before one of them sank his fangs into my neck.

I've been in bad spots before, but not quite this difficult. Better to go down fighting than cowering, though. With a pivot in what I hoped was an unexpected direction, I drove the point of my saber through a Vampire chest. It wasn't a silver stake, but it should work the same way.

The Vampire shuddered and collapsed. Where its body had been was a pile of moldering bones. I didn't even have to bother freeing my blade. The circle around me backed up a foot or so.

My breath came in ragged pants. I swung about and skewered another one. This Vamp was younger. Blood spurted from it, blackish ichor that outdid any charnel pit for stink.

Motion from the corner of my eye was the only warning I got. Swinging blind, I beheaded the Vamp trying to close on me from one side. Bones clattered as he hit the floor.

They could do this all night. I couldn't. I was already woozy from six months of barely sleeping. Where was Death? She'd always come before when I called her. I'm a Reaper, not a soldier. Reaping is usually peaceful.

I silenced my mind. Feeling sorry for myself—or expecting help to materialize—were dead ends. At least it was late enough, no mortals were likely to show up. I didn't want to be the cause of anyone joining the ranks of the Undead.

Time passed. I stabbed, swung, stabbed some more. My head hurt. My hands hurt. My eyes were giving me trouble, refusing to focus. I can build wards, but not against the dead. It would be counterproductive since I'm supposed to be a beacon for them.

A burst of furious Old Gaelic battered my ears. Great. A Celtic Vampire. Just peachy. Had this bunch summoned the Undead version of someone like Sir Lancelot? I narrowed my eyes, but my vision was a joke. Blurry and caught up in the half-light common to the dead, I couldn't see a thing.

"Move over, Ms. Carrick," a familiar voice ordered just before a man slinging magic burst through a portal. I blinked against the glare arcing from his fingers.

"Liam?"

"Who in the bloody fuck did you expect? Santa Claus?"

Intent on beheading Vamps with Sidhe magic, he didn't so much as glance my way.

I admit, I was slow on the uptake, but once it sank in I might not end up turned tonight, I waded into the fray, swinging my saber with renewed energy. Maybe Liam did something, but my lethargy dropped away. Once I had enough oomph to drag all of me back to the land of the living, my vision returned to normal.

My mind was firing on all cylinders again, and I didn't care for its conclusions. Liam wanted something. He must have wanted it pretty damned bad to show up now. Surely, his Sidhe magic told him what he was walking into.

I was grateful, sure I was, but also suspicious as hell. Why did I have the feeling death by Vampire might be preferable to the favor Liam was about to call in?

Tough to refuse someone who'd just saved my bacon. Tough, but not impossible. I cautioned myself to wait. Once we were out of this, I'd keep as open a mind as possible. At least listen to him before I said no.

Keep right on reading. Click here for info and buy links.

ABOUT THE AUTHOR

Ann Gimpel is a USA Today bestselling author. A lifelong aficionado of the unusual, she began writing speculative fiction a few years ago. Since then her short fiction has appeared in many webzines and anthologies. Her longer books run the gamut from urban fantasy to paranormal romance. Once upon a time, she nurtured clients. Now she nurtures dark, gritty fantasy stories that push hard against reality. When she's not writing, she's in the backcountry getting down and dirty with her camera. She's published over 75 books to date, with several more planned for 2020 and beyond. A husband, grown children, grandchildren, and wolf hybrids round out her family.

Keep up with her at www.anngimpel.com or http://anngimpel.blogspot.com

If you enjoyed what you read, get in line for special offers and pre-release special reads. Newsletter Signup!

Rebel Reaper

Untamed Reaper

GenTech Rebellion

Winning Glory

Honor Bound

Claiming Charity

Loving Hope

Keeping Faith

Ice Dragon

Feral Ice

Cursed Ice

Primal Ice

Magick and Misfits (Coming Fall and Winter 2020)

Court of Rogues

Midnight Court

Court of the Fallen

Court of Destiny

Rubicon International

Garen

Lars

Soul Dance

Tarnished Beginnings

Tarnished Legacy

Tarnished Prophecy

Tarnished Journey

Soul Storm

Dark Prophecy

Dark Pursuit

Dark Promise

Underground Heat

Roman's Gold

Wolf Born

Blood Bond

Wolf Clan Shifters

Alice's Alphas

Megan's Mates

Sophie's Shifters

Wylde Magick

Gemstone

Lion's Lair

Unbalanced

STANDALONE BOOKS

Branded, That Old Black Magic Romance (paranormal romance)

Edge of Night (short story collection, paranormal and horror)

Grit is a 4-Letter Word (nonfiction)

Heart's Flame (post-apocalyptic romance)

Icy Passage (science fiction romance)

Marked by Fortune (post-apocalyptic coming of age story)

Melis's Gambit (historical paranormal romance)

Midnight Magic (paranormal romance)

Red Dawn (post-apocalyptic paranormal romance)

Shadow Play (historical paranormal romance)

Shadows in Time (Highland time travel romance)

Since We Fell (contemporary romance)

Warin's War (paranormal romance)